# Beguiled by the Highlander

**Daughters of the Isle**

**Book 1**

## Christina Phillips

© Copyright 2025 by Christina Phillips
Text by Christina Phillips
Cover by Kim Killion Designs

Dragonblade Publishing, Inc. is an imprint of Kathryn Le Veque Novels, Inc.
P.O. Box 23
Moreno Valley, CA 92556
ceo@dragonbladepublishing.com

Produced in the United States of America

First Edition June 2025
Print Edition

Reproduction of any kind except where it pertains to short quotes in relation to advertising or promotion is strictly prohibited.

All Rights Reserved.

The characters and events portrayed in this book are fictitious. Any similarity to real persons, living or dead, is purely coincidental and not intended by the author.

## ARE YOU SIGNED UP FOR DRAGONBLADE'S BLOG?

You'll get the latest news and information on exclusive giveaways, exclusive excerpts, coming releases, sales, free books, cover reveals and more.

Check out our complete list of authors, too!

No spam, no junk. That's a promise!

### Sign Up Here

www.dragonbladepublishing.com

---

*Dearest Reader;*

*Thank you for your support of a small press. At Dragonblade Publishing, we strive to bring you the highest quality Historical Romance from some of the best authors in the business. Without your support, there is no 'us', so we sincerely hope you adore these stories and find some new favorite authors along the way.*

*Happy Reading!*

*CEO, Dragonblade Publishing*

# Prologue

*Isle of Skye, Winter 1565*

"The Earl of Argyll appreciates yer support." William Campbell grasped the arm of John MacDonald, laird of Fincaith Castle, to seal the deal they had just made.

The older man merely grunted in response.

William had arrived at the castle on Skye the previous day and, although his mission had been successful, he had the feeling the MacDonalds were lukewarm at best when it came to appeasing the earl. He tried a different tact. "As do I."

"Aye." John rolled his shoulders and glanced around the great hall of his castle, where William's men mingled with his own. "We have no love for the MacGregors. They'll find no support with Clan MacDonald of Sleat."

Thank God for that. The MacDonalds might no longer be Lords of the Isles, but their influence was great, and knowing Clan Campbell could rely on them as allies in this bloodied feud with the MacGregors on the mainland was a relief.

His cousin Hugh strolled over, the keen gleam in his eyes belying his casual approach, and William gave an imperceptible nod to convey all was well. Hugh, with his easy charm, and tankards of ale all around, soon loosened John MacDonald's prickly reserve, and the older man turned to William with a knowing grin.

"I hear ye're promised to the wild MacDonald lass of Sgur. How much longer are ye going to keep her waiting, lad? Ten years is a mighty long time."

William's mood instantly soured, and he hid his irritation by taking a long swallow of ale. The issue of his betrothal to Isolde MacDonald of Sgur Castle wasn't one he enjoyed discussing. Especially with a stranger.

Especially when that stranger clearly knew more about his intended than he did himself.

He wasn't best pleased at being called *lad*, either.

"Soon." Next spring if his second cousin, the earl, had his way. The prospect of his MacDonald bride had shadowed him since he was fifteen, and when, three years ago, Isolde had refused his invitation to visit his newly acquired castle, Creagdoun, it had merely strengthened his doubts.

It was clear she had no wish to unite their clans, or any interest in attempting to make the best of their situation. It wasn't as though either of them had a choice. The contract made between her grandmother and his father was, alas, binding.

"I wish ye well with that," John said with relish. It was obvious he wished for anything but. "Isolde of the Isle is no Campbell lass ye can bend to yer will. I told her father many times, God rest his soul, she should have been a lad with her love for the sword. Her Norse blood runs deep, and that's a fact."

It was clear John MacDonald was trying to goad him. William offered him a grim smile instead. Many rumors of Isolde of the Isle had reached him over the years, and this latest remark merely confirmed them.

All he wanted was a gentle lass content to run his castle and bear his bairns. His bride-to-be was, God help him, the last woman he could imagine settling to such womanly tasks, and his future hovered as gray in his mind as the clouds that had obscured the jagged mountain peaks of Skye since they'd arrived.

But he'd rip out his tongue before confessing such to this MacDonald.

"That's good to know," he said but the smirk on the other man's face assured him MacDonald wasn't falling for his act. Perversely, the fact John was so sure the idea of wedding Isolde was so distasteful irked him, and before he could stop himself, he added, "A strong woman is always an asset. I'd rather a wife with fire in her veins than milk."

What the hell had possessed him to say that? He hoped to God it didn't get back to Isolde. The way Hugh snorted into his tankard only proved he should have kept his mouth shut.

"Ye'll get fire, sure enough." John appeared to find the idea most entertaining. "It will be interesting to see if a Campbell can handle a spirited MacDonald woman from the Isles. The odds are not in yer favor."

※

LATER THAT AFTERNOON William and his men returned to their ship, docked in a sheltered loch, connected to the sea by a canal. It was, he had to admit, an impressive improvement on leaving ships in unprotected harbors, exposed to the unforgiving winter elements.

"There's a storm brewing." John MacDonald eyed the sky. "Are ye sure ye're equipped for it?"

"We are." William kept his voice level. There was nothing to be gained by reminding the other man that although the Campbells might not have the advantage of being a seafaring clan, they were far from novices when it came to navigating the seas.

After the obligatory farewells, they weighed anchor and set sail through the canal. William stood at the prow as they headed south, in the direction of the Small Isles and narrowed his eyes against the dense mist that rose from the sea. The salt-tinged wind was bitterly cold, and waves smashed against the bow as the lowering clouds turned ominously dark.

Damn. He hoped they reached the safety of the port of Oban before the promised storm hit. But he was not one for taking chances.

He swung about and caught sight of his childhood friend, Alasdair, and hailed him.

"Lower the sails," he yelled, above the roar of the wind, just as the skies opened and icy rain drenched them. Swiping his hair from his eyes, he made his way across the pitching deck to the helm, where Hugh fought to keep the ship steady. He gripped the handles, and together they battled against the might of the tempest.

He lost track of time, but night had long since fallen, and still the storm raged. There was no telling how far from their destination they were until dawn broke, but finally the ceaseless battering began to ease, and he clasped Hugh's arm. "I'm going to check on the men."

Hugh gave a brief nod, his attention fixed on the roiling sea ahead. "Watch yerself."

Through the slashing rain and shadows that obscured his vision, William counted the men who were busy keeping the ship seaworthy.

Shit.

There was one missing. He couldn't tell who, but that was of no consequence. He would not lose any man under his command. With a muttered curse he braced his weight into the howling wind and headed towards the stern.

He couldn't see anyone. With a sinking sensation in the pit of his stomach, he grasped the gunwale and peered into the churning sea. Not that he expected to see anyone in this weather. If a man had fallen overboard, there was no hope for him.

A muffled creak behind him sent trepidation spiking through his blood. Although God knew why. The ship groaned like a living thing against the battering of the storm. And yet—

Something heavy smashed against his temple, and the world turned black.

# Chapter One

*Isle of Eigg*

Isolde MacDonald stealthily eased herself out of the bed, so as not to wake her two younger sisters, who snuggled beneath the covers with barely their noses showing. She wrapped her thick shawl around her shoulders and shivered, even though the fire still glowed in the grate, staving off the worst of the chill in the air.

Grear, their young serving girl, lay wrapped in a great sheepskin at the foot of the bed, but Isolde did not wake her, either. She was well able to ready herself for the day without help, and besides, Grear's assistance would inevitably awaken her sisters, and her plan to slip out of the castle unhindered would dissolve.

And despite how much she loved her home, the castle of her foremothers, she dearly needed to escape it this morn. There was nothing she loved more than breathing in the sharp tang of sea and earth after a fierce storm, or marveling at the ancient power of the elements that lingered in the crisp air.

She went to the fire and dipped her finger into the pitcher of water that stood by the hearth. It was cold, but at least it wasn't covered with a crust of ice, and, bracing herself, she hastily washed before pulling on a fresh woolen kirtle and leine.

Her precious dagger, in its worn leather sheath, lay on the table beside the hearth, and she secured it within the folds of her gown, the way she had for the last five years since her beloved grandmother had given it to her on the seventeenth anniversary of her birth.

With a quick glance at the bed, she picked up her boots and left the chamber.

As soon as she closed the door, three small bodies charged across the antechamber towards her.

"Hush, lads," she whispered, before any of them could start their barking, and they obediently fell back, tails wagging. She dropped her boots to the floor and gave them each a hug, stifling laughter when they enthusiastically tried to lick her face off. "Enough, now."

She pulled on her boots, found her gloves and hood, and then eyed the three terriers who gazed at her expectantly. They were littermates, and although each dog belonged to one sister, it was unthinkable that she take sweet Sjor with her and leave the other two behind.

The three dogs were at her heels as she opened the antechamber door and made her way to the stairs that led down to the ground floor. The servants were already at their tasks, and she crossed the great hall to the kitchens to find something to break her fast.

Grabbing a satchel, she gathered some oatcakes and warm bannocks before tossing the dogs three slices of choice, fresh meat.

"Come," she called to the dogs as she picked up a lantern and left the castle. It was still dark, and the heavy clouds allowed no glimpse of the moon or stars. The air was damp, and as she made her way across the courtyard a dark shadow emerged from the stables and tailed her.

She sighed. Even without turning, she knew who he was. "There's no need to accompany me, Patric. I'll only venture as far as Sgur beach."

"No swordplay this morn, then?" His voice was grim, but she heard the hint of amusement in his voice. After her father's untimely death ten years ago, his faithful warrior and lifelong friend had stepped in as a surrogate father and continued her unconventional lessons, a fact for which she loved him dearly.

But it didn't mean she wanted him to shadow her every time she stepped foot outside the castle ramparts.

"Not until after the sun rises. I prefer to see my opponent."

"Where's the challenge in that?"

She shook her head. Clearly, he had no intention of allowing her to escape his watchful eye. "I'm ready for any challenge, as ye well know, Patric." She slung him a glance over her shoulder. "Sundown, then. And I will have ye eat yer words, make no mistake."

His low laugh warmed her as she picked her way down the mighty hill and headed to the beach with Patric following in her wake. The sound of waves crashing against the rocks grew louder with every passing moment and the scent of salt and seaweed drenched the air.

In the distance, lightning flashed, illuminating the heavy clouds and stormy sea. She paused and held her lantern higher as she gazed at the breathtaking sight. The tempest raged, yet here, on her beloved Isle, an illusory cocoon of calm settled across the land.

Either the storm would blow itself out over the sea or it would sweep around and return to the Isle. As though confirming her thoughts, the wind picked up and pinpricks of frost spattered her face in welcoming familiarity.

With the dogs at her heels, she tramped across the bracken moorlands before reaching the beach and inhaling a deep breath. In truth, winter was her favorite season, when the wind howled and waves lashed as though Njord himself, the powerful Norse god of the sea, had awoken after his timeless slumber.

She smiled at her fanciful thoughts, as she always did. The old gods of her ancestors were only myths, yet how she had loved hearing the stories from her grandmother when she was a bairn.

But her devotion to Eigg went far deeper than simply enjoying the tales from the past, when the Norse had planted their roots in the Small Isles. It was in her blood, a part of her, and how her grandmother could imagine for one moment that she'd give all of this up and wed some Campbell stranger . . .

Panic churned through her, the way it always did when the specter of leaving Sgur Castle assailed her, and her grip on the lantern tightened.

*No.* She would not dwell on such thoughts. She had been born on this Isle. And by God, and all the gods of her ancestors, she intended to die here, too.

There was only one way to calm her racing heart and the alarming sensation that the beach was spinning beneath her feet. She sank to her knees, and after placing the lantern to one side, tore off her gloves, and pushed her palms into the chilled sand.

With a ragged breath, she closed her eyes. The cold ate into her fingers and the tiny grains scratched her skin, but an ethereal whisper of calm inched along her arms and into her blood. The erratic thudding of her heart eased, the dark dread that hovered on the edges of her mind receded, and the wailing of the storm wrapped itself around her in a misty caress.

Aye. This was where she belonged. Her Isle was her anchor and her strength and no matter what had possessed her grandmother to make such an agreement with a damn Campbell, they both knew it could never happen. She and her sisters were destined to remain on Eigg, just as their foremothers had.

Somehow, she had to find a way to get through to her grandmother. And soon. Before summer arrived, and with it, the prospect of an Argyll bridegroom.

She opened her eyes and from the dull glow of her lantern watched the dogs as they darted between the bracken and sand, chasing real or imaginary vermin. And then, without warning, the three of them froze, their noses pointed towards the sea.

Frowning, she followed their gaze, but the storm still raged, and lightning still split the sky asunder. It was fierce, to be sure, but it took more than a winter's tempest to cause the dogs to act in so unnatural a manner.

Before she could call them to heel, they took off, barking wildly, disappearing into the twilight, and she scrambled to her feet and grabbed the lantern, before glancing at Patric.

He shrugged, anticipating her question without the need for her to voice it.

"The storm might have thrown a dolphin ashore." He sounded skeptical at the notion, but it was always a possibility, and something untoward had certainly set the dogs off.

"Then we'd best return it to the sea," she said, and Patric fell into step beside her as they trudged towards the shore, following the sound of the dogs.

Once more, lightning rent the cloud-laden heavens, revealing the dogs standing beside an indistinguishable figure sprawled upon the sand. Thunder rumbled in the distance and a shiver raced over Isolde's arms.

"That doesn't look like a dolphin." Her words were whipped away in the wind, but the way Patric stiffened by her side was answer enough that he, also, knew what they were looking at.

"Poor soul." His voice was grim. "Wait here."

She followed him as he strode across the sand, since there was no need to protect her from the sight of a dead man, and Patric was well aware of that. But every now and then he recalled his pledged fatherly duty towards her to shield her from the harsher side of life.

It didn't mean she had to abide by his commands.

Together, they stared at the victim of the storm. The lantern cast a glow around him, creating eerie shadows and the illusion that the man still breathed. Face-down in the sand, his midnight hair was a tangled mass, and it was a miracle he hadn't merely sunk without trace considering he still wore both mantle and surcoat.

Patric grunted. "I'll haul him further onto the beach and get the men to take him to the kirk at first light."

It was a sound plan. And yet...

She frowned and crouched, swinging the lantern over the back of his head. "Look." She pushed aside his hair, and dark blood coated her gloved fingers. "Tis a fresh wound."

Which meant he hadn't spent endless hours in the unforgiving sea.

Without waiting for Patric's reply, she set the lantern down and heaved the man onto his back. At least, that was her intention, but it was harder than she'd anticipated. With a long-suffering sigh, Patric gave her a hand, and she caught sight of the man's face.

A sharp pain pierced through her breast, which was inexplicably odd, since she didn't recognize him as a MacDonald from any of the Isles. But that didn't mean he wasn't one. Perhaps he came from their clan on the mainland, and it was their shared blood connection with their ancestors that recognized him as kin.

It seemed far-fetched, and she wasn't prone to making such fantastical leaps of logic, but why else would the glimpse of his admittedly handsome face cause such unfathomable sorrow?

His eyelids flickered.

Shock stabbed through her. Had she imagined it?

She leaned over him, scrutinizing his features, before pulling off one glove and tentatively placing a finger beneath his nose.

The icy weather snaked around her finger. But she scarcely felt it, for a faint whisper of warmth also dusted her skin.

"God's teeth." She wiped his hair back from his cheeks. "Can ye hear me, man?"

Patric placed his hand on the man's chest and uttered a low curse. "Stand back. We need to get him inside the castle."

This time she did as he bid, and after he pulled off the mantle and surcoat, she picked up the heavy, sodden garments. With obvious effort, Patric, who was one of the strongest warriors she knew, hefted the stranger over his shoulder and staggered across the beach.

There was no way he could get the stranger up to the castle without help. But typical man, he would never admit it. She grabbed his arm and yelled in his ear.

"Wait here before ye crack yer back. I'll bring help."

Patric muttered under his breath, but she didn't wait to hear his inevitable affronted protests. With the dogs chasing circles around her, she hastened back to the castle and hailed the warriors who stood guard. Within moments, three of them left the courtyard to assist Patric.

Still clutching the stranger's soaking clothes, she hurried to the great hall, where a young serving girl had just finished setting the fire. Isolde set two stools before the hearth and draped the clothes over them. Water pooled over the stone floor, and she sighed. In truth, the garments needed a good wash to rid them of the sea, and she glanced at the serving girl, who was gazing at her in avid curiosity as she petted the dogs.

Isolde peeled off her wet gloves and rubbed her hands together in the heat of the fire. "We have a guest," she told the girl. "Ensure the fire is set in the solar, and we shall need hot broth."

"Aye, milady." She bobbed a curtsey before leaving the hall, and Isolde ineffectually tried drying her damp skirt in front of the fire before abandoning the task. Instead, she went back outside and peered anxiously into the darkness, although she had no idea why all her senses were on edge.

To be sure, it was unnerving to rescue an insensible stranger washed up on the beach, but there was no earthly reason why she was now standing in the cold, waiting for his safe arrival. Especially when he was in no fit state to appreciate her consideration.

In the distance, a pinprick of light came into view as the men, with a single lantern held aloft, returned. Quickly, she directed them to take him to the solar, since it was on the ground floor and easily accessible, unlike the bedchambers upstairs.

As she followed the men across the great hall, her grandmother appeared and came to her side. Clearly, her grandmother's serving woman had informed her of events. "A stranger?" she said by way of greeting, before kissing Isolde's cheek. "Still alive?"

"Tis a miracle, and that's for sure. But perhaps ye'll recognize him, Amma."

They entered the solar, where he was lying on the floor before the fire. Several oil lamps lit the chamber, and for the first time she got a good look at her stranger from the sea.

The breath caught in her chest, an inexplicable constriction, as she gazed, entranced, at the vision before her. Even battered and grazed from the savagery of the storm-tossed sea, his starkly chiseled features were utterly compelling.

His torn shirt revealed tantalizing glimpses of his broad shoulders, and the drenched linen molded his impressive biceps like a second skin. Her mouth dried and she took a hasty step back, lest anyone—her grandmother, in particular—noticed her indefensible reaction to an unconscious man.

Heat blasted through her, burning her cheeks, but thankfully everyone was focused on their unexpected guest. She swung about and threw another slab of peat onto the fire, but the reprieve did little to calm her racing heart.

She took a deep breath. Whatever foolishness was gripping her, she would not allow it to distract her from her duty. She was the eldest daughter of Sgur Castle, and she would never give cause for anyone to question her integrity.

Carefully, she folded her cloak over a stool before placing her hood on top.

"I've never seen this man before," her grandmother pronounced, and Isolde gave a silent sigh. She could procrastinate no longer.

"Whoever he is, we must tend the wound on his head," she said, as she returned to her grandmother, who was on her knees beside the man. "And ensure he has no other injuries."

"No bones appear to be broken." Her grandmother stood and gave Isolde an inscrutable look. "Have the maids dry him while ye attend to his head."

One of the maids brought warm water, and Isolde steadfastly kept her eyes on her task of cleaning the gash on his head, and not at his expanse of naked chest as the maids vigorously rubbed life back into his chilled body.

The wound did not look too bad and fortunately was no longer bleeding. Likely they could thank the sea water for that, otherwise the poor man would've been at the mercy of her sewing skills as she stitched his head together.

She rolled back on her knees and focused on his face as the maids finished their task and wrapped thick blankets around him. Now he was dry, they could move him into the box bed, but she had to confess she was a little concerned he was still insensible.

"Can ye hear me?" She leaned closer and frowned when her whisper elicited no response. Trepidation licked through her. Certainly, he wasn't dead, but suppose he never awoke again?

It was foolish to think she could wake him from oblivion when the journey from the beach, and the less than gentle ministrations of the maids, hadn't evoked even a groan from him. But she had to try.

She grasped his shoulder through the blanket and gave him a good shake. "Wake up. Ye're safe now, but ye must open yer eyes."

His impossibly long black lashes flickered, and for a reason she could not fathom, she held her breath, as he slowly did as she had bid him.

His eyes were a captivating swirl of blue and gray. Like a stormy sea.

*How apt.*

She scarcely had the wits to chide herself for such a fanciful notion.

Instead, she smiled at him. A comforting smile, to assure him all was well.

At least, she hoped it conveyed comfort, and not a scandalous lack of sense due to his enchanting eyes.

"Where am I?" His voice was hoarse. There was no reason for the sound of it to send delicious shivers along her arms.

"Sgur Castle. We found ye on the beach. Tis lucky ye're alive."

Confusion clouded his eyes. "The beach?" he echoed, as though he had never encountered the word before.

"Aye. We can only guess ye went overboard during the storm. Although we found no shipwreck," she added hastily, but now the thought had occurred to her, they would need to search at daybreak for any wreckage.

He gazed at her as though he was unaware of anyone else in the chamber. It was a novel sensation and undeniably thrilling. "Who are ye?" he whispered.

"Isolde MacDonald." She refrained from giving him her full title. Besides, she'd already told him he was at Sgur Castle. "What is yer name?"

His lips parted, and then an expression of disbelief, no, horror rippled over his face, and he struggled to sit up, the blanket falling to his lap, revealing his breathtaking chest. By sheer force of will, she refused to look and instead gave him an encouraging smile.

"I can't... I cannot recall." The words sounded as though he'd ripped them from the bowels of hell itself.

Her smile slipped. "What?"

He sucked in a jagged breath, his fierce gaze never leaving hers. "I don't know who I am."

# Chapter Two

His stomach churned and chest tightened, as though an iron band wrapped around him, crushing his ribs. How could he not know who he was?

A wild rushing filled his head, an unwelcome counterpoint to the incessant throbbing of his brain. God help him. What had happened?

"Try not to worry." The beautiful, flame-haired lass who knelt by his side patted his shoulder before snatching her hand back as though his skin burned. "Ye cracked yer head. That's why ye don't remember. But ye'll be right as rain after a good sleep."

He hoped to God she was right. And yet, as he gazed into her enchanting green eyes, the panic that consumed him ebbed. Of course she was right. Whatever had happened, this was a temporary loss of memory.

"Thank ye." Christ, was that raspy sound really his voice? Did he always sound as though his throat was flayed raw, or was it a consequence of his accident?

"Well, ye're more than welcome. 'Tis fortunate we found ye when we did. I doubt ye would've survived until daybreak."

Bemused, he cocked his head. "Lucky me."

Her smile was like a flash of sunlight in a dank cave. What the hell? Did he usually indulge in such bizarre imaginings, or was it another result of his head injury?

Cautiously, he touched the back of his head. It was a relief not to encounter a gaping hole. As he let out a thankful breath, he caught sight of three terriers sitting beside the hearth, their avid attention fixed on him.

"Aye, ye were lucky indeed, and that's a fact. If not for the dogs, we may have passed right by ye without even knowing it."

The dogs thumped their tails, as if in acknowledgement of their part in his rescue.

"Isolde." The commanding voice caused him to squint up at the older lady who stood beside his unlikely savior. Although her hair had faded with age, there was no mistaking the hint of auburn, and her eyes were the same piercing green as Isolde's. Neither was there any mistaking her authority. She was the matriarch of this Sgur Castle, wherever that might be. "Our guest must be made comfortable, now."

Intriguingly, Isolde did not jump to her feet at the implied command. Instead, she once again smiled at him, and despite the alarming blankness that filled his head, he grinned back.

"Can ye stand?" she enquired. "Ye'll be more comfortable on the bed. And once ye've some good hot broth inside ye, maybe yer memory will return."

The spinning in his head wasn't too bad. He was certain he could stand. And then realization struck.

Where the hell were his clothes? Gingerly, he lifted the edge of the blanket that draped across the top of his thighs.

He was stark naked.

He cast a wary glance around the chamber. Besides Isolde and her older relative, four grim warriors eyed him with varying degrees of distrust, and three young serving maids huddled by the open door, clearly agog by the proceedings.

Dull heat washed through him. What had possessed him, to imagine he and Isolde had been alone?

Had she been the one to strip him?

Even in his befuddled state, the possibility that she had touched his body in so intimate a manner caused his cock to thicken. At least some things still worked the way they should. Except he'd much rather be in full possession of his senses, so he could recall such a pleasurable interlude.

What in the name of God was he thinking? He resisted the urge to groan and involuntarily tightened his grip on the blanket. He was certain that, in the normal course of his shadowed life, he didn't care who saw his naked body. But Isolde aside, the prospect of having been in so vulnerable a state before a chamber full of strangers was most disconcerting.

"Oh." A faint blush swept across her cheeks, and he could not tear his gaze from her. "Maybe Patric could give ye a hand? The bed is just there, behind ye." Then she waved her finger in the vague direction of his legs and avoided his eyes. "We, uh, had to dry yer clothes, ye see."

He grunted in acknowledgement, but when one of the burly warriors approached, apparently to make good on Isolde's offer of assistance, he forced his tongue to work. "I can manage on my own."

The warrior folded his arms, and Isolde hastily rose from her knees as he attempted to stand without losing whatever slight dignity he retained. Once on his feet, gripping the blanket around him as if his life depended on it, the chamber swayed as though he stood on the deck of a storm-tossed ship.

For a hazy moment the sensation was so visceral he staggered. A ship. A storm? Yet when he tried to hold onto the fleeting fragment it dissolved, as if it had never existed.

Isolde gasped and grasped his biceps. "Are ye certain ye can walk?"

The temptation was great to say no, just so she would assist him, but it was more likely her burly warrior would intervene instead. "Aye. I simply stood up too fast."

She released him, although she appeared reluctant. But that was likely only his own warped perception. A box bed stood against the far wall, and he concentrated on putting one foot in front of the other until, with barely concealed relief, he reached it and sat down.

As Isolde brought over a small table, the warriors and serving maids left the chamber, although the older lady remained by the fire, her keen gaze never leaving him. And then she spoke.

"Ye have no recollection of how ye washed up on Sgur Beach?" She raised her eyebrows as if she found the notion somewhat unbelievable.

Not that he blamed her. Until this moment, he would never have believed it possible to lose all memory of who one truly was.

"Aye, milady." The honorific fell automatically from his tongue, even if he did not know who she was. "I wish I could tell ye more, but there's a dark cloud I cannot shift inside my head."

"It's not surprising," Isolde said. "Ye banged yer head badly on rocks or some such. Tis fortunate ye didn't drown. Truly, Njord favors ye, and that's a fact."

He stared at her blankly. "Njord?" The name was faintly familiar, but he couldn't fathom why.

"The ancient Norse god of the sea." She smiled, and he damn near forgot how to breathe at the sight. "How else could ye have survived that storm, if he hadn't watched over ye?"

"I confess, I know little of this god." And he had the feeling it wasn't because of his memory loss, either. Had he washed up on some forgotten foreign shore, where the inhabitants worshipped old, pagan ways? He was sure the prospect should alarm him more than it did.

"Ah, do not fret. We will not sacrifice ye for yer ignorance."

"That's gratifying. It'd be a waste, after ye went to so much trouble to save my life."

"Aye, that's true. Although it could've been worse. At least ye're awake."

He acknowledged the truth of that. "Awake, aye. But still no closer to knowing who I am."

She glanced at the door, where a servant entered with a bowl. "Ye'd best have this broth now, while it's hot. It might help bring yer memories back."

He couldn't see how, but he hoped to God it did.

⁂

ISOLDE HOVERED WHILE the stranger took a spoonful of broth. She knew she ought to leave him in peace to eat since, aside from the wound on his head and lack of memory, there didn't appear to be anything else afflicting him, and yet here she was.

Hovering, like a besotted scullery maid.

"Isolde." Her grandmother's voice was an unwelcome intrusion, especially as she'd forgotten she was still in the solar with them. "Ye'll catch yer death."

Curses. Surreptitiously, she patted her skirt, which was soaked due to carrying the man's mantle and surcoat. Alas, her grandmother was right. She would need to change into dry clothes if she wanted to avoid catching a chill.

Her stormy-eyed stranger glanced up at her and consternation flashed across his face. "My apologies, Lady Isolde. I confess I don't recall how, but it's certain I'm the cause for yer discomfort."

Charmed by his concern, she shook her head. "'Tis nothing. And don't tell Patric, for his pride will never recover, but if I hadn't taken yer outer garments, the poor man would never have managed to hike ye over his shoulder, never mind taken a single step forward."

"Then I'm in Patric's debt, also."

"I'm sure we'll think of some way ye can repay us, once ye're fighting fit again."

Without warning, the vivid image of her stranger from the sea cradling her face in his hands flooded through her mind. And if that wasn't disgraceful enough, she could almost *feel* his lips brushing hers, and a strangled gulp lodged in her throat.

To be sure, she wouldn't in the least bit mind if he decided to kiss her. But not as repayment for having saved him from death.

"Ye have my word, my lady."

Was there a thread of amusement in his tone? Had he somehow guessed her thoughts?

She released an exasperated huff. What a fanciful notion. "Good. There's always work to be done maintaining the castle."

From the corner of her eye, she saw her grandmother arrow a piercing look her way, from where she now stood at the door. Isolde smothered a sigh. Much as she wanted to continue conversing with this enigmatic stranger, her legs were slowly freezing beneath the weight of her sodden skirts.

And that reminded her. "We cannot keep calling ye the stranger from the sea." Wait. Maybe she was the only one who thought of him that way? Before he had the chance to question her about it, she hurried on. "So, until yer memory returns"—after he'd finished his broth, good Lord, what nonsense was she spouting here? Yet somehow, she could not stop her unruly tongue. "How do ye feel about me calling ye Njord?"

His beautiful mouth twitched, as though he held in laughter. "After the god of the sea? Are ye sure he won't rescind his benevolence and find another way to claim my soul?"

"Not at all. It's a token of reverence for how he looked over ye while ye were in peril in his domain."

"I'll take yer word for it. God knows, I'm thankful however I ended up here." And then a frown creased his admirable brow. "Ye mention Sgur Castle. But where is this place?"

"We are on the Isle of Eigg." When no flicker of recognition lit his features, a shaft of sorrow pierced her breast. Poor man, to have no recollection of the Small Isles. For wherever he came from, he was a Scot, and all Scots knew of the Isles. She couldn't even begin to fathom how adrift he must feel, unable to remember even the most basic facts of his life.

With a small smile, she left him to his thoughts.

"I cannot believe ye didn't wake us." Isolde's younger sister, Freyja, shot her a vexed glance as she pulled on her boots in their bedchamber. "I should've at least examined him for further injury."

"By all means, offer to examine him if ye wish." Isolde took a fresh gown from Grear. "But Amma examined him and found nothing. Besides, there wasn't time to tell ye. It's not my fault the pair of ye like to laze abed until all hours."

"But how thrilling." Her youngest sister, Roisin, gave a great sigh as Grear began to braid her hair. "A mysterious stranger who cannot recall a thing about himself. It's sure to be a sign, Isolde."

"Aye, a sign that it's foolish to sail in a tempest." Freyja planted her hands on her hips. "Let's hope he soon regains his senses, so he can return to his kin."

"The weather may have been calm when they set sail," Isolde pointed out. "The storm was sudden, Frey."

"And washed him right onto our beach. What are the chances? I know it means something."

Isolde shook her head in mock despair at Roisin, even though, in a hidden corner of her mind, she couldn't help wondering the very same thing. "All it means is he was damn fortunate not to drown. Don't go losing yer senses over him, Roisin."

Even if she was perilously close to losing her own.

"I cannot promise that," Roisin said, and Freyja laughed. "Is he *very* handsome?"

"Handsome like the fantastical Tuatha de Danann ye love so well?" Freyja gave their youngest sister a teasing smile. Roisin was entranced by the legends of the mythical folk from Eire. "Alas, no mortal man can live up to such perfection."

"He's no immortal," Isolde said. "Another hour at most, and his body would be in the kirk, awaiting burial."

"'Tis very romantic, ye must admit."

Freyja groaned. "Nearly drowning is romantic? I'm certain Isolde's stranger would think differently."

"But he didn't drown," Roisin pointed out. "That would've been a tragedy. Perhaps he is yer soulmate, sent here to save ye from a disastrous match with the Campbell."

At the reminder of the unwelcome understanding her grandmother had brokered with Clan Campbell—which as far as she was concerned meant exactly *nothing*—her mood deflated. And she wasn't best pleased by Roisin's assumption that she needed a man to save her from an arranged marriage, either.

"I don't believe in soulmates. And I can save myself, thank ye very much."

"If ye shared yer plans with us, we could help." There was no longer any hint of amusement in Freyja's voice. "Ye cannot leave the Isle. None of us can."

If she actually had a solid plan, she'd be only too happy to share it with her sisters. Unfortunately, despite having had ten years to scheme, the best she'd come up with was to challenge William Campbell. The chances were high he'd refuse, for a single reason.

No Campbell would want to risk being bested in a sword fight by a woman.

When the prospect of this cursed marriage had been little more than a specter in her future, her plan had seemed good enough. But lately, she saw nothing but flaws in it.

Suppose William Campbell didn't give a damn about her challenge? The prospect of him gaining a foothold on Eigg through her might well prove too enticing to care what sort of wife she'd make.

One thing was certain, though. If they wed, he'd expect her to leave her beloved Isle, and that simply couldn't happen.

Once again, the panic coiled deep in her gut, and this time there was no comforting Sgur Beach where she could sink her hands into the sand and ground herself. Instead, she grasped her skirt tight, willing the insidious fear to slither back to the dark crevices in her soul.

Roisin came to her side and slid her fingers through hers. For a moment she said nothing, and slowly, slowly, the panic ebbed. Her youngest sister was fanciful, and half the time lived in her own imagined world, but sometimes, like now, she saw far too much.

"All will be well," Roisin said. "Don't fret, Izzie. I knew ye and Frey laugh at me, but I feel this in my heart. There's a reason ye found this stranger, a man with no past. How could it be otherwise?"

Isolde squeezed her sister's fingers. She knew what Roisin was hinting at. But her sister was a dreamer and believed in old tales brought to the Isles long ago from France, of chivalry and how love conquered all.

It wasn't real. And her stranger from the sea, her Njord, hadn't washed up on her beach because he was her destiny. He was just a fortunate man who hadn't drowned.

## Chapter Three

He finished the broth and exhaled a long sigh. Finally, the last remnants of ice melted from his veins and his stomach was full. But his mind was as dark as ever.

Not that he'd truly believed anything as simple as food would help regain his memories, but Isolde's optimism had been hard to resist.

Lady Isolde of Sgur Castle. He probed the fog that swallowed the essence of who he was, but nothing was forthcoming. And yet the unassailable certainty hovered on the edges of his mind that he should know of her.

That he should know of Eigg.

Christ, would he ever recover knowledge of his past?

He pressed his fingers to his temples, but it didn't help ease the fire eating through his brain. Although, to be fair, it wasn't as fierce as when he'd first regained his senses. All he wanted to do was fall back on the bed and welcome oblivion, but that luxury would need to wait. He needed to find out as much as he could about where he was, and where he might have come from.

But first, he needed his clothes.

With a pained grunt, he pushed himself from the bed and, gripping the blanket around himself, made his way to the hearth. The chamber wasn't large, with thick rugs on the floor and tapestries on the walls to keep out the damp. One of the shutters was partially open, revealing a glazed window, through which shards of dawn illuminated the chamber. The elusive master of Sgur Castle, it appeared, was prosperous.

Thank God, the chamber no longer spun around him.

It didn't stop him from propping his shoulder against the wall beside the hearth for additional support. He might no longer feel dizzy, but the short walk had made his surroundings oddly disconnected. Almost as though he wasn't standing here, on solid ground, but instead floating just outside his body.

He cast a furtive glance at the bed. Maybe he shouldn't have been too hasty to leave it.

A distraction at the open door caught his attention. Isolde stood there, with two young women, and she smiled at him, which caused a bolt of heat to fire his loins.

Thank Christ the blanket was thick.

"Are we disturbing ye? My sisters wished to meet ye."

With more effort than he liked, he relinquished the support of the wall. "Ye're not disturbing me."

At least, not in the way she imagined.

"Freyja, Roisin, may I introduce the stranger from the sea, Njord." She flashed him another irresistible smile, and he couldn't help but return it. "Unless ye have recalled yer own name?"

"I have not." He hoped he didn't sound as frustrated by that fact as he felt.

"'Tis early days." Isolde waved at the young women who flanked her. "Njord, my sisters: Freyja and Roisin."

"'Tis an honor." He bowed his head and gritted his teeth at the pain that stabbed through his brain.

One of the sisters, Freyja, frowned, and stepped forward. "May I examine yer wound?"

He stared at her, unnerved by the unexpected question. Before he could formulate a denial that wouldn't cause offense, Isolde gave an impatient tut.

"Frey, really."

Freyja ignored her, focusing on him. "There's no need to look so alarmed."

Involuntarily, his grip tightened on the blanket. Hellfire. Did he look alarmed?

"Isolde and our amma are more than adequate, of course," Freyja continued, apparently oblivious to how Isolde glared at her. "But my calling as a healer compels me to ensure nothing further needs to be done for yer wellbeing."

He hiked the blanket from where it had draped around his hips, so it was secure at his waist. Certainly, he was aware he'd been prodded and probed while unconscious, and washed, God help him, since he didn't smell of the sea, but he wasn't unconscious now, and the prospect of a young woman further examining him wasn't something he relished.

Did these people not have a physician in their castle? He couldn't say how he knew that was how things were done. He only knew it was.

"If he wants a third opinion," Isolde said, "I'm sure he would ask for it. Wouldn't ye?" she added, pointedly, to him.

There was no way out of this. Whatever he said, he risked offending one of the sisters. "I'm greatly obliged by yer concern, my lady," he said to Freyja. "If I experience any worrisome symptoms, might I share them with ye?"

"Hmm." Interestingly, Freyja didn't appear affronted by his response. "Ye appear lucid enough. If ye fall into a fever I shall be back, make no mistake."

"He would have already succumbed to a fever by now," Isolde said.

"Aye, but 'tis always wise to be cautious," returned her sister.

The third sister had yet to speak, but she stood slightly behind both Isolde and Freyja and clearly had no insight to add on the state of his health.

He returned his attention to Isolde. "Yer kindness to a stranger is much appreciated. I should like to convey my thanks to the master of Sgur Castle, at his convenience."

"Our grandmother, Lady Helga, is the mistress of the castle." There was no mistaking the pride that infused Isolde's words. "She's happy to accommodate ye until ye regain yer strength."

"Or yer memories." Freyja cast her sister a sideways glance before looking back at him. "Yer kin must be worried by yer absence."

His kin. Christ, who were his kin? Was he wed? Did he have bairns? Surely, he wouldn't forget *that*?

"Alas, the storm still rages on the sea." Concern wreathed Isolde's face. "We cannot send word to the other Isles until it calms."

He released a tortured breath. It was true that nothing could be done until it was safe to leave this Isle and search for his homeland. But where was he meant to begin such a journey, when he had no idea where to start?

"Since it's plain ye're not in need of my skills, I wish ye well, Njord from the sea." Freyja smiled at him, and although the resemblance was strong between the three sisters, her smile did not stir him the way Isolde's smile did. "Come, Roisin."

Roisin didn't follow her sister, although one of the dogs did. Instead, she tugged Isolde's sleeve. "My books," she whispered.

Isolde nodded in understanding before going to a desk with a paneled front that stood in front of the window and opened a cupboard door in its back. "Here," she said, handing Roisin a pile of what looked like manuscripts. "Is that everything?"

Fascinated, he watched Roisin pick up a few more things before stowing them in the folds of her skirt.

"Aye, that's it." She avoided looking at him and made her way to Freyja, taking another of the dogs at her heels, who waited at the door for her. Once they'd left, he turned back to Isolde, whose brindle terrier sat by her feet.

"It seems I've displaced Lady Roisin from her chamber."

"Ah, 'tis fine. Roisin took over the solar a few years back because the chamber is so full of light, even during the winter. But she cannot bear to be parted from her work, even for a day or so. They are her treasures."

"She's a scribe?" He'd never heard of a young woman being such a thing. But then, maybe he had, and simply couldn't recall it. Damn his faulty brain. He could believe nothing he thought he knew or didn't know.

"Well, in a manner of speaking I suppose she is. Even since she was a child, she's documented the histories of our bloodlines. There are some wild stories I could tell ye, and that's a fact."

"Wild stories of Sgur Castle?" He grinned at her and surreptitiously leaned his weight against the wall. He would not disrupt this conversation by any indication that he needed to sit, in case she decided he should recuperate in peace. Even if the stone *was* cold and damp.

"Aye, and I'm certain the walls hold many more secrets that we shall never uncover. Even before the Norse built their mighty halls on this mountain, it was a place of worship for the ancient Picts. And our bloodline runs through them all."

"An impressive heritage." He hoped he would soon recall his own.

"It is one we're destined to keep upon the Isle, no matter what. If we leave—" She cut herself off, and for the first time since he'd met her, looked flustered. "Ah, well, never mind that. I came to tell ye that yer clothes are ruined, so we will find ye a spare plaid." Her glance slid down his body to his bare feet. "And boots. I fear yers are sodden."

"That would be most welcome, Lady Isolde. It's somewhat undignified being wrapped in nothing but a blanket."

"Yet ye carry it so well."

He laughed, which caused a bolt of pain to shoot through his head, but the discomfort was worth it to witness Isolde's smile. "I hope my circumstances are such that when I regain my senses, I'm able to repay the kindness of ye and yer kin."

"There's no need for repayment, if ye're speaking of goods and chattels. Clan MacDonald will always help those in need. Especially those thrown onto their beach by the sea."

Clan MacDonald. Did he know of them? He tried pushing deeper into the dense fog inside his head, but no flash of recognition ignited. Only a dull throb, a warning to go easy.

Frustration reared its head again, which only made his brain throb harder. It went against all his instincts, but it seemed he had no choice but to let his memories return in their own time.

There was a knock at the open door, and a young serving maid entered. Relief rolled through him at the sight of her arms ladened with a plaid and faded yellow leine. She carefully laid the clothes on the bed, and a pair of boots on the floor, before picking up the bowl he'd used earlier and leaving the chamber.

"Well, I'd best leave ye to it." Isolde eyed the clothes. "Once ye're decent, if ye feel up to it, I'll show ye around the castle. I'm still holding ye to yer promise to help out, once ye're properly back on ye feet."

"I gave ye my word. I'm not about to break it."

She nodded, before glancing at her dog. "Come, Sjor."

He watched her leave the chamber, the solar, she'd called it, and close the door behind her. With a heavy sigh he returned to the bed and pulled on the leine. The plaid proved a harder task, and by the time he was done, exhaustion hovered.

He sat on the edge of the bed and closed his eyes, willing his heart to slow its frantic hammer. There was no denying it. His injury had sucked his strength, and despite how he wanted to spend time with Isolde, the prospect of exploring her castle when he could scarcely even dress himself was daunting.

He'd rip out his tongue before confessing such a thing to her.

The silence wrapped around him. A bed had never appeared so enticing before. Maybe he'd rest his eyes for a few moments and hope it eased the incessant throb between his temples.

He lay on the bed, angling his head so he didn't inadvertently worsen his injury, and closed his eyes. Blessed relief enfolded him, a soothing wave, and the tension in his shoulders faded.

Aye, just a few moments, that's all he needed. And then he'd be fine to explore Isolde's castle.

Except it wasn't her castle he wanted to explore.

It was Isolde.

## Chapter Four

"And I'm telling ye," Freyja said, as the sisters made their way to their grandmother's private chamber, "the man needs to rest."

Irritated that her sister appeared to be implying she gave no heed to Njord's recent injury, Isolde gave her an aggrieved glance. "I know that. I don't intend to drag him about the castle until he's fully recovered. I simply thought he might like the distraction."

"I believe it's distraction enough that he's lost his memories," her sister retorted.

"Aye, and maybe he'll recover them faster if he strolls in the courtyard. The fresh air might blow aside the fog in his mind."

Good Lord, could she not just shut up? She wasn't even fooling herself as to why she wanted to spend more time with her enigmatic stranger, so there was no surprise she wasn't fooling Freyja.

Her sister rolled her eyes. "Aye. I'm not denying fresh air will do him good. But not today. If ye wish to coddle him, ye'll need to do so in the solar."

"I have no wish to *coddle* him." Kiss him, aye. Curses. Why did she keep thinking of his delectable mouth?

"I do not think he'd object, if ye offered." Roisin gave a sweet smile when Isolde turned to her, startled that her sister appeared to have heard her unwary thoughts. "And he *is* very handsome, after all."

"What?" she blurted. It was one thing to find him unaccountably irresistible. It was quite another for her sisters to guess how constantly he'd been on her mind since the moment she'd found him upon the beach.

"Handsome," Roisin repeated. "Although not in the way of the Tuatha de Danann. But 'tis obvious he finds yer company agreeable, Izzie. I'm certain he'd have no objection to ye keeping him company while he recovers."

Ah. Roisin spoke of coddling. Not kissing.

What a relief.

Thankfully, she didn't need to answer since they had arrived at their grandmother's chamber, and after they entered, they sat on their usual stools before the fire.

Their grandmother regarded them in silence from her carved chair behind her desk. The same desk that had been passed down through generations of Sgur MacDonalds and would, one day far in the future, pass into her own safekeeping.

"There's something I cannot fathom about this mysterious visitor of ours."

"There's nothing to fathom, Amma," Isolde assured her. "He's a lost soul, nothing more."

"That I do not deny." Their grandmother drew in a great breath, but a frown marred her brow. "Yet still, something feels amiss."

Isolde kept a placid smile upon her face. Like Roisin, their grandmother often saw far more than anyone would wish. And the last thing Isolde wanted was for her beloved amma to suspect she held anything more than conventional concern for the stranger from the sea.

"Do ye think he feigns his memory loss?" Freyja sounded curious, and Isolde gave her an incredulous glance at the accusation.

"Why would he feign such a thing?" She looked back at their grandmother, but it was impossible to guess her thoughts. "Amma, surely ye cannot believe this of him?"

Their grandmother focused on Freyja. "What is yer view?"

Isolde pressed her lips together. Generally, her grandmother's deference to Freyja in such matters wouldn't bother her. Frey was, after all, an esteemed healer and midwife. But this concerned the stranger. *Her* stranger. And she did not care for how his honor was being questioned.

"Certainly, his injury could cause his memory to fragment." Freyja paused, as though considering the matter. "I believe his story is genuine. I cannot imagine why anyone should fabricate such a tale, especially when the circumstances put their own life in such peril."

Isolde let out a disbelieving *huh*. "Aye, for if Patric and I hadn't ventured onto the beach this morn, the poor man would've died of exposure. A fine plan that would be if he was truly a spy or—or whatever it is ye're insinuating."

"Why would a spy come to Eigg?" Roisin sounded flummoxed by the notion. "And a spy from where?"

"Child, spies are everywhere." Their grandmother sighed and gazed into space, as Isolde and her sisters exchanged startled glances.

Spies were everywhere? Certainly, she'd made the accusation, but she hadn't really meant it. To be sure, one always had to be wary when dealing with other clans, but the Isles were predominately MacDonald, and suspicious behavior by others was never a secret for long.

She shook her head, as if that might clarify things. Of course, she couldn't know for *sure* that her stranger was of Clan MacDonald, but would she feel such an affinity for him, if he were not?

"What are ye suggesting we do, Amma?" Isolde said. "We cannot turn him out into the storm, can we?"

Her grandmother caught her gaze. "I'm suggesting ye be wary, Isolde. That is all. Remember, ye are promised to the son of Bruce Campbell, baron of Dunstrunage."

And just like that, her mood plummeted. Why did her grandmother have to bring that up now? Why did she need to bring it up at all?

So many times during the last ten years she'd questioned her on the vexatious subject, and not once had she received a satisfactory explanation. Well, she deserved one, and if Amma wished to drag Bruce Campbell's son into this conversation, then so would she.

"I've never consented to the match with the Campbell, and I cannot fathom why ye ever agreed to it. All the Campbells want is to strengthen their foothold in the Isles, and why ye seem eager to assist them by sacrificing me into their barbarous clutches is beyond my ken."

Her grandmother's jaw tightened, but it was the only indication Isolde's words had affected her. Until she spoke.

"Ye misunderstand, Isolde. This match isn't for the benefit of Clan Campbell. It is to keep ye safe."

Keep her safe? Of anything she'd imagined her grandmother might say, this wasn't it. It did not even make any sense. The only way to remain safe, to ensure Eigg was protected and prospered, was to stay on the Isle.

"How am I in danger in Eigg? Our foremothers have lived on this Isle for generations without number."

"Truly, Amma," Freyja sounded troubled. "Ye are the one who taught us all how Eigg was known in ancient times as the island of the powerful women, right up until ye were a girl. It's our destiny to protect Eigg and strengthen alliances within our own clan from the other Isles."

"Aye. But we cannot always live in the past."

Something akin to alarm threaded through Isolde's breast. If danger threatened their Isle, why hadn't she shared it with them—or at least, with her, as the eldest?

"But what of the Deep Knowing?" Roisin's voice was hushed, and instinctively Isolde took her hand and gave her fingers a comforting squeeze. Both their mother, before she'd died, and Amma, had often shared the old stories of their ancestors, and the origin of the creed they lived by.

*The bloodline of the Isle must prevail beyond quietus.*

The meaning was plain. Their bloodline could not leave the Isle.

"I cannot explain it to ye, child." Their grandmother gave Roisin a sad smile. "All I know is the path for Isolde does not lie on the Small Isles."

And what kind of answer was that? Isolde pressed her lips together, to keep her retort locked inside. No good would come of it should she tell her grandmother what she thought of such airy-fae nonsense.

But a kernel of disquiet lingered, all the same. For her grandmother was a pragmatic, canny woman, respected throughout the Isles, and not given to flights of fancy. To be sure, an outsider might consider the Deep Knowing, that had been passed from mother to daughter for the last nine hundred years, to be a little strange.

But it was a secret known only to the MacDonald women of Sgur Castle. And there was nothing fantastical about it. It was simply the essence of who they were, and how they were inextricably entwined within the fabric of Eigg herself.

No. She wouldn't let her grandmother's odd insistence that the reason she had to wed the Campbell was to keep herself safe sway her view.

She belonged in Eigg, and nothing would change her mind.

---

HE STIRRED, GROANED, and opened his eyes. The unfamiliar timber ceiling was uncommonly low, disorienting him, and alarm flashed through him.

*Why am I in a box?*

It took but a moment for realization to seep through his fogged brain, and he turned his head, where the doors to the box bed were open, revealing the solar.

He frowned and pushed himself upright. His eyes were gritty, but his head wasn't too bad. Although light streamed into the solar, it wasn't as bright as when he'd discarded the blanket for the borrowed clothes. It seemed his few moments of resting his eyes had turned into something far longer.

Instinctively, he glanced at the door, but it remained shut. Had Isolde returned to take him on the promised tour, only to find him passed out on the bed?

It wasn't a pleasing notion. She'd already seen him at his worst, which was bad enough. He didn't want her thinking he'd lost all his strength to the sea.

The boots were a little tight, but they would do until his own had dried out. Dizziness no longer assailed him as he strode to the door, opened it, and eyed the dark corridor that greeted him.

Now what?

Luckily, a serving maid was approaching with a basket filled with peat slabs. He offered her a friendly nod, which caused her to stop dead in her tracks and stare at him as though he possessed two heads.

He cleared his throat. "I'm searching for Lady Isolde. Do ye know where I might find her?"

"In the courtyard." She jerked her head in the direction from which she'd come. "Do ye want someone to give milady a message?"

"'Tis fine. I'll find her."

He made his way along the dimly lit corridor, which led to the great hall. A fire burned in the large hearth and splendid tapestries adorned the walls, which reinforced his notion that the MacDonalds of Sgur Castle were wealthy indeed. Servants were at their daily tasks, and he felt their sideways glances as he headed towards the far end of the hall.

He pulled open one of the double doors, and the chilled air of twilight hit him. He puffed out a breath and stepped outside. The courtyard spread out before him, but he couldn't spy Isolde among the castle inhabitants who went about their business.

A walk in the brisk air would do him good. He set off, although his pace wasn't as swift as he'd like. Maybe there was no need to march, after all, and he slowed down, taking his time, and the throb in his head receded.

The sky was gray, heavy with clouds, but it wasn't raining, for which he was thankful, although the mighty crashing of waves echoed across the land and the scent of salt permeated the air. He glanced back at the castle and then paused in his tracks as he took in the sight of the massive rocky outcrop beyond the castle. It towered high above the entire keep on the mountain upon which the castle was constructed, a magnificent backdrop that stalled the air in his lungs.

It was unlike anything he'd seen before.

And inevitably, a mocking whisper brushed through his mind.

*Is it, though?*

As he passed by the dovecote, he caught sight of Isolde. She was on the far side of the stables in what looked like a smaller, self-contained courtyard, and he smothered a grin as anticipation fired his blood.

Even the wind didn't feel as bitterly cold.

To his left was the farrier, and to his right the stables, creating a wide alley that led to where Isolde stood in the distance, her back to him. From the corner of his eye, he saw a figure emerge from the shadows of the courtyard, a blade glinting in his hands.

What the hell? Acidic shock spiked through his blood. Christ, the man was about to assassinate her. A woman. An unarmed woman. In her *own goddamn castle*.

He broke into a run, even though he was too far away to save her from injury. Or worse. He'd never reach her in time, but that bastard would never crawl out of here alive. Where was his sword? His dagger? For God's sake, there had to be something—

Isolde swung about, and he came to a skidding halt. She gripped a claymore, and in a flawless arc of beauty, the blade clashed against the man's, sending him reeling back.

She took immediate advantage, following through with another forceful sweep of the weapon. The man recovered instantly, and he watched, staggered to the depths of his soul, as Isolde held her own against the warrior.

Through his stunned brain, comprehension belatedly dawned.

This was a training ground. And Lady Isolde was no mere novice.

He couldn't recall ever seeing a woman with such excellent swordsmanship, and this time he didn't qualify his thought to take account of his faulty memories.

Noblewomen didn't take the sword. Nevertheless, Isolde was magnificent.

Finally, she and the warrior clasped each other's arms, and he stepped forward. Isolde turned to him, and her smile warmed him deep inside. As he drew closer, he recognized the other man as Patric, who, according to Isolde, had helped save his life.

"Ye're looking well," she said, casting her warm gaze over him. Her cheeks were flushed by her exertions, and wisps of fiery hair had become loosened from their bindings and whipped across her face. He had never witnessed a more enchanting vision.

"Aye. And I have ye both to thank for that." He nodded at Patric, who grunted in response. He returned his attention to Isolde. "Yer skill is admirable, my lady. My fear for yer life was unfounded."

She laughed. Even Patric cracked a grin. "'Tis my passion. Patric is a good teacher, and that's a fact."

"Are all noblewomen as skilled with the sword on this isle?"

"They are not." Pride threaded through Patric's response. "Lady Isolde has the blood of her Norse forefathers in her veins."

"Aye," she said, her mesmerizing green eyes sparkling with mirth. "But don't ye forget my formidable Pict foremothers, Patric, lest ye draw their curses upon yer head."

He knew of the Norse. Hell, he knew of the Picts. Why then could he not recall the simple matter of who *he* was?

"No one on Eigg could forget yer Pict foremothers, lass."

It wasn't Patric's familiarity that caused him to give the man a sharp glance. It was the way he said Eigg.

To be sure, Isolde had already told him where they were. But now, incomprehensibly, the name stirred an ember of recognition.

"The Isle of Eigg." Long ago, the Norse had conquered the Small Isles. And before that, they'd been occupied by the Picts. "The Highlands."

"Are ye recalling yer past?" Isolde gazed at him, the hope clear in her eyes.

He pushed harder at the fog, but all that did was cause the pain to return, and he exhaled a frustrated breath. "The history of the Highlands is familiar. But I cannot recall what I did before I awoke in the castle's solar."

"It will come in time." She sounded so certain. "After all, ye know more than the last time we spoke."

It was true. It just wasn't enough. And although Isolde was sympathetic to his plight, he didn't want to discuss it with her. The holes in his awareness, of things he should instinctively know, was demeaning, and the truth was, he didn't want her sympathy, God damn it.

He nodded to the claymore. "'Tis a fine weapon ye wield."

"It belonged to my father. When I was a child, he always said one day it would be mine, but I didn't think to inherit it so soon."

"I'm sorry for yer loss, my lady." Damn his big mouth.

"Ah." She brushed aside his condolences. "I thank ye, but 'tis not recent. Ten years ago, my parents were on the mainland when they succumbed to the fever." Her smile faltered, before she took a great breath and offered him another smile. "It was a shock, I'll not deny. Sometimes, even now, I still think they will return. I know such sentiments are folly."

"Not folly." Briefly, he wondered if he still had parents. Was he close to them in the way it seemed Isolde had been with hers? "Ye must've been but a child at the time."

"We were fortunate. We've always lived here in the castle, with our parents and Amma, so at least we didn't lose our home."

"Ye have no brothers?"

"We do not." Her lips twitched, as though she held back a smile. "I know what ye're thinking. But ye'd be wrong. Even with a brother, Amma would still be the mistress of the castle. It descends through the female line, ye see, from the time of our Pict queen foremother."

"An illustrious lineage. Ye have royal blood, then."

"Aye, but she was a warrior too."

"And that's more important?"

"One day I might tell ye about that queen." There was a thread of laughter in her voice now, and despite how he was slowly freezing to the spot, he grinned back. "Ye'd be awestruck, I have no doubt."

Patric held out his hand to Isolde. "I'll return the claymore. Ye best take him back to the castle to warm up before Freyja discovers he's escaped the fireside."

Isolde looked stricken as she passed the weapon to the older man. "Ye're right. What was I thinking?" She turned to him. "I should not have kept ye out in the cold. Ye're scarcely dressed for it. My sister will have my hide if she finds out. She's of the opinion ye need to rest."

"I have rested. For most of the day, by the looks of it." He fell into step beside her, as her dog quit chasing shadows and came to heel. "And missed the tour of the castle ye promised."

"Never let it be said I don't keep my promises. How does the morrow sound to ye?"

"It sounds grand." Anything that involved spending time with Isolde was fine by him.

"Good. Well, let's see about getting something hot inside ye."

## Chapter Five

Isolde was relieved the darkening day concealed her burning cheeks. Her words were innocent, and yet they echoed around her head, sounding vaguely indecent. Thankfully, her stranger—Njord—appeared to find nothing untoward about her unthinking response.

He strolled beside her, and she slowed her normal pace to accommodate him. He had suffered a head injury, and, as her sister had reminded her, he needed to take things easy.

But it was hard to recall such things when he cut such a fine figure in her father's plaid. No one would guess, simply by looking at him, that he wasn't in the best of health. His shoulders strained against the confines of the linen shirt, and she curled her fingers into fists lest she accidentally stroke his breathtaking biceps.

As they approached the castle entrance, he paused. "That," he said, "is an impressive rock."

And so was his profile. Especially in the twilight, which threw shades of purple across his beautiful bone structure. Without following his gaze—after all, she knew exactly what had captured his attention—she said,

"Aye. Tis An Sgurr, the great ridge of Eigg. The views from the castle are exceptional, but from the peak of An Sgurr, ye feel ye're on top of the world. As soon as ye are able, when the weather is fine, I'll take ye up there and ye'll see for yerself."

They entered the castle and made their way to the fire. Guilt ate through her at how he rubbed his hands together in the heat. She should've brought him straight back here when she'd finished her session with Patric, instead of standing in the cold air flirting with him.

Although, in her defense, she hadn't flirted, had she? They'd simply been talking. But still. The result was the same. The poor man was almost blue.

"There ye are." Freyja's voice, only slightly censorious, cut through her thoughts. "Amma wishes to know if our guest is joining us for supper."

"I should be honored," he said and bowed his head.

Entranced by his bearing, Isolde gazed at him as he responded to her sister's questions on his wellbeing. The mystery of his identity enthralled her. He was certainly the son of a laird, at the very least, which should make finding his kin easier than if he were a serf.

It was bad luck to wish such things, but it didn't stop her from hoping the storm on the sea might rage for just a few days longer, so she could spend more time with her enigmatic Njord.

⸛

THAT NIGHT, AS she and her sisters readied for bed, Roisin sat before the fire, hugging her knees. "The stranger is quite smitten with ye, Izzie."

An illicit thrill raced through her, even though it was foolish to suppose it was true. "His manners are very pretty, and that's a fact."

"I'm not speaking of his manners." Roisin gave a silent laugh. "He is most polite to Amma, but I'd not suggest anything more. Do ye not see the way he looks at ye? Like," she gave a great sigh, and a faraway look glazed her eyes. "Like he cannot believe the truth of his eyes."

Freyja snorted. "Let's not forget the man has a head injury and cannot even recall his own name. It would be foolish to read anything into anything he says or does until his memory returns."

Isolde knew her sister was right. But sometimes, Roisin's view of the world was far more exciting.

"No one is doing that, Frey," she told her sister, even if it wasn't quite the truth. Because, for sure, she had noticed the way he looked at her. With admiration.

And something more.

Heat bloomed between her thighs, and as she combed her hair, she averted her burning face from Freyja. It was odd how deeply he affected her when they scarcely knew anything about each other. Certainly, no other man caused the blood to fire in her veins or breath stall in her throat the way he did. Even when they weren't in the same chamber. And she'd met plenty of MacDonald men from the Isles who were easy on the eye.

"Suppose he never regains his memory?" Roisin rested her cheek on her knees and regarded Freyja. "What will we do with him then?"

"Word will spread among the Isles and to the mainland. Someone will claim him."

"Ye make him sound like a lost puppy." Isolde wasn't sure why Freyja's flippant dismissal of Njord's fate irked her so.

"He *is* lost," Freyja reminded her. "And if he cannot recall his life, what else can we do but try and find his kin for him?"

It was a perfectly reasonable response. But it still rubbed her the wrong way.

Yet what was the alternative? He couldn't remain here on Eigg, in the castle, forever, could he?

FOR THREE DAYS the storm howled across the Isle, making all but essential forays beyond the castle walls folly. On the fourth morning after her stranger had washed up on the beach, the skies finally cleared, and Isolde heaved a sigh of relief as she stood by the window in the bedchamber, the shutters open, breathing in the fresh, cold air.

Being confined within the castle for days on end always made her restless. Although, admittedly, the company of Njord had livened things up considerably. But they had never been alone, and she had the sneaking suspicion her grandmother was behind that.

Which was somewhat insulting. Didn't Amma trust her alone with Njord?

Well, it didn't matter. The weather was fine, and she would show him her beloved Isle. A leisurely walk, to blow away the cobwebs. Even Freyja would approve of that, now the wound on his head had healed so beautifully.

Roisin groaned and pulled the wool coverlet over her head. Freyja sat up, blinking in the light from the lamps. "Is the storm passed?"

"Aye." Isolde leaned through the narrow window and peered out to sea. While the windows on the ground floor had been glazed when her grandmother had been a young woman, such extravagance had not been deemed necessary for the bedchambers. "I believe it's finally blown itself out."

Which meant word could be sent to the other Isles. She tried to tell herself she was glad for it, but that was a lie. Because as soon as Njord's kin knew where he was, he would leave.

Freyja flung back the bedcovers, grabbed her shawl, and rushed to the fire. "I must visit Laoise. Her time is almost upon her, poor wee lass."

Isolde closed the shutters and went over to her sister. "'Tis a pity ye cannot geld her brute of a husband."

Freyja sighed. "After her last babe, I went through all the ancient remedies with her. But I fear she simply cannot remember to take the teas as often as she needs to."

"'Tis not teas she needs. 'Tis a sharp dagger. That'd solve the problem of his unfettered lust well enough."

"I don't disagree with the sentiment, Izzie. But I can scarcely prescribe that remedy, can I? He's not a horse."

Isolde shook her head. Laoise, wife of one of their farmers, was barely twenty, and this was her fourth confinement in as many years. But it wasn't the frequency of her pregnancies that raised her ire. She knew many women across the Isles who reveled in displaying their fecundity and ability to regain their health after confinement.

It was how her husband treated her. As though she were beneath him and her only worth lay in her capability to produce bairns.

Whether she wanted to or not.

"I know what ye're thinking." Freyja eyed her as she pulled on her boots. "But even if the worse thing happens, and ye end up wedded to the Campbell, ye know well enough how to regulate yer moon cycles. Ye'll not be a brood mare, Izzie."

No, she certainly would not. Not for any man. And besides, she hadn't yet abandoned hope that their grandmother would come to her senses about the whole distasteful matter. But even if she didn't, she still did not intend to wed the cursed Campbell.

HE OPENED THE shutters on the windows. It was still dark, but the roar of the storm that had raged for the last three days had died during the night. Had it also calmed over the sea?

The notion was oddly unsettling. Once it was safe to sail, ships would come to the Isle. And with them came the chance of discovering his identity.

God knew, he wanted to find out who he was. And yet he couldn't dismiss the lingering disquiet that, once the truth was revealed, nothing would be the same between him and Isolde.

His nights were filled with scorching fantasies of her climbing into the box bed with him. Enveloping them in their own sensual cocoon.

Of how she would look, by the flickering light of the fire, her hair unbound across his pillows, as he made her his.

He swallowed a groan as the image burned through his mind. It was madness, to want her so, when he had no idea if he had anything worth offering her. Just because she teased him constantly that he had to be the son of a great laird, did not make it so.

She had noble blood in her veins. Hell, royal blood, even.

Distractedly, he raked his fingers through his hair. Even if his lineage was as noble as hers, for all he knew he could be wed.

It no longer hurt his head when he pressed the fog for answers, but the answers he sought were still as elusive as ever. There was nothing he could do about his missing memories. But maybe there was something he could do to help regain a sense of who he was.

Maybe, with a sword in his hand, the fog would recede.

As on the previous mornings, they broke their fast in the great hall, and after Lady Helga left, he turned to Isolde. "I need to assess my skill with the sword. Do ye have a practice target I might use?"

And a spare sword, God damn it. It went against the grain to ask for everything he needed, but there was no help for it if he wanted to discover the level of his abilities.

She gave him an assessing look, a small smile playing on her lips.

*Don't think about her lips.* Inevitably, he could do nothing else, considering what he had fantasized about her doing with her mouth last night. Somehow, he managed to swallow his frustrated groan.

"We do," she confirmed. "But ye'd be far better practicing against a flesh and blood opponent."

"Aye. But I doubt Patric has the time nor inclination to assist in this matter."

"I wasn't thinking about Patric."

It took a moment for him to understand her meaning. "Lady Isolde, are ye offering yerself as my opponent?"

"Why not? I won't go easy on ye, if that's what ye're afraid of."

She was laughing at him. He was still too taken aback by her offer to fully appreciate the way her beautiful eyes sparkled in mirth at him.

"I'd never raise a blade against a woman."

"Ah." She waved her hand at him in mock disgust. "'Tis simply a training session, nothing more. We'll use wooden swords, so I don't injure ye too terribly."

He wasn't in the least concerned that she might injure him, terribly or otherwise. "'Tis still a weapon. I'd never forgive myself if I hurt ye."

She laughed and turned to Roisin. "Hear that? Njord has a high opinion of his swordsmanship."

"Then ye are equally matched," her sister said in her soft voice, but mischief lurked in her eyes, and he laughed when Isolde gasped in mock outrage.

"My honor has been slighted," she said, returning her gaze to him. "Twice over. What will ye do about it?"

"I won't fight ye."

"Why not?"

Was she serious? He'd already told her why not. "It doesn't sit right with me."

Her laughter vanished. "Ye object to a woman learning how to defend herself and her castle?"

What? He hadn't said that at all. "Ye're putting words in my mouth. I'm not attacking ye or yer castle." He recalled the training session he'd witnessed the day he'd arrived at Sgur. "And before ye ask, I think ye'd defend both admirably."

"Aye, but only because I *practice*."

He saw the trap she was setting but with a sense of inevitability, seemed unable to avoid it. "With Patric."

"Not every warrior fights the same. I need variety. Are ye denying me the opportunity to improve my skills?"

"Will ye never let this go unless I pick up a sword against ye?"

"It would show appropriate gratitude for me having saved yer life, don't ye think?"

He shook his head, fairly flummoxed by her. "Ye save my life and want me to attack ye for it. I'm certain I've never met a woman like ye, my lady."

"I shall take that as a compliment, even if ye didn't mean it as such."

"It was a compliment," he admitted. "How could it be otherwise?"

Her smile damn near took his breath away. She looked soft and sweet, as though there wasn't a fierce thought in her head, nor sharp word on her tongue. But he knew different, and thank God for that. A meek and biddable lass would never fire his blood the way Isolde of Sgur Castle did.

"Then we must choose our weapons. The challenge will be set at sunrise."

He could scarcely believe he'd agreed to this madness.

"Wooden swords," he reminded her. At least then the worst he could inflict upon her was bruises, rather than an unwary cut from a blade.

"Indeed. I shouldn't wish to scar yer handsome face, now would I?"

"Don't think to put me off my stride with pretty words, my lady."

She laughed, before dropping a kiss on Roisin's cheek. "Best not to let Amma know of my challenge," she said to her sister, who shook her head in what appeared to be resigned agreement. As though she were well used to Isolde's unlikely escapades. Isolde straightened and looked him in the eye. "Come. I'll take ye to the armory."

The armory was situated next to the farrier's, and when Isolde unlocked the door and showed him inside, he inhaled an appreciative breath at the impressive display of weapons. Sgur Castle was well fortified, and that was a fact.

"Here. See how this suits ye." She handed him a wooden sword, a mocking smile on her face, and he gave a few practice thrusts. He'd far rather use a real weapon, so he could properly judge his skill, but there was no way on God's earth he'd let her know that. She'd likely be only too pleased to exchange the wood for steel.

"It suits me well enough," he told her, but the way she rolled her eyes told him plainly she knew exactly what he really thought.

When they left the armory, the sun had risen, and glimpses of pale blue sky could be seen between the gray clouds. He was glad of his surcoat as they made their way to the smaller courtyard where he'd seen Isolde and Patric the other day, for although the rain had stopped, the temperature had plummeted.

She turned to face him. The morning sunlight glinted on her hair, enhancing the fiery curls that escaped her plait and danced in the brisk wind that whirled about them.

"Are ye ready?" she enquired, and he scarcely had time to confirm before she attacked him.

Her swift assault sent him reeling, and just as swiftly, she backed off, giving him a moment to recalibrate, which didn't exactly soothe his wounded pride at having been so woefully unprepared.

He blocked her next thrust, but she didn't stumble when his momentum shoved her back. Instead, she danced out of reach, a wild gleam in her eyes, and damn if it wasn't the most arousing thing he'd ever seen.

Brutally, he pulled his senses back into line. Isolde wasn't playacting, and if his mind wandered, she would have him. Her next strike hit its target, and the air whooshed from his lungs.

God's blood. In the edges of his mind, he'd assumed Patric had tempered his swordplay with Isolde. That he'd pandered to her whims, and ensured she appeared excellent to onlookers. But as he parried another well aimed thrust, he realized the folly of that assumption.

Isolde was not merely quick on her feet, nor able to give an admirable show of competence. She truly was good. Better than he'd anticipated. Far from allowing her latitude so she might presume they fought on a fair footing, he needed all his innate skill to keep up with her.

Whatever she lacked in brute strength, she made up for with agility. Admiration clawed through him, even while his pride recoiled at the notion of losing to a woman.

Strange. In the armory, he'd harbored the vague notion of yielding beneath her attack. But now, actively defending his position, it struck him as dishonorable.

Besides, he had the strongest suspicion that if she suspected, for even a moment, that he'd allowed her to best him, she'd never forgive him.

He surged forward, catching her off guard. She staggered back under the force of his attack, and he didn't hesitate to take advantage.

He pressed the blunt tip of his sword to her throat. "Do ye yield?"

## Chapter Six

Isolde panted, her heart racing from her exertions, as Njord's wicked grin sent sparks of awareness skittering over her skin. His stormy eyes glinted with triumph, and she had to confess it was more than the swordplay that caused her erratic breath to catch in her throat.

"I yield." Her voice rasped, but she couldn't help that. Instead of easing its frantic hammer, her heartbeat echoed through her bones and filled her head. It should have been alarming, but instead it was intoxicating, and even the knowledge she had lost the challenge faded into insignificance beneath the heat in her stranger's eyes.

With a flourish, he swept the sword aside and then bowed. It was utterly charming, as though he had stepped from the stories Roisin so loved when chivalry had ruled France.

"Yer skill is formidable. Sgur Castle is safe in yer hands."

She shook her head and took his sword from him. "Believe it or not, I know my limitations. But it's good to know I can at least protect myself and my sisters, should the need arise."

"I trust the need will never arise."

"Aye, but at least here, on Eigg, I'm prepared."

He gave her a curious glance as they returned to the armory. Their challenge hadn't gone unnoticed, and she knew within moments the tale of how she had been vanquished would be common knowledge across the Isle. Her handsome stranger had bested her, but she hadn't disgraced herself.

And the next time they fought, she would use what she had learned about his skills this morn against him.

"What do ye mean, here on Eigg?" He held the door of the armory open for her as she returned the swords. "Ye can defend yerself anywhere, Isolde."

An illicit ribbon of warmth flickered through her at how he spoke her name so informally. Her grandmother wouldn't approve of such familiarity, but Amma wasn't here.

He stood beside her as she locked the door from the key on her chatelaine. "I'm bound to this land, Njord." She turned to look at him. He was so close, they were all but touching. How easy it would be to press her hand against his chest. She swallowed, her mouth uncommonly dry, and tried to harness her scrambled thoughts. "Tis the blood of my foremothers in the very earth beneath my feet that gives me my skill with the sword."

He didn't appear convinced. "Maybe 'tis the blood of yer foremothers in yer veins. But I cannot see how the land has anything to do with it."

She sighed. There was no reason why he should understand, yet she wished he did. They turned from the armory, and instead of returning to the castle, they strolled across the courtyard.

"We can trace our Sgur lineage back nine hundred years to our Pict queen ancestor, and all our foremothers since her have spent their lives on Eigg. It is who we are."

"All of them?" Skepticism threaded through each word. "Do women never leave the Isle?"

"Of course." As they made their way down the great hill, Sjor dashed ahead, barking at mist-shrouded shadows. "Doubtless they traveled between the Western Isles, as my sisters and I do. But we know our future lies here. Our bloodline must prevail."

"Tis an illustrious bloodline. But it would prevail whether ye remain on Eigg or not."

They crossed the moorland, but she didn't head to the beach where she'd found him. There was something she wanted him to see.

"I shall tell ye a strange thing." It was something she had never said before, since on the Isles, it was common knowledge. "From time immemorial, the MacDonalds of Sgur Castle had only one daughter in each generation. As I told ye before, the castle and lands pass from mother to daughter. It has always been the way, and the men of the Isles who wed into Sgur understand this."

He gave her a sharp glance. "Ye have two sisters."

"Aye. But in the course of time, it will come to me as the eldest daughter."

"So, yer two younger sisters can leave the Isle if they wish, but ye cannot?"

"'Tis not a question of whether we wish to leave or not. We *don't* wish to leave. But even if we did, we're bound to our beloved land by the word of our foremothers."

He grunted. "But what if one of ye wishes to wed a man who cannot give up his own estates to live here on the Isle?"

"Then he's not the right man."

"This seems a harsh binding."

"Not for me. I could never be happy away from Eigg."

"'Tis beautiful, for sure." But he wasn't looking at her beloved land. He gazed at her, and her cheeks heated, despite the chilled breeze. "But still, Isolde. Yer strength and skill with the sword come from ye, not from the land ye stand upon."

She smiled. How could she not? He was wrong, but she appreciated his compliments on the results of her years of hard work. "Well, 'tis not something I will compromise on."

The specter of the Campell her grandmother wished her to wed hovered in the back of her mind, like a ghoul from the pit of hell. She shoved it aside. She would not think of that now, when her enigmatic stranger from the sea was by her side, his smile an irresistible combination of admiration and intrigue.

It was clear he did not quite believe in the strength of her resolve, but she could excuse him for that when he was still searching for his own origins.

"Forgive me." His voice dropped to a deep rumble, and his hand brushed against hers as they skirted the woodlands. It may have been an accidental touch as they walked side by side, but delightful shivers raced through her, nonetheless.

Especially when he didn't instantly put more distance between them.

Keeping her gaze ahead, she brushed her own knuckles against his. And this time his fingers slipped between hers, capturing her in an illicit embrace.

Her breath caught in her throat, and she looked at him. He gave her an inscrutable smile, as the wind tossed his dark hair across his face with careless abandon. She wasn't quite sure how they ended up in the shadow of the trees, for she had no recollection of moving in that direction. Yet here they were. Half hidden from view, should anyone else be following the same path they had taken.

"Forgive ye?" Her voice was husky, and despite her best intentions, her gaze slipped to his mouth. Dear God. Was he about to kiss her? She held her breath in anticipation, and scarcely stopped herself from rising onto her toes, so as to meet him halfway.

"Aye. 'Tis none of my business, I know." His voice was a bone-melting growl across her senses, and heat bloomed low inside. It was scandalous, and utterly thrilling. "But are ye spoken for, Isolde? Is there a man from the islands who has captured yer heart?"

It wasn't a kiss, but the implication behind his question was almost—no, perhaps even better. A kiss could be fleeting. But what her stranger from the sea was asking . . .

That could mean something far deeper.

"No." It was a whisper. It was all she could manage. "There is no one from the Isles."

*Only a Campbell from the mainland.*

But she wasn't spoken for. It was an agreement made between her grandmother and the Baron of Dunstrunage. She had not given consent to wed William Campbell. They were not officially betrothed.

There was no need for the twist of guilt in her chest.

His fingers tightened around hers, and his calloused hand cradled her cheek. A thousand butterflies filled her breast, and strangest of all, the wind that buffeted them felt as warm as sunlight.

"No one," he murmured, and she could not fathom if he was repeating her words to himself or asking her for clarification. His thumb stroked her warm cheek, and his eyes darkened. It was exhilarating, and yet that cursed twist of guilt would not die.

It was no good. She could not lie to him, even by omission.

"No one I can stomach," she whispered. "My grandmother harbors a mystifying desire to see me wed to a Campbell from Argyll. But we've never met, and I shall not wed a man not of my own choosing."

A frown slashed his brow as though the notion of a Campbell expecting to claim her hand irked him. Ah, how she hoped the notion irked him. The very thought of it made her lightheaded.

"A Campbell?" His gaze was intense, but there was the faintest note of uncertainty in his tone, as though he tried to place the name. Then he expelled a sharp breath, and his fingers slid from her cheek and caressed her throat. Sparks ignited beneath her skin, and before she could stop herself, she grasped the front of his surcoat.

"Is the name familiar?" But in truth, she didn't care, and it was terrible, for the most important thing was that he regained his memories. Yet right now all she wanted was for this moment to never end.

"No."

She heard the frustration in that word. And her heart ached for him. But then he pressed his forehead against hers, and she forgot about everything but him.

"Ye shouldn't wed a man ye don't care for." His breath fanned her face, and a delicious shiver ran through her. "Ye deserve so much more than that, Isolde."

She tipped her head back, and his fingers raked into her hair. "I've no intention of wedding him. He only wants me for my lands, and to breed countless bairns. And I shall tell ye this, I won't be any man's broodmare, least of all a cursed Campbell's. The very notion of it fills me with dread."

"Don't say such things." There was a harsh note in his voice, and his fingers tightened in her hair. "No man should treat ye with such little regard."

Her heart warmed at his vehemence on her behalf. "Don't worry. I'll find a way to stay on my Isle, ye'll see."

"If I knew who I was." He bit off his words and ground his teeth. "I cannot offer ye anything when I can't even recall my own name."

Holy God, was he suggesting he would court her, if he knew his past? Her heart thundered against her ribs, but somehow, she pushed out the words that needed to be said.

"I don't need anything. I have Sgur Castle."

"But what do I have? A man should have his own legacy. That's only right."

"I'm certain ye do. And I know ye'll remember one day, when ye least expect it." She knew no such thing, but it was a small lie, to keep hope alive. "Don't fret about it, Njord."

The dark clouds of frustration that wreathed him faded, and he smiled at her. "How can I fret about anything, with ye in my arms? I thank God every day that ye found me on the beach. How easily I could've perished."

He stepped closer, until there was no space between them. If she held her breath, she fancied she could feel his heartbeat echo through her blood, but of course, that could not be. Not when they both wore so many layers of wool and linen.

Logic didn't stop a ripple of delight coursing through her, though.

He released her hand and cradled her face, his intense gaze roving over her as though memorizing every feature. Then his lips brushed hers, in a kiss as ethereal as a butterfly's touch, and she gave a soft gasp.

He didn't pull back. His hot breath dusted her in an evocative caress before his mouth once again claimed hers, and this time, he wasn't seeking permission.

The tip of his tongue teased the seam of her lips and she opened to him, needing whatever he offered. His tongue pushed into her mouth, a shocking invasion, and thrills spilled across her flesh as he explored and tasted as though he could not get enough of her.

She wound her arms around his shoulders, hugging him tight, loving the way his big body crushed against hers. If only they were not hampered by endless lengths of plaid.

Panting, he broke the kiss, and she clutched fruitlessly at his shoulders, trying to pull him back. His groan vibrated through her, a throbbing counterpoint to her own. "Ye make me lose my mind." He grimaced. "Whatever mind I retain."

"There's nothing wrong with yer mind." She sucked in a great breath, that chilled her down to her lungs. But it didn't help calm her erratic heartbeat. "Just a few holes in yer memory."

His laugh sounded pained. "Aye. And 'tis those holes that prevent me from—" He snapped his jaw shut and shook his head.

She longed to know what he could not say, but her imagination was more than up to the task. Her hands slid from his shoulders to his biceps, and she lingered there, entranced by the solid muscle beneath her fingers. How she would love to glide her palms over them in all their naked glory.

Sjord's wild barking tore her from her bewitching reverie, and she frowned in his direction. In the distance, several women were heading towards them, clearly on their way to the village.

"Ah, curses." With more reluctance than she'd ever admit, she forced herself to release Njord. To be sure, the trees might hide them from view. On the other hand, they might not. And either way was irrelevant since Sjord had already made his presence known. "Unless ye wish to be subject to even more gossip than ye are already, we had best be on our way."

He straightened, glanced over his shoulder, and a dark frown slashed his brow. "I cannot allow yer reputation to be sullied because of me. I'll go further into the woods and wait until the danger's passed."

She laughed. "There's no need for such dramatics, man. Come, we can cut through the trees and rejoin the path up ahead. They'll never know we were skulking in the shadows."

Without waiting for his reply, she took his hand and darted through the trees. Beside her, he laughed, and the uninhibited sound of mirth warmed her heart. She glanced at him, and he winked at her, and for some reason she found it vastly amusing.

They rejoined the path just beyond the rocky outcrop that shielded them from the women and continued onto the village which lay directly ahead. She supposed she ought to release his hand, since the news would certainly reach her grandmother's ears. But the prospect of a reprimand wasn't enough to forego the exhilaration of having Njord's fingers interlaced with hers.

As they reached the village, he shot her a sideways grin before releasing her hand, and she smothered a sigh. He had noble manners, and she could scarcely fault him for it. Even if she secretly wished otherwise.

"A fine village," he said. "I see why ye wished to show it to me."

"Indeed. 'Tis the finest village in Eigg. But that isn't the reason I brought ye here."

"I'm agog with anticipation."

"I feel ye may be mocking me, and considering what I'm about to show ye, that is *not* a good idea."

"Let me guess. We've come to pay our respects at the tomb of yer Pict queen ancestor."

She cast him an approving glance as the kirk of Kildonnan came into view. "Not bad. Except there is no tomb."

They went around the side of the old stone kirk, which had been constructed two hundred years ago or more with an impressively grand arched window that looked out over the graveyard. "Are ye sure ye're ready to learn of my Pict queen ancestor?"

"I feel ye are very like her in nature, so aye, I'm ready to learn about her."

She laughed. "I like to believe I have her fighting spirit. But ye may change yer mind about the rest." She turned and pressed her palm against the stone wall of the kirk. "This has been a place of worship for over a thousand years, ye ken. The Norse, and before them, the Picts, built shrines to their gods. And who knows who were here before them?"

"Don't look at me. I don't even know where I was last week."

She smiled and couldn't resist giving his forearm a comforting pat. "Before the Norse claimed the Isles, Eigg was ruled by a powerful Pict queen. Some say she was a druid from ancient times. Her legacy had passed onto her from her mother, and in turn, she passed it onto her daughter."

"Huh." He gave her another of his bone-melting smiles. "Could she have known her legacy would prevail for so long?"

"I'm certain she wanted it to." The Deep Knowing was proof of that. But the Deep Knowing was something that could not be shared outside her family, no matter how she wished to tell Njord of it. "However, Saint Donnan from Eire took this holy place and built his monastery upon it. But the queen refused to convert to the new religion."

"Damn. Did the saint kill her?"

"He did not. When he refused to relinquish what he had stolen, the queen gathered her warriors—all women, mark ye—and slaughtered the saint and his monks in his newly built monastery."

"A warrior queen, indeed." He appeared amused by the story, as though he thought it nothing more than an intriguing legend. "Ye do have her spirit, I'm sure of it."

She planted her hands on her hips in mock outrage. "Ye do not appear sufficiently awed by how the queen avenged the wrongs inflicted upon her land."

"I'm sure she was a fierce queen. But it was a long time ago."

She sighed. "Aye. But 'tis more than a story. She was willing to sacrifice everything for the love of this Isle. As her descendants, we are blood bound to ensure her legacy endures."

The daughters of Sgur's bloodline could not leave the Isle. She had known this since the first time her mother had told her of the Deep Knowing, when she had been but five years old.

But since she was forbidden to share the Deep Knowing with him, she could scarcely tell him of her conviction of its meaning. And it troubled her more than it surely should.

"Isolde."

She swung about at the sound of Freyja's voice. Her sister looked exhausted.

"How is Laoise?" She took Freyja's hand, and her sister exhaled a weary sigh.

"Poor lass was in labor all last night. Her idiot husband did not think to send word to the castle for me, since he didn't wish to battle the storm in the dark. Thank God I arrived when I did. Her mother and sister were doing their best, but it was a close thing." She drew in a ragged breath. "Thankfully, she is safely delivered of another daughter."

"That's good news, indeed." Although she was certain Laoise's repulsive husband would rage that, once again, his wife had not produced his much-wanted son. "I'll gather a gift basket for her as soon as we return to the castle."

Freyja gave a brief nod before turning to Njord.

"How's yer head after yer fine walk?"

"No pain," he confirmed. "No revelations, either, alas."

"Now the storm's broke, we'll send word to the other Isles. We'll soon discover who ye are."

Isolde smiled and nodded agreeably at her sister's comment. It was, after all, a perfectly sensible comment. It didn't mean she had to like it.

The three of them began the walk back to the castle and had barely left the village when they saw Roisin and Grear heading their way.

"I'm glad we found ye." Rosin fell into step beside Freyja. "Colban MacDonald has just arrived. They're on their way to Skye, but he wanted to stop here and see ye, Frey."

Aye, she bet he did. Colban MacDonald wasted no opportunity to spend time with Freyja, and yet her sister appeared oblivious that he might have an ulterior motive than the usual friendly clan concern. Not that she wanted Frey to end up with the man. Something about him rubbed her the wrong way, although she couldn't for the life of her explain why.

"Well, there ye are." Freyja gave Njord a bright smile. "Maybe Colban can shed light on this mystery."

Aye, maybe he could. And she should be glad of it. But deep in a hidden part of her soul, the unsavory truth lurked.

She was afraid that when they discovered the truth of Njord's past, it would shatter forever any slender hope of them forging a future together.

# Chapter Seven

"So ye're the mindless one they saved from the storm."

They'd returned to the castle, and Colban MacDonald and his men were in the great hall, drinking mead and warming themselves by the fire. He didn't bother smiling at MacDonald's jibe. The malicious gleam in the other man's eye made it clear his remark wasn't said in jest.

"Being unable to recall a few things hardly makes a man mindless, Colban." Isolde sent Colban a smile that should've frozen the man's heart in his chest.

"But ye don't recognize him?" Disappointment threaded through Freyja's voice as she passed a cup of warm mead to her younger sister.

"Can't say I do. He's not from Islay. We don't breed the weak of mind there."

Much as it burned, he bit back the caustic retort on his tongue. The man was an uncouth oaf, but he wouldn't disrespect Lady Helga or her granddaughters by starting a brawl in their home.

Instead, he turned to Isolde, and a spark of amusement flashed through him at the glare of thunder she sent Colban. Not that the man noticed. He appeared unable to drag his gaze from Freyja.

"Ye're quite wrong," Freyja said. "Tis only Njord's strength of mind that pulled him through."

Isolde caught his eye and a smile tugged at her lips at her sister's reprimand. While Colban attempted to justify his comment, he was having the hardest time dragging his bewitched gaze from Isolde's mouth.

God, what had possessed him to kiss her in the woods? Anyone could've caught them, and daughter of the castle or not, she was still an unwed maid and the risk to her reputation was only too real.

Yet the fact remained: given the chance, he would do it again.

"Well," Isolde's voice was low, for his ears only. "We can celebrate that ye're not related to Colban, at least."

He took a swig of mead to hide his grin. "Small mercies," he agreed, and God help him, it took all his strength not to wrap his arm around her shoulders and pull her close.

The truth was, it was a blow that Colban didn't know him. How could he ask anything of Isolde before he discovered his birthright?

"How did ye arrive so early? 'Tis a fair stretch from Islay." Freyja took another long sip of her mead.

"When the storm hit, we took shelter in Muck. We've been stranded there the last few days."

He tried to place the name but couldn't, and familiar frustration ripped through him. If he hadn't taken such an instant dislike to Colban, he'd request to accompany him to Skye, in the hope of finding some answers there.

Yet an insistent voice in the back of his mind would not be silent.

*Would ye?*

If the truth to his identity lay on Skye, and it was unpalatable, he could never return to Eigg.

He'd never see Isolde again.

Isolde leaned in close, pulling him from his wretched thoughts. "'Tis one of the Small Isles, south of us. Ye can see it clearly from here, on a fine day."

"Another MacDonald Isle?" He was only half jesting. During the last few days, he'd learned a lot about the powerful MacDonald clan.

"The Western Isles are MacDonald territory." And then her teasing smile faded, and she sighed. "Ah, well, they were at one time. The cursed Campbells claim more of our land with each passing year."

Just like when she'd told him of the Campbell her grandmother wanted her to wed, a dull flicker of something just out of reach flashed through the darkness clouding his mind. He frowned, trying to hold onto the elusive sense of somehow *knowing*.

Knowing what?

That he was a Campbell?

Unease slithered through him at the possibility. If he were a Campbell, did he know the man Lady Helga wished her eldest granddaughter to wed?

LATER THAT MORNING, Isolde and her sisters returned to the village, ladened with baskets of provisions for Laoise and her wee ones, while Njord accompanied Patric on his daily inspection of the castle's fortifications.

It meant the faithful warrior approved of him.

She knew she risked heartache with the gossamer dreams she could not help but weave about him. Of all the men she'd met across the Western Isles since she'd turned fourteen and began to see them in a different light, not one of them had filled her thoughts while she went about her everyday tasks. Or caused her pulse to race simply by recalling their conversation or how his laugh warmed the very core of her soul.

"Good Eir." Freyja's exasperated voice, tinged with amusement, filtered through her daydreams, and she tossed her sister a good-natured smile. Frey only ever invoked the name of the ancient Norse goddess of healing when the three of them were alone, and for good reason. Not everyone, even on the Small Isles, was comfortable with reminders of gods long since vanquished in the stream of time.

"What?" she responded, and Roisin laughed as she and Frey exchanged looks.

"Ye've not heard a word Roisin and I have said. Which means yer thoughts are far more exciting than overseeing to the castle's administration."

"Ye've had a glow ever since yer walk with Njord," Roisin added. "Did he profess undying love for ye?"

She laughed. "He did not. Nor would I expect him to."

*But how I wish he would.*

"Undying love, indeed." Frey threw their younger sister an indulgent glance. "I suspect he stole a kiss. Or tried to, at least. Am I right?"

She tried to hide her smile at the recollection but failed. "No stealing was involved, I assure ye."

Roisin expelled a great sigh. "I knew it. If only he could recall his past, he could challenge the Campbell for yer hand."

"Those barbarous days are long gone, Roisin," Freyja said. "Besides, if any challenging is to be had, Izzie will undertake it herself, I'm sure."

"I hear he bested ye, Izzie." Roisin shook her head, as though in wonder. "He's a fine champion, which can only mean he's a worthy opponent for any Campbell."

Isolde felt compelled to defend herself. "He's a grand warrior, and that's a fact. I'll be ready for him the next time we fight."

"Do ye think he'll leave with Colban in the morn?" Freyja glanced at her. "'Tis possible John MacDonald of Fincaith might know who our Njord really is. Skye sees far more travelers than we do here."

"I doubt it. Did ye not hear the disrespect Colban displayed?" Isolde shook her head in disbelief that Freyja had missed Colban's bad manners.

Freyja shrugged. "That's just his way. I cannot see that would stop Njord from requesting passage, if it means he might discover his missing memories."

"Well, I can't speak for him and his plans." Isolde flashed her sister a bright smile to hide her uneasy thoughts. Because although it was clear Njord found Colban disagreeable, that didn't mean he wouldn't ask for passage.

She'd simply assumed he wouldn't.

---

ON ACCOUNT OF Colban and his men's arrival, dinner was a more lavish affair than usual, with three courses instead of the customary two. An extra table had been added to their high table in the great hall to accommodate the additional guests, and in the presence of their grandmother, Colban was on his best behavior.

Njord who, as usual, she had managed to seat beside her, raised his tankard, but instead of taking a swig of ale, he said under his breath, "Does Colban think to win Lady Freyja's hand by sweet talking Lady Helga?"

"He can try. But unless Frey changes her mind about seeing him as nothing more than a neighbor, he's wasting his time."

"Lady Helga wouldn't insist on a match between them? I've heard he's well respected in Islay."

Maybe Patric had mentioned it to Njord while she and her sisters were in the village earlier. And considering Patric's view of Colban wasn't far from her own, she could imagine how that conversation had gone.

"He is. But I'm certain Amma wouldn't force the match if Frey is unwilling."

"Yet Lady Helga is determined for ye to wed against yer wishes."

Her mood deflated at the reminder. "I cannot understand her insistence."

Beneath the table, out of sight of everyone, he threaded his fingers through hers, and lightning streaked through her. Hastily, she grabbed her goblet to occupy her free hand so no one might wonder why she'd stopped eating.

"Is it possible," he began, his voice dropping even lower, and she stealthily leaned closer so she might not miss a word. What a hardship. His scent of soap and fresh woodland filled her head, and it was hard to concentrate, especially when his thumb stroked a mesmeric circle over her hand. "That the Campbell from Argyll is forcing Lady Helga's acceptance by outside means?"

She risked looking at him. And could not tear her gaze away. Concern filled his stormy blue-gray eyes, and with his black hair tamed by a length of velvet, he was breathtakingly dashing.

Somehow, she forced herself to answer. "The women of Sgur Castle are not easily pressured by outside forces. I cannot imagine the Campbell is forcing this match." And then, as Njord's frown deepened, the ugly possibility that he might be right snaked through her mind. "What could he threaten that is so bad she would agree to this match?"

Before he could respond, her grandmother spoke. "Ye must be greatly relieved, Njord, that the weather has turned. We have a ship leaving for Oban—on the mainland—at the end of the week. God willing, someone there will know of ye."

Greatly irked, Isolde could not hold her tongue. "Ye cannot expect Njord to travel to Oban when there's no guarantee he'll discover his origins there. What will he do if his kin don't just happen to be at the docks waiting for news of him?"

"I'm not suggesting he should be on the ship, Isolde. Unless he wishes to be."

Curses. She took a sip of her ale, but thankfully it seemed the entire table had not taken note of the exchange between her grandmother and herself. Carefully, she replaced the goblet on the table and tried not to react when Njord gave her fingers a comforting squeeze.

"Thank ye, my lady," he said to her grandmother. "I should be greatly obliged if I might remain in Eigg for a little longer, until my memories return. I'm willing to move from the castle and find lodging elsewhere."

Isolde let out a frustrated huff, but her grandmother merely smiled.

"There's no need for that," she said. "My granddaughter saved yer life, and for that we are obliged to do all we can to return ye to full health. Ye may stay in the castle until we've exhausted all possible means of discovering who ye might be. After that, we will consider further."

LATER THAT AFTERNOON, as twilight settled across the horizon, he stood on the beach where Isolde had told him she'd found him, and breathed in deep as he gazed at the waves that broke on the shore.

Disquiet gnawed his gut, a relentless reminder that, despite being on solid land, in truth, he remained lost at sea, tossed by the uncaring winds of fate.

His senses prickled, a familiar sensation, although he couldn't recall ever feeling it before. But danger spiced the air, and instinctively he swung about.

Colban MacDonald was striding across the sand towards him.

The man stopped short a sword's length from him and regarded him with hostile eyes. "Who are ye?"

Irritation clawed through his chest at what Colban implied. "If I knew the answer to that, so would ye."

Colban's lip curled into a sneer. "Ye might fool the ladies of Sgur Castle, but ye cannot fool me. What do ye hope to gain by this deception?"

Ever since meeting the man, he'd put up with the unsubtle jibes and insults. But they were no longer under Lady Helga's roof, and he'd be damned if he'd let this oaf disparage his word without consequence.

He took a step towards Colban, and the other man visibly stiffened as if the action had taken him aback.

"Are ye calling me a liar, MacDonald?" He didn't raise his voice. He didn't need to. His intent was plain.

Colban stood his ground. It was obvious the sword on his hip gave him a sense of invulnerability, considering *he* possessed nothing more than a basic dagger.

Borrowed, at that.

The knowledge didn't improve his mood.

"I've seen the way ye look at Lady Isolde. I won't stand by and allow a transient opportunist to take advantage of Lady Helga's good nature. So, I'll ask ye again. Who the hell are ye?"

White rage burned through him at the implication he sought to entrap Isolde by dishonorable means. "If ye have issues with me, fine. But keep Lady Isolde out of it."

"Keep her out of it, when 'tis clear ye've set yer sights on her?"

He inhaled a long breath, striving for calm. The man was determined to provoke him for his own twisted reasons, but he wouldn't rise to the bait. "We're done."

"No. Ye're done with yer lying. Since when does a bump on the head cause a man to lose his mind? Are ye here to spy for the Crown?"

The *Crown*? "Ye're the one out of his mind, MacDonald. I'm no spy."

How could he be so sure? Yet in his bones, he knew it was the truth. Nothing would persuade him otherwise.

"Ye know that for certain?" There was a lick of triumph in the man's voice, as though Colban believed he'd caught him in a lie. "When ye cannot recall yer own name?"

"I don't answer to ye." He loaded each word with the scorn the other man deserved, even though, in a discordant corner of his mind, he found it hard to dispute the logic of Colban's accusation. Why was he so sure of some things, yet still in the dark as ever about others?

"There're other ways to make ye talk."

It happened so fast. He reacted on pure instinct, and MacDonald had scarcely gripped the hilt of his sword before his palm slammed onto MacDonald's knuckles, pinning his hand to his hilt, while his fist smashed into the underside of the man's jaw. Colban staggered back, lost his balance, and fell on his arse.

He stepped back, flexing his fingers, as Colban spat blood onto the sand and sent him a glare of loathing. Without another word he turned on his heel and made his way across the beach. From the gathering shadows a figure appeared from the moorland and raised his arm.

"Colban," Patric said, and he couldn't work out whether it was said in greeting or as a warning.

He glanced over his shoulder, but the other man was striding along the beach in the opposite direction. Patric came to his side.

"Watch yer back," he said. "I don't interfere between men's disagreements, but there's no honor attacking an unarmed opponent, whatever the provocation."

He shot Patric a sharp glance, but it was too dark to see his expression. Not that he needed to. For the second time, it seemed Patric had been instrumental in saving his life.

"Aye." His voice was gruff. It hadn't occurred to him Colban wouldn't hesitate to run him through when his back was turned, yet here they were.

God damn it, he needed to regain his memories. Even if the truth wasn't as he hoped, at least he'd know whether he was worthy to fight for Isolde's hand against the faceless Campbell.

When the ship left for Oban at the end of the week, he would be on it.

# Chapter Eight

The following morning Isolde and her sisters, with Grear in attendance, were in the great hall when she saw Colban marching towards them. She stifled an impatient sigh. He had disappeared after dinner the day before and hadn't joined his men for supper, but he now gave the impression of a man on a mission. And doubtless, Freyja was that mission.

"Yer admirer approaches," she told her sister, who flashed her an aggrieved glance.

"He admires my healing skill, that's all. He's told me so many times."

"'Tis a form of flattery," remarked Roisin. "But I'm not convinced he means it."

"He can mean it or not." Freyja sounded irked. "'Tis nothing to me."

She was on her way to meet with her grandmother in the kitchens, to evaluate their winter stocks, but it would be impolite to walk away when a guest was arrowing their way. Even if his target was Freyja, she was the eldest granddaughter and therefore obligated to remain.

Her smile of welcome dropped into a shocked gasp as he drew close, and she caught sight of his livid jaw. "God's teeth, man, what happened?"

He offered her a grim smile. "I shouldn't wish to trouble yer ears about it."

Freyja went up to him and examined his injury. He appeared not to mind when she ran her finger over his jaw. Then her sister stepped back and planted her hands on her hips. "From my observations it seems ye were involved in a fight, Colban."

"Aye, my lady. A man cannot be condemned for defending himself."

Isolde narrowed her eyes as suspicion slithered through her. "Ye were attacked?"

"I'll not cast shade on an unfortunate that Lady Helga has offered charity to."

Irritation burned through her at his remark. It was obvious to whom he referred. "Are ye telling us Njord attacked ye without provocation?"

Colban's jaw tightened. He clearly took offense that she hadn't immediately believed his tale. "'Tis not in my nature to stand by when I see injustice. There's something about him that doesn't ring true. He's out to entrap ye, Lady Isolde. Why else did he wash up on yer beach and claim he'd lost his mind?"

Only when Freyja wrapped her hand around her wrist did she realize she'd taken a step forward. Not that there was any danger of her injuring Colban, since her claymore was stored in the armory.

She drew in a calming breath before she said something to disgrace her foremothers' legacy of ensuring justice prevailed on the Isle, and even managed a chilly smile.

"We appreciate yer concern, Colban. But only a fool would give himself a head injury and risk drowning in an icy sea for no other reason than to . . ." she hesitated. What exactly was Colban implying? It certainly bore no resemblance to the intoxicating lightning that sparked between her and Njord whenever they met. Nothing would convince her that he was deceiving them all, and Colban's veiled denigration of Njord's honor irked her greatly. "Well, do whatever nefarious deed ye are imagining. Lady Freyja examined him herself and proclaimed it was a miracle he survived."

"It's true he would have died on the beach if he hadn't been found until the morn," Freyja confirmed, and Colban's expression darkened further before he swiftly bowed his head.

"I hope ye are right. Lady Freyja, might I entice ye into walking with me before we set sail to Skye?"

"'Tis kind of ye, but I'm on my way to see a patient. Safe travels, Colban." With that, Freyja inclined her head in farewell and departed.

Since it was expected, Isolde forced the words out. "I'll speak with Lady Helga about yer accusation. Now, ye must excuse us. If we don't see ye before ye leave, we wish ye safe passage."

With that, she continued on her way to the kitchens, while Roisin and Grear made their way to the solar to work on their embroidery. She was still quietly seething when she came upon her grandmother in the buttery, cataloguing the wine.

Her mood didn't improve when Amma didn't instantly dismiss Colban's accusations as nonsense.

"For whatever reason, Colban took an immediate dislike to Njord, and this is his way of trying to turn us against him." Isolde flashed her grandmother an annoyed glance. "I wouldn't put it past him to have punched himself in the face to gain our sympathy."

"That's most unlikely."

Aye, it was, but it was surely *more* likely than Njord attacking him for no reason.

"What is it to him who we take into the sanctuary of the castle, anyway?" She knew she sounded waspish but couldn't help herself. "The MacDonalds of the Western Isles never turn their back on their kin."

"That's true." Her grandmother turned to face her. "I've known Colban since he was a babe. I know his character, Isolde. But ye must remember something: the stranger from the sea is likely not a MacDonald, and not our kin. Ye must learn to keep perspective in all matters to be a fair judge of truth."

Isolde pressed her lips together, but the injustice burned deep. She didn't need to ask Njord what had happened. She knew he hadn't attacked Colban. She may not have known her stranger from the sea for long, but she knew enough about him that he possessed honor, and he wouldn't tarnish that honor by punching Colban for no reason.

It didn't stop her from confronting Njord when she next saw him at dinner. He'd once again spent the morning with Patric, and when he took his place beside her at the table, he looked delectably windswept, and the scent of the fresh sea wind clung to him. His smile of greeting sent shivers racing to the pit of her stomach, where they collided into streaks of pleasure, and it was all she could do not to squirm on the bench in disgraceful reaction.

It took her far longer than it should have to realize there were no bruises on his face.

As he dug into his stew with clear relish, she buttered a wedge of bannock and waited until the conversation around the table reached a pitch where they wouldn't be overheard. Then she leaned in his direction and used the bannock as a shield to hide her words from any curious eyes.

"Colban and his men left for Skye this morn."

Njord grunted but appeared disinclined to discuss the other man further. She tried again, even though it went against the grain to mention the subject with him, when she knew Colban had fabricated the entire story.

But she would not have anyone accuse her of being unjust in her dealings.

"He told a fine tale that ye had attacked him without provocation. I only mention this so ye're aware, should anyone else confront ye with it."

She had the uneasy feeling she hadn't been quite as neutral in laying out the facts to him as her grandmother would have wished, but it was too late now. Besides, she didn't need him to deny it. She already knew he was innocent.

Njord gave her a sideways look, his stormy eyes filled with such primal heat it was a miracle she didn't melt into a puddle of molten need at his feet. Hastily, she bit into the bannock to occupy her lustful thoughts, but it might as well have been hay for all she could taste of it.

"I punched him on the jaw, but only in self-defense."

A piece of bannock became stuck in her throat, and she coughed, grabbing her cup, and taking a mighty sip to wash the offending particle away. Njord patted her on the back, which was highly ineffective in preventing her from choking, but she appreciated the gesture, especially when accompanied by the concerned expression on his face.

She waved away the curious glances from the others at the table to assure them all was well, before once again turning to Njord.

"He claims ye were both in a fight and he was the one acting in self-defense." Then she couldn't help herself. "Did he attack ye without provocation, Njord?"

He sighed. "It's done, Isolde, and now he's left Eigg it's unlikely we'll meet again. I don't wish to cause any trouble between MacDonalds."

"Ye may be a MacDonald yerself."

"Aye. But I might not. And that's why I've decided to seek passage on the ship leaving for Oban at the end of the week."

Her appetite fled and she stared at him, aghast. "But ye are not well enough. How can ye travel when ye have no idea if ye have kin waiting for ye at Oban?"

"I can't stay here, hoping a visitor to the Isle might hold the secret to my identity. But one thing I promise ye: as soon as I regain my memories, I'll return to Eigg for ye." Then he leaned closer, his gaze intense, and all she could see was him. "That's if I have anything worth offering ye, Isolde."

Heat suffused her heart, unlike anything she'd experienced before, and it was hard not to simply smile at him like a besotted maid of fourteen. No matter how she longed for everyone in the hall to know Njord had all but proposed to her, now was not the time to share that thrilling news.

But she had to make him understand that regardless of his heritage, he was enough.

"Ye can be the sixth son of an impoverished laird, and not own a strip of land to yer name, and ye'd still have plenty to offer me. After all, I cannot leave Eigg even if ye do discover ye're the laird of a fine castle in the Highlands."

She expected him to grin, not for a dark frown slash his brow. "That's not the point. If I possess a fine castle in the Highlands, then I'm worthy to fight for ye, Isolde. I won't be beholden to Lady Helga's charity."

Colban had thrown the word charity in her face when he'd spoken of Njord. She liked it even less when Njord himself uttered the word.

"'Tis not charity," she hissed. "We're merely helping ye get back on yer feet. What's so bad about that?"

He expelled a measured breath. It was clear he was greatly conflicted, and to be sure, she understood that. But right now, he was simply being stubborn.

"Nothing." He sounded as though he meant the opposite. "But I can't spend the rest of my life indebted to the benevolence of the ladies of Sgur Castle. How can ye not want to know what kind of man I am, Isolde?'

"I do know what kind of man ye are." Except she also understood his frustration. If she had lost her memories, wouldn't she do anything she could to regain them?

Aye, she would. And of course she wanted Njord to discover his past. But she couldn't shake the sense of dread that if he left Eigg at the end of the week, she would never see him again.

FOR THE FOLLOWING three days Isolde went about her daily tasks at the castle, assisting her grandmother in the management of their estates, and practicing her swordplay with Patric as usual. Yet even during the most mundane of duties, a frisson of awareness danced through her blood as though she had overindulged on the finest imported wine from France.

Even when Njord was out of her sight, he was never out of her mind. Their stolen kisses lingered long after they'd parted, and it was becoming harder by the hour to conceal how she truly felt about him.

That afternoon, Roisin joined her in the vault beneath the great hall to assist with the midwinter check of the castle's non-perishables. They worked in companionable silence for a while until finally her sister let out a great sigh.

"Is Njord still determined to leave when the ship sails?"

Isolde sat on a broken barrel and contemplated the half-completed inventory on her lap.

"He won't be persuaded otherwise." She couldn't help the frustration in her voice. It didn't matter how often they spoke of it. He would not change his mind. "It's a foolhardy mission, don't ye agree?"

"He should stay here, with ye."

Isolde gave a faint smile at her sister's impassioned response. So different to Freyja, who thought Njord had set himself a noble undertaking. "Aye. 'Tis a pity his honor is such he won't contemplate doing that."

Although, in truth, that wasn't quite fair. She admired his honor. If only he hadn't decided to tie it so irrevocably with his need to leave Eigg and discover his identity.

"I'm convinced ye're meant to be together, Izzie. If he leaves Eigg, he will return, I just know it."

She wished she had Roisin's faith.

"I'm sure ye're right. But I cannot help but fear..." her voice trailed away, and she shook her head. If, God forbid, he discovered something unsavory about himself, she feared he wouldn't come back to tell her of it. He'd disappear, and she would be left forever wondering.

Roisin grasped her hand. "There's no need to fear." She sounded so sure. "He's yer destiny, and yer key to escaping the Campbell forever."

# Chapter Nine

He was rinsing his hands when Isolde came into the stables and shut the door behind her. She carried a lantern, which she hung on a hook, before making her way to him, her faithful dog at her heels. In the flickering light, her hair was a mesmeric reddish-gold glow, and a burning pain stabbed through him at the knowledge of how easily she could slip through his fingers.

"There's no need to be working in the stables." She smiled, but there was a note of censure, too.

He shrugged and dried his hands. "I like to make myself useful. Besides, it's a balm to my soul, being with the horses."

She glanced around, as though ensuring they were alone. He took her hands and pulled her close, savoring her elusive scent of lavender, and with a barely repressed groan, captured her lips.

Her arms locked around his shoulders and her sigh vibrated inside his mouth. She tasted of the forbidden, of a prize out of reach, but he couldn't release her. He could never release her in the scarce moments when they found themselves alone.

He plunged his fingers through her glorious hair, holding her head as he trailed hot kisses along the delicate line of her jaw. She tipped her head back, and he grazed her throat with his teeth, and her shudders of pleasure sent bolts of fire arrowing straight to his cock.

"Christ, Isolde." For a fleeting moment, sanity returned, and he buried his face in the sweet curve between her neck and shoulder. Lust roared through him like a ravenous beast, and he squeezed his eyes shut, grasping for control, but with every frantic thud of his heart, restraint slid further from his reach. "Ye've bewitched me. I cannot get ye out of my mind."

"Then ye've bewitched me too." Her teasing smile faded, and he braced himself for what he knew was to come. "Please, Njord, don't leave. Stay a little longer. Yer memories will return. There's no need to leave to find them."

He pressed his forehead against hers, as his hand slid beneath her surcoat and hugged her waist. "I must." His throat was raw. Surely, she knew he had no choice but to leave. "I want to know who I am, Isolde. I want to hear ye call me by my God-given name when I finally make ye mine."

The vivid image of her lying on his bed, her hair spread across his pillows, filled his mind, and it was so real, so visceral, the breath stalled in his throat.

"Then let me come with ye," she whispered, and he frowned, trying to process her words. Had lust caused him to hear things?

"To the mainland?" He gazed into her beautiful green eyes and all but forgot why he'd asked the question. What else could possibly matter, when Isolde was in his arms, begging him to stay? God, if only things could be that simple.

"We could travel in the spring," she said, her hands cupping his face as though she feared he might pull back. But even though he had to leave, in this moment, he was powerless beneath her spell. "And take a small contingent with us. Patric will come, I'm certain of it. And then ye'll not be alone while ye search for yer kin."

It was tempting. Too damn tempting. But spring was months away. And in the meantime, he'd endure the ceaseless gnaw deep in his chest of not knowing his own worth. The irresistible vision of Isolde would haunt him whether he stayed or not, but at least if he left Eigg the danger of one day losing what little control he retained when they were alone together would no longer hang over his head like a poisoned fog.

He wound his arm around her waist, securing her, and silently cursed at the twist of fate that had brought him to a woman he couldn't imagine living the rest of his life without—and yet the very circumstances under which they had met was why he had to leave her.

"I must do this without yer help, mo chridhe."

She gave a choked gasp at his endearment, and her fingers tangled in his hair. The words had slipped out, unintended, but he meant them.

She was his heart. He hoped he might one day deserve hers.

The stable door creaked, and they sprung apart as though the fire that scorched his blood had burst into flame between them. Frustration roared through him, and he sucked in a shuddering breath before grabbing the lantern he'd brought with him earlier and handing it to her.

He'd be damned if their clandestine kisses caused her reputation to be tarnished. No one would conclude he had taken advantage of her if she held a lantern.

A stable lad entered, and after a quick glance in their direction, hastened to his tasks. Isolde stepped back, but her gaze never wavered from him, and her smile told him she knew exactly what was on his mind and found it amusing.

"Then we shall see ye shortly, Njord," she said, as though finishing a conversation that had been interrupted, and loud enough for the lad to hear without straining his ears. "Good eve to ye."

※

As Isolde and her sisters stood by the fire in the great hall after supper, their grandmother came to her side. There was a familiar, unsmiling expression on her face which meant she had serious issues on her mind. "Isolde, we must speak."

She hid her flare of impatience as best she could. She'd planned on spending some time with Njord. Even if they weren't alone in the great hall, and even if her sisters joined their conversation, it was far better than the alternative of not seeing him at all.

Certainly, better by far than enduring an audience with Amma. There was no doubt in her mind that her grandmother wanted to discuss Njord's imminent departure and how she, Isolde, now needed to resign herself to a future with Bruce Campbell's son.

As if *that* would ever happen. And there was even less likelihood of it happening now she knew for sure how Njord felt about her.

As she accompanied her grandmother to her private chamber, his husky endearment echoed through her mind and sent delightful ripples of desire between her thighs. Before he left Eigg, she would extract an oath from him, that he would return to her, no matter what he discovered about himself.

His honor would not allow him to break such a promise. And whatever the outcome of his visit to Oban, she was determined they'd end up together.

"Isolde." Her grandmother's voice, with a hint of ice, pulled her brutally back to the present, and she sat on her usual stool before the fire, Sjor at her feet, as Amma took her place on her chair. "Ye were observed leaving the stables shortly before the stranger from the sea."

Taken aback by the statement, Isolde stared at her grandmother. Who had told her? And whose business was it to tell tales on her anyway?

"Is that a crime?" Curses. Why did she sound so defensive?

"To be alone in the stables with a man we know nothing about? 'Tis not a crime. But 'tis hardly prudent."

"We weren't alone. A stable lad was in there." Had he spoken to Amma? It was so unlikely as to be laughable, yet she couldn't think of any other possibility.

"Child."

She couldn't recall the last time her grandmother had called her that. Generally, she used it when addressing Roisin, and it was a term of endearment. But now it was nothing less than a reproach.

"Aye?" And she still sounded defensive. As though she had something to hide. But she wasn't guilty of anything, and neither was Njord.

"I watched ye enter the stables. And I saw ye leave."

The injustice seething in her chest flooded her cheeks with mortified heat. Was her grandmother spying on her now?

"We did nothing wrong." It burned her that she even felt the need to say that, but she wouldn't have her grandmother thinking Njord had besmirched his honor.

"He will be gone in two days." Her grandmother's voice was gentle, and somehow that was even worse than if she'd shouted at her. "That's his choice, Isolde, and I respect him for it. I don't doubt he has feelings for ye, but he cannot offer ye the future ye need. The future ye deserve as a daughter of Sgur."

Isolde pounced on her grandmother's last words. "And a daughter of Sgur can never abandon the Isle. I don't care what ye've promised Bruce Campbell. I have no use for his son, and I shall not wed him."

"We've discussed this before—"

"But we haven't." She knew she was being unforgivably rude, but she would no longer pander to this inexplicable whim of her grandmother's. "The most ye've ever shared with me was the other day, when ye said it was for my benefit, and not Clan Campbell's. How can it benefit me when I don't want it?"

"Ye must trust me. I can say no more."

Frustration clawed through her. She loved Amma, and they had rarely disagreed until the shattering revelation ten years ago when her grandmother told her what she expected from her.

"Will ye hog tie me and have me dragged from Eigg to fulfil this promise ye made the Campbell?"

Her grandmother blanched, and for a fleeting moment Isolde regretted her harsh words. But it was only for a moment. Because when Lady Helga angled her jaw in that regal way she had, Isolde knew there was no hope in changing her convictions.

"Ye're a MacDonald of Sgur. Ye'll never disgrace yer foremothers in such a manner."

It was true, but it was also infuriating to have that fact flung in her face. She drew in a deep, calming, breath, and Sjor gave a soft whine, centering her. She'd never learn the truth by antagonizing Amma.

"Forgive me. Ye know I'd never bring shame upon our lineage. But I must know. Why are ye so set on this alliance?" And then a terrible possibility occurred to her, and she gasped. "Do they threaten war if I don't agree?"

God help them, that must be why her grandmother was so determined for this match to go ahead. Njord had been right. Why hadn't she realized it before?

Amma closed her eyes and drew in a long breath and Isolde gripped her fingers together in dread. Then her grandmother looked at her.

"Clan Campbell holds no such threat over my head, Isolde. It was I who approached Bruce Campbell with this proposition."

Her anger against the Campbells seeped from her as anguish squeezed her heart. "But why?" she whispered. "Why would ye turn from the Deep Knowing?"

*Why would ye turn yer back on me?*

Her grandmother pressed her lips together. She wasn't going to say anything more. Yet somehow, it no longer mattered. There was no great conspiracy among Clan Campbell to claim the MacDonalds of Sgur's lands.

Her own Amma had offered her to them on a gilded platter.

"I didn't turn my back on the Deep Knowing." Her voice was scarcely above a whisper. "This is the will of the Deep Knowing,

Isolde. The dreams that plagued me from the night of yer birth ended only after I pledged ye to William Campbell. I cannot tell ye why. I can only tell ye that, for a reason I don't understand, yer bloodline must prevail away from Eigg."

※

ISOLDE COULD NOT sleep, and neither could she toss or turn, since that would awaken her sisters. Instead, she lay rigid on her back, glaring into the darkness, as her grandmother's enigmatic confession thundered around her head.

She had never mentioned dreams before. What did she mean, anyway? No one made life-altering decisions simply based on a *dream*.

Especially when that decision concerned someone else.

For ten years she'd assumed Bruce Campbell had somehow persuaded Lady Helga, and most likely by foul means, to agree to a match between his son and her eldest granddaughter. Which was bad enough.

But the truth was far worse.

She wouldn't wed the Campbell to satisfy her grandmother's incomprehensible conviction that doing so was somehow the answer to vanquish Amma's bad dreams. She'd never heard such nonsense in her *life*.

The injustice and, she couldn't deny it, the sense of betrayal burned through her, twisting her stomach into knots. She hadn't even had the chance to speak with Njord last night, as when she'd finally escaped her grandmother's clutches, he had disappeared. And although she could have confided in her sisters, for the first time in her life she hadn't, and she still couldn't quite understand why.

Roisin would be completely sympathetic, and Freyja would, no doubt, dismiss the whole dream thing as a strange aberrance on their grandmother's part.

But she hadn't been able to find the words.

No, that wasn't true. At least, it wasn't the whole truth. Because it wasn't her sisters she wanted with her when she spilled out her hurt. It was Njord.

Ah, this was unendurable. Stealthily, she eased out of the bed, picked up her shawl, and wrapped it tightly about herself. The fire had burned low, which meant it was the early hours of the morn. Too early for any of the servants to be about to witness her nocturnal visit.

It was scandalous to even contemplate going to see Njord now, but she was too wound up to sleep, and if she didn't speak to him soon she'd go mad.

In the antechamber, she lit an oil lamp, and bade Sjor to stay, before she cautiously made her way down the stairs and to the solar. At the door she hesitated and glanced over her shoulder. Although she was often up in the early hours, the castle was never this still, and it felt strange not to encounter even a single servant.

But then, that was just as well, considering what she was doing.

Gently, she tapped on the door, but he didn't bid her to enter. She bit her lip and pressed her ear against the wood. Was he asleep? It was most likely. Why wouldn't he? Most sane people would be.

Curses. Now what? Should she knock again, or creep back to her own chamber and pretend this madness had never assailed her?

Since she was wider awake than ever, and still as churned up over her grandmother's revelations, she took a deep breath and raised her fist to knock on the door once again.

She never got the chance. The door swung open, and Njord stood there, holding a candle, and wearing an expression of supreme astonishment.

"Isolde?" His hushed voice sent shivers along her arms. Although perhaps the fact he wore only his shirt, with his hair deliciously disheveled, had something to do with it too. "What in the name of God are ye doing here?" He sent a swift glance over her shoulder, before returning his gaze to her. "Is anything amiss?"

"No," she whispered. Good Lord, wasn't he going to invite her inside? "May I come in?"

For a moment he stared at her as if he had no idea what she was talking about. Then he stood back, before shutting the door behind her. Shadows wreathed the chamber, and it was very different, being here alone with him in the solar at night, than it was during the day.

Her mouth dried and her heart hammered in her breast. With only the dull glow from his candle and her small oil lamp, he appeared so much bigger than he did in daylight, and towered over her in a way that was both breathtaking and a little alarming.

It had seemed such a grand idea to come and speak with him when she had been safely in her bed. But now she was here, she could scarcely believe she'd carried through on her harebrained scheme.

She should have waited until the morning. But it was too late to change her mind now and truth be told, she didn't want to.

She needed his arms around her. His kisses to reassure her all would be well. Most of all, she needed him to promise that he would return to Eigg—to her—when he'd discovered his past.

To return to her even if his memories never came back.

# Chapter Ten

Isolde stood before him, the lamplight flickering over the delicate features of her face, and he expelled a tortured breath. When he'd opened the door to her, he'd feared he had fallen into a fevered dream, but she was no nighttime fantasy. She had come to him, despite all the risks that entailed, and he could scarcely fathom it.

Her plait trailed over her shoulder and errant red-gold curls brushed her cheeks and she gazed at him, more tempting than any of the forbidden visions that haunted him whenever they were apart.

He should send her away, while he still could. But instead, he remained mute, drinking in the reality that Isolde was in his chamber, and there could be only one reason for it. Especially since her faithful dog did not shadow her heels as he usually did.

"Did I wake ye?" Her voice was hushed.

"No." It wasn't quite the truth. He'd been half asleep, his mind filled with lustful images of seducing Isolde, but he wasn't going to tell her that. "But it wouldn't matter if ye had."

He took her lamp and placed it, and his candle, on the table beside the box bed, before taking her hand and pulling her close. Lust thundered through his veins and pounded at his temples, and he was so damn hard he feared for his sanity.

His honor was all he possessed. The only thing he had in the world, to prove to Isolde he was worthy of the trust she put in him. But he feared it wasn't strong enough to resist her when she melted against him, and when the beat of her heart sank into his blood like a powerful aphrodisiac from the dawn of time.

She released a shaky breath. "I should have waited until the morn. Ye'll think me foolish, but I cannot help the hurt I feel."

"Hurt?" With more difficulty than he'd ever admit, he hauled his rabid hunger back and tried to focus his desire fogged brain. What had he missed? And then a possessive wave of outrage boiled through him, and he cupped her jaw, tilting her head back so she looked at him. "Who's hurt ye?"

She shuddered before taking a great breath, and he steeled himself for her revelation. No one had the right to upset his Isolde and, stranger from the sea or not, he'd ensure justice prevailed.

"I cannot believe Amma would do such a thing, but she told me so herself."

He knew she called Lady Helga *amma*, an old Norse word for grandmother, and his righteous anger ebbed. Whatever Lady Helga had said paled to insignificance against the myriad insults against Isolde he'd imagined during these last few moments.

"What did she do?" Tenderly, he brushed an irresistible curl from her cheek. Her skin was soft and warm, and he swallowed, battling against the urge to sweep her into his arms and take her to bed.

It seemed she hadn't appeared at his door for the reason he'd imagined.

Her fingers traced along the front of his shirt, and he tensed. She wasn't being provocative on purpose. The reminder didn't help cool the fire licking through his blood.

And then she grasped his shirt and a frustrated groan lodged in his throat.

"It was her." Her whisper was agonized, and he forced himself to focus on what she was saying, and not what she was doing to his body. "It was Amma who approached Bruce Campbell about an alliance. How could she betray everything we believe in?"

He knew how little Isolde thought of Clan Campbell, and over the last few days he'd learned—relearned, most likely—how the Campbells had eroded the MacDonalds' power over the Western Isles.

The possibility that Lady Helga had been coerced into agreeing to an alliance between Isolde and Bruce Campbell's son had lodged in the back of his mind. Only a laird from an equally powerful clan stood a hope of challenging such an alliance. It was the reason why he needed to leave Eigg and find out who he truly was.

But if Lady Helga was the driving force behind it, how did that change things? He couldn't challenge a noblewoman with ancient royal blood in her veins. A lady who'd allowed him to recover in her own castle.

Frustration curdled deep in his gut. "So it's not the Campbells holding ye to this betrothal?"

"Ah." She gave a bitter laugh. "The alliance with the MacDonalds of Sgur is too enticing for any Campbell to disregard. Amma may have made the first approach—and I'm not certain I can ever forgive her for it—but ye can be assured Bruce Campbell won't let the prospect of digging his claws into Eigg slip through his fingers."

"I swear to ye, Isolde, if I have the bloodline, I'll challenge every damn Campbell for the right to make ye mine."

She hitched in a jagged breath. "I don't care about yer bloodline."

His smile was grim. If only it could be that simple. "I do. And so will Lady Helga."

"Promise ye'll return to me, Njord." There was a note of desperation in her voice, that tore through him like a barbed lance. "No matter what ye discover, whoever ye turn out to be, ye must return to Eigg and let me know. Don't leave me wondering for the rest of my life."

"I wouldn't do that to ye." His voice was rough, and guilt ate through him. Because if he discovered he wasn't fit to wipe her boots, he'd no intention of seeing her again. Or of facing Lady Helga, with the knowledge he had nothing to offer her granddaughter. Only humiliation waited for him on that path.

But she clung to him, her bottom lip trembling. How could he deny her anything when she gazed at him with such faith? Before he could stop himself, he raked his fingers through her hair and cradled her head. "I promise I'll return."

She gave a ragged sigh and gave him a tremulous smile. "Thank ye. I could not bear it if ye deserted me."

He pressed his forehead against hers and tried to ignore the hammer of his heart that filled his head and made coherent thought so hard. The last thing he wanted to do was hurt her. And how would returning, only to tell her they had no chance of a future together, do anything but hurt them both?

But now he'd promised her. Even if it killed him inside, he'd keep that promise.

She wound her arms around him, and he tugged her close. Too close. Unlike every other time when they'd been together, they weren't wearing heavy plaids, and he screwed his eyes shut and savored the sensation of her body melting against his.

She sighed and her shawl slipped from her shoulders. Roughly, he shoved it to the floor. She wore only a shift, and there was no way on God's earth that she couldn't feel his erection burning against her through his shirt, but he couldn't pull back. It was a sweet torture, but he'd rather this, than nothing.

Her hands slid over his back, coming to rest just above his backside, and she tipped her head back, catching his gaze. Her eyes were dark with passion, her uneven breath warmed his jaw, and then she went onto her toes and kissed him.

---

ISOLDE'S EYES CLOSED in bliss as Njord responded, his mouth claiming hers in a kiss that vibrated to the core of her being. It was reckless, and she should leave before she entirely lost her senses, but surely one more kiss would not hurt.

His fingers tangled in her hair, a savage gesture, and sparks of desire prickled along her skin as he freed her hair from its bindings. Her breath caught in her throat as he ravished her mouth, his tongue teasing and exploring as though he had never tasted her before.

It was heady and magical, and her fingers grasped his shirt, tugging at the material until she felt bare flesh. A strangled groan escaped, but she could scarcely tell if it was her or Njord. Her heart thundered and his hard length dug into her stomach, hot and thick, and she had the dizzy sensation that if his strong arms were not about her, she'd sink to the floor in a boneless heap.

She traced her fingertips over his naked buttocks and his hips flexed, pushing his magnificent erection even more securely against her. A shudder raced through her as she palmed his tight arse, and in response, he tore his mouth from her and panted in her face.

For the last week, his face had haunted her dreams, and she could recall every aspect of his features when they were apart. But now, as he gazed at her with raw lust glowing in his eyes, a fierce, predatory determination emanated from him, and she scarcely recognized him at all.

It was utterly thrilling.

"Ye should go, Isolde." His voice rasped in the heated space between them, but he made no move to release her. "If ye stay, I cannot trust myself..."

He didn't finish his thought, but it didn't matter. "I trust ye," she whispered. And she wasn't certain whether she meant she trusted him not to compromise her, or she trusted him to compromise her in the most breathtaking way imaginable. And then, because his honor was so much a part of who he was, and he would never take her if he suspected she harbored even a slender doubt, she rose onto her toes and murmured against his lips. "There is no one else I'll ever want to give myself to but ye, Njord."

A shudder rippled through him, and although surely it was not possible, his manhood pressed harder than ever against her.

"I cannot take yer maidenhead. Not like this." His hoarse words, an attempt to dissuade her, failed when his hands roamed down her back and cradled her bottom.

She gasped, her fingers involuntarily digging into his flesh, and his grin verged on madness as he stroked her in an intimate caress. Somehow, she found her voice.

"Ye cannot take it if I give it freely."

He gave a rough laugh before he grasped her shift and inched the material up her legs. How could the delicate slide of her hem against her skin feel so decadent?

"I've dreamed of this." He kissed her, a deep, exploring kiss, that sent quivers of need cascading through her vitals. His knuckles skimmed her back, and belatedly she realized what he was doing.

Her gaze caught his and slowly she released him. With infinite care, he tugged her shift over her head before dropping it to the floor.

And she was naked before him.

Her mouth dried as his hungry gaze raked over her. The fire had burned low in the hearth, and although the lamp and candle threw out a golden glow, most of the solar was in darkness, but there was surely enough light for him to see every curve of her body.

Heat washed through her, but she had scarcely moved to cover herself when he threaded his fingers through hers, preventing any show of belated modesty.

"My dreams were sadly lacking." Had she imagined that note of awe in his voice? Her tense muscles relaxed, and she offered him a small smile. But it seemed he hadn't finished. "Ye're beautiful, Isolde. I can scarcely believe my good fortune in having found ye."

"We found each other," she whispered, and he kissed her, tenderly, almost reverently, and she quivered as desire licked through her like a molten flame.

"Ye're cold," he muttered but she didn't feel cold. Not when the heat from Njord's body swirled around her like an ethereal embrace.

He swept her into his arms, and she gasped, clutching at his shoulders as he strode to the bed. "Don't want ye catching a chill."

"I'm certain it would be worth it."

His smile took her breath away, before he gently lowered her to the bed. "I'd never forgive myself."

He followed her onto the bed, kneeling over her, entrapping her between his muscular thighs. The wooden sides and ceiling of the box bed wove an aura of intimacy around them, and Njord was scarcely more than a dark shadow above her. Yet somehow, not being able to see every feature of his face made this illicit rendezvous exquisitely intoxicating.

"Why are ye still robed?" She tugged at his shirt, and for answer, his teeth gleamed in a wicked smile before he ripped the offending article over his head and flung it onto the floor.

She sucked in a wonderstruck breath as the flickering light enhanced the intriguing shadows across his magnificent chest. Daringly, she traced a finger from his throat to his navel, delighting in how he tensed his muscles in reaction to her touch.

Before she could explore further, his mouth crashed down on hers, and his hard body pinned her to the bed. She pulled her hand free and ran her fingers along his back. His groan vibrated inside her mouth, sending featherlike flutters of need arrowing to her core, and she writhed beneath his unyielding strength.

When he braced his weight on his knees, she clawed his hair in protest. "Njord." Her voice was so husky she scarcely recognized it.

He gave a grunt of amusement, or maybe pain, she wasn't sure. "I'm not going anywhere, mo chridhe."

Her heart melted at the endearment. There was no other explanation for why warmth flooded her breast and surged through her blood and she loosened her death grip on his hair.

He lowered his head and trailed kisses along her throat, as he cupped her breasts and teased her nipples with his thumbs. She arched into his touch, and gasped in pleasure as he took her sensitive peak into his mouth.

Her fingers tangled in his hair, a silent encouragement, and he sucked her tender nipple, and her ragged breath filled the chamber.

When he inched down her body, his fingers skimmed her waist and hips in a featherlight touch that left ribbons of fire in his wake. His hot, uneven, breath dusted her flesh in a sensual caress, and she shuddered, desperately needing more.

And then he shifted, rising above her, bracing his weight on his hands as he kneed her thighs apart. The breath stalled in her throat as his calloused fingertips traced across her stomach and the tops of her thighs, igniting a wild craving deep inside that she'd never imagined could exist.

Restlessly, she stirred beneath him, her legs wrapping around his thighs in a futile effort to pull him down on her body again. But he was immovable, keeping his distance as though he enjoyed hearing her sighs of protest.

Her eyes closed as his fingers teased her thighs, circling higher with every stroke. And then his tongue licked her slit. Shock spiked through her, and instinctively she pushed herself upright. His dark head was buried between her thighs. She had never seen a more mesmerizing sight.

"Njord." Her whisper was hoarse, and when he didn't answer, but instead slid his tongue inside her, she collapsed back onto the bed, panting erratically.

Somewhere in the back of her pleasure-fogged mind a small voice of reason urged caution. But she was beyond rational thought as fiery spirals ignited wherever his magical tongue explored.

He gripped her bottom, and her fingers dug into the mattress as his mouth worshipped her. She hovered on the precipice, so close to something she could scarcely imagine, yet clinging to what she already knew. And then his tongue pushed against her clit and her reason liquified. Involuntarily, her muscles tensed, and she gave a choked gasp as unimaginable bliss consumed her.

Before she had time to catch her breath, he imprisoned her hips between his knees and pressed her breasts together. Dazed, she could only watch as he pushed his thick manhood into the deep valley he'd created, and renewed ripples of desire claimed her at this most unexpected move.

"But . . ." she gasped. Was he not going to claim her maidenhead?

"Isolde." He sounded wild, primitive, and as he rocked between her breasts her questions fled as need consumed her. "Hold me."

Enthralled by his command, she threaded her fingers through his, and the sensation of her hands covering his while he cupped her breasts pushed her perilously close to the edge once again. He gave a strangled groan and then went rigid before his hot seed flooded her.

Gasping, she wrapped her arms around him as he collapsed on top of her. Her heart thundered, and his harsh breathing filled her head. Time lost meaning as she clung onto him until, at last, he raised his head and gazed at her.

"Don't move." His voice was hoarse as he left the bed, before returning with a damp cloth. Tenderly, he wiped her breasts and throat and then dried her with another cloth. Spellbound, she watched his face as he concentrated on his task, as though ensuring her comfort was the most important task he'd ever undertaken.

Finally, he was satisfied, and once again lay beside her, pulling her into his arms and dropping a lingering kiss upon her head. She snuggled close, her fingers playing with his sprinkling of chest hair, loving how he idly caressed her shoulder.

"I didn't imagine a man could be so heedful," she whispered.

"I would never risk getting ye with child." Tenderly he cradled her face, and she mirrored his actions, loving how his day-old beard chafed her palm.

She didn't tell him her moon time was due in two days, which would wash out his seed before any consequences could arise. Or that she knew full well how to regulate her menses even during her fertile phases.

That was women's knowledge, and besides, there was no need. He'd taken it upon himself to protect her, and even though she wished his honor had not been quite so immovable, she couldn't deny his strength of will left her breathless with admiration.

"Only a man of honor would take such care." She brushed a soft kiss across his lips. "When ye return to Eigg, there'll be no need to hold back."

"Aye. I pray ye're right, Isolde." Then he sighed heavily. "I don't want ye to leave, but we cannot risk ye being found here."

She slumped against him. He was right, but the last thing she wanted to do was leave.

With clear reluctance he untangled himself from her and gathered her clothes. She pulled on her shift and shivered as the cold linen slithered over her skin, and Njord wrapped her shawl around her before pulling her into a rough hug.

He walked with her to the door and peered outside into the gloom before turning to her. "No one is around. Dream of me until dawn, Isolde."

## Chapter Eleven

The following morning it was hard for Isolde to keep the besotted smile from her face. Thankfully, her sisters had still been asleep when she'd returned to their chamber, but after she had slid into bed beside Roisin, slumber had eluded her.

Doubtless she would pay for her lack of sleep later, but today was Njord's last day before he left Eigg, and she intended to spend the entire time with him.

"Ye don't look too sad that Njord is leaving on the morrow." Roisin gave her a concerned glance as they dressed in front of the fire in their chamber.

"Ye don't look sad at *all*." Freyja raised her eyebrows, and while Isolde didn't especially want to keep the wondrous hour she had spent in Njord's arms from them, it was something she would share once he had sailed.

But for now, it was a magical secret she hugged close to her heart.

"He's determined to discover his past," she said, scrutinizing her boots so she didn't have to look at her sister. She had the feeling that, if she wasn't careful, Freyja might very well guess what she'd been doing earlier this morn. "But he's grown fond of Eigg, and I'm certain he could be happy living here, should he wish."

And after what they'd shared, she was more than certain he'd be happy to remain on Eigg. Once his memories had returned.

*Or even if they don't.*

"Eigg is not the only thing he's grown fond of." Roisin gave a dreamy sigh. "And if he decides to stay, it won't be because he's fallen in love with the Isle."

It was only when Freyja gave her a keen glance that Isolde realized she was smiling like a smitten fool. It was too late to try and hide it, but she did her best by opening the door and letting the dogs in.

※

As they broke their fast, she assiduously avoided her grandmother's pointed glances and kept her attention on Njord.

"'Tis predicted to be a fine day," she told him. "I shall take ye to the peak of An Sgurr, just as I promised. When ye take in the magnificent view, ye might change yer mind about leaving."

She knew he wouldn't. But he had promised he would return, and she believed him.

His stormy eyes were so full of heat when he caught her gaze, the warmth made her very toes curl inside her boots.

"Ye know there's only one reason why I'm leaving." His husky whisper caused havoc to her insides, and it took all her willpower not to slide her fingers between his. But her grandmother was already giving her wary glances, and she'd do nothing to raise her suspicions further and risk being ordered to attend to some mundane tasks within the castle, instead of spending the day with Njord.

"Aye. But if ye haven't returned before the first sign of spring, ye can be certain I'll gather a contingent and follow ye to the mainland."

"I'd expect nothing less." His amused grin fairly took her breath away. "God willing, I'll have found my kin and have my own contingent by then."

She was certain he would. But despite how deeply she believed in him and his word, it didn't stop a tiny sliver of doubt in the back of her mind. If he discovered he had nothing to his name, would his pride overcome his honor, and instead of fulfilling his promise to return, would he disappear into the Highland mountains?

⚛

DAWN WAS JUST breaking as they left the castle, and they made their way through the heather and bracken moorland, with Njord carrying a satchel she'd filled with a picnic. He also carried a thick blanket on his back, and once again he'd tied his black hair with a length of velvet.

It was hard to keep her eyes on the rocky track when he presented such a delectable figure by her side. But since she had no wish to fall and injure her pride, never mind break a bone, she had to be content with frequent sideways glances.

He paused, tipped back his head, and eyed the formidable wedge that dominated the landscape. Its steep face that towered over the castle was impossible to climb, but by following the rugged furrow that wound around the far side of the ridge, they would eventually reach the final slopes that led to the summit.

"I've never seen a mountain like it," he said.

She didn't ask if some of his memories had returned, the way she had earlier in the week when he made similar comments. It seemed his mind remembered certain things, and it was only the most important elements of his life that remained swathed in fog.

"That's because there is no other mountain like it," she teased. "And no other isle like Eigg, either."

"I believe ye." He tossed another bone-melting grin her way, and heat bloomed between her thighs as she recalled the magic his mouth had kindled when she'd been in his bed. The breath caught in her throat and her heart quickened, sending delightful ripples of awareness across her skin. She had never imagined such rapture could exist, and without him taking her maidenhead, too.

She swallowed a groan of frustration, grateful that the incessant wind that blew across the moor snatched the sound away before Njord heard it. How would she survive the following months without him?

But there was still tonight. And she planned on visiting him, aa soon as the castle fell silent, so they could enjoy such bliss again.

His arm slipped around her waist, and he brushed a possessive kiss against her temple. She released a sigh and leaned against his welcoming strength. "When ye look at me with such passion, the only thing on my mind is how much I want to ravish ye."

"That's good to know," she responded. "I should be mortified if I was alone in wishing to ravish ye within an inch of yer life."

He laughed, and the sound sank deep into her blood, warming her from the inside out.

"Ye're far too tempting for my peace of mind, Isolde. A man can only take so much."

How she loved it when he said such things to her. How odd that she'd never craved any man to profess such devotion for her, until she'd met Njord.

And how easy it was to believe Roisin was right, when she said it had been a sign that Njord had washed up on their beach. They *were* meant to be together. And in her heart, she was certain he was of Clan MacDonald.

As they scrambled over the slippery rocks, laughing and pulling each other onward, a bittersweet pain pierced her breast at the knowledge that by this time tomorrow, he would be on his way to Oban.

She'd give anything if only he decided not to board the ship and sail away from her.

At last, they reached the summit, and the plateau spread out before them. The sun glinted on the calm, azure sea, with a clear view of the archipelago of the beautiful Small Isles. It was truly the perfect winter's day, with only a few light clouds and no dense fog to spoil the panorama, and Njord expelled a breath of appreciation as he surveyed the view.

"Worth the climb?" she enquired as she unstrapped the blanket from his back and laid it on the ground. They would likely still get damp, but it would surely be worth it to spend time alone with him.

"'Tis certainly a sight." He cast his gaze to their close neighbor, the Isle of Rum, its mountainous terrain rising through the sea mist and seemingly touching the clouds above. "I see why ye love yer isle, Isolde."

"Ye should see it in spring." And, with a little luck, he would. "Come, hand me the satchel. I'm famished."

They sat on the blanket, and she pulled out the oatcakes and pasties she'd packed earlier, as Sjor chased elusive scents to hidden burrows. And when they'd eaten their fill, Njord wrapped his arm around her shoulders and gave her a lingering kiss.

She snuggled against him, sliding her arm around his waist and holding him tight. Could this day be any more perfect?

His sigh echoed through her, reaching places inside she didn't even know existed.

"Will ye still want me if it turns out I'm one of the cursed Campbells?"

She laughed and rubbed her cheek against his shoulder. "I'd do my best. But I still hold out hope ye're a MacDonald."

He grunted and pulled her on top of himself as he lay back on the blanket. "No MacDonald, nor Campbell neither, could care for ye the way I do."

Her heart melted. "Ye care for me, do ye?"

"Ye saved my life."

She gave him a mock frown. "I don't want yer gratitude."

He leered at her. It was most enchanting. "What do ye want from me, my lady?"

"That would be telling. Ye must work it out for yerself."

"An impossible task."

She folded her arms across his chest and dropped a kiss upon his lips. "I'm certain ye'll manage it."

His hands roamed down her body and gripped her bottom. Even through all the layers she wore, she fancied she could feel the heat of his palms branding her skin.

The way he had branded her in the night.

Thrills raced through her at the memory, and desire stirred, strong and hot. Lord, she wanted him so.

"Stop yer wriggling." His voice was raw. She wriggled again, even though she hadn't been doing it on purpose before. He let out a tortured groan. "Ye're killing me, woman."

"There are worse ways to go, I'm sure."

"And better ones, too, I've no doubt." He gave her a feral grin. "But I'd rather not think of such things when I'm with ye."

"Tell me what ye think when ye're with me."

"'Tis not fit for a lady's ears."

"I promise I won't be shocked."

He wrapped his arms around her hips, so securely she imagined she could feel his magnificent rod, even beneath the thickness of his plaid. A jagged breath escaped, as she recalled how his wondrous body had felt beneath her exploring fingers.

How desperately she wished to touch him again.

"Ye're doing it again." His groan was the most alluring sound she'd ever heard. "I believe ye only brought me up here so ye could torture me in peace."

"Ye could be right." She shook with silent laughter as she stole another kiss. He plunged his fingers through her hair, anchoring her head, and plundered her mouth until she could scarcely breathe, never mind think.

The frenzied thunder of her heart filled her head, and only when Njord broke their kiss and swore under his breath did the sound of Sjor's barking penetrate her passion-drenched senses.

"Someone's coming," he muttered as he rolled her onto her side and clumsily straightened her skirts. She sucked in a sharp breath and glanced hastily around. Sjor was at one side of the plateau, barking out to sea.

She expelled a relieved breath. "No one can climb that sheer cliff. There's only one way to reach this summit, and that's the way we came."

He was already on his feet, casting a grim glare at the way they had come. With a sigh, she stood, too, and taking his hand led him over to her dog. "What is it, my bonny lad?"

She shielded her eyes from the glare of the sun. A ship was sailing in the waters far below, heading directly for Eigg.

Unaccountably, a shiver raced along her arms.

"Huh." Njord turned to her. "More visitors. Maybe they can shed light on my origins." The skeptical smile that accompanied his words belied his optimism, but she smiled back, since he clearly expected it.

"That would be good." And then she brightened. It would be more than good. It would mean he would no longer feel the need to leave tomorrow. "We need to head back, anyway, if we want to reach the castle before dusk falls."

The sun was already dropping below the horizon as they entered the great hall. Aside from the usual castle servants and warriors, her sisters and grandmother were also present, standing beside the fire.

And so were a dozen foreign Scots.

Once again, unease shivered through her, and she had the mad urge to grab Njord's hand and run back out into the night. But even if she had planned on following such foolishness, it was too late now, as her grandmother had seen them.

She took a deep breath. Whether these men knew Njord or not, all would be well.

One of the strangers swung about, and Njord faltered by her side. She cast him a searching look. Did he recognize this man?

"God's bones, William." The stranger strode across the hall and grasped Njord's arm, before pulling him into a bear hug and thumping his back with his fist. "We thought ye were dead, man. We've been searching the islands for ye since the storm broke."

The stranger released him and stared intently into Njord's face. A slow frown crossed his features. And then he spoke.

"Hugh?"

"Aye." Hugh sounded vastly relieved, and Isolde gripped her fingers together as her stomach churned with sudden nerves. Njord did know this man. What else could he recall of his life? Nothing?

Everything?

"Christ." Njord sucked in a ragged breath. "The storm. Someone hit me on the head, Hugh, and tossed me overboard. It was no accident."

Someone had tried to *kill* him? She stared at him in horror. There had been many things she'd wondered about him, but it had never occurred to her he'd ended up in the sea because someone had tried to murder him.

Hugh's voice dropped. "We'll find the man responsible." Then he appeared to notice her and bowed his head. "Forgive me, my lady. My actions are unpardonable, but I'm so relieved to discover my cousin is alive and well."

Njord gave Hugh—his cousin—a friendly and obviously familiar punch on his arm. His grin was entirely inappropriate, considering he'd just discovered someone had tried to kill him, and another ripple of unease snaked along her spine.

*What am I missing?*

Then he turned to her. "Lady Isolde, allow me to introduce ye to my cousin, Hugh Campbell."

Hugh bowed, but she scarcely heard his formal response. A loud buzzing filled her head, and only one word penetrated.

*Campbell.*

Njord's cousin was a Campbell.

*God's bones, William.* That was what Hugh had said when he caught sight of Njord, and the churning in her stomach turned nauseous.

William Campbell.

Of Argyll?

"Aye," he responded to whatever Hugh had said. "Lady Isolde of Sgur Castle, the lady who saved my life. And my intended bride."

No. *No.* This could not be happening. Her noble Njord could not have deceived her so. Yet he stood beside her, a satisfied grin on his face, as he claimed her for his bride in front of the entire hall.

When he attempted to take her hand, her wits returned, and she hastily stepped back, out of reach. He frowned, as if he didn't understand, and a great vise squeezed inside her chest, making it all but impossible to drag air into her starved lungs.

She'd always believed Clan Campbell would stoop to any depths to secure what they coveted. The history of their isles, and how Campbells of the past had pledged allegiance to the Crown, told that story plain enough.

But to feign memory loss, to invoke her sympathy and lead her on a dance of deception . . . ah, God. She could scarcely fathom it.

"Isolde?" He sounded so concerned. Didn't he realize his masquerade had cracked open, and now she could see him for what he truly was? Nothing more than a liar. "Are ye well?"

All eyes were upon her. If only the floor would open so she could disappear and not have to face this utter humiliation. But she was the eldest granddaughter of Sgur Castle, and the honor of her foremothers rested upon her shoulders.

She summoned up the frostiest glare she could muster, and despite his great height did her best to look down her nose at him. He would never discover just how deeply his pretense had shattered her.

"Quite well." Thank God her voice didn't quiver with the turmoil shredding her breast. "Alas, it's no comfort to discover the Campbells are as lacking in honor as I always feared."

With that, she turned on her heel and left the hall before she disgraced herself for all time by allowing a tear to escape.

# Chapter Twelve

William stared after Isolde as she regally stalked from the hall, her scathing words ringing in his ears. Aye, he knew she despised the name Campbell. But that was when she'd been betrothed to a faceless man. Everything was different now that they both knew the truth.

"William."

"What?" He didn't turn to his cousin, although God knew how relieved he was to see him. The insidious sense of being cast adrift in an incomprehensible sea no longer haunted him like a shadowy specter. When he'd recognized Hugh as his kin, and recalled who he was and all that entailed, the revelation had streaked through him like lightning, incinerating all the doubts he'd harbored.

His heritage was worthy of seeking Isolde's hand.

Except it was only too clear she wanted nothing to do with him.

Hugh was speaking, but there was something of more importance he needed to address. He gripped his cousin's arm. "Later, Hugh."

Hugh nodded, and William strode after Isolde.

By the glow from the lanterns that lit the forecourt, he saw her striding to the armory. He grabbed a lantern and let out a curse under his breath as he quickened his pace. "Isolde, wait."

She didn't even pause. He reached her side just as she thrust the key into the lock of the armory.

"Are ye planning to run me through with ye father's claymore?" It was only half in jest. She certainly looked irate enough to challenge him.

She snatched her hand away before he could grasp her fingers but kept her glare firmly on the door. "Ye deserve nothing less."

The bitterness in her voice hit him right in the gut. She sounded as if she couldn't bear the very sight of him.

"Why?" He grabbed her arm and swung her about, so she had no choice but to face him. "Because I'm a Campbell? Christ, Isolde. I even asked ye if ye would feel any differently about me if I discovered I was a Campbell. But ye're not even trying. Ye're condemning me for something I have no power over."

"Not even trying?" She all but spat the words in his face, and it took more willpower than he cared to admit not to recoil from her anger. "Don't make me laugh, William Campbell." His name fell from her tongue as if the sound of it sickened her. "Ye knew who ye were all along. What a fine jest, to pretend ye recalled nothing, when all the time ye were merely spinning a web around me."

"I never lied to ye." His voice was harsh, but he could scarcely believe she leveled such an accusation at him. "Have ye forgotten how it was ye who found me half dead on the beach?"

"I remember. And I remember how Patric and I thought it a miracle a man could survive such a thing. But it was no miracle. It was all part of yer despicable plan to ensnare me."

He almost laughed at her outrageous claim. Except he'd never felt less like laughing in his life. "Why would I plan to be attacked on my own ship and thrown overboard in a raging storm? Only a madman would fabricate such a foolhardy scheme."

She gave a mirthless laugh, and something sharp and hot stabbed through his chest. "Stop. I'll not fall for any more of yer tales. I'm disgusted that I ever did."

"Tales?" He pulled her closer, and her gasp of outrage fueled his own. "Did I imagine that bash on my head?"

"'Tis likely yer cousin Hugh gave it to ye, to lend credence to yer falsehood."

"Will ye listen to yerself, woman? Yer accusations are madness."

Aye, utter madness, yet he still wanted to wrap his arms around her and kiss her until all her groundless recriminations fled.

She wrenched her arm free and glared at him. "My only madness was not listening to those with more sense. Even Colban MacDonald saw through ye, but I wouldn't heed his warning."

Having Colban MacDonald's name thrown in his face after the man had tried to murder him while his back was turned was too much.

"Colban MacDonald is a worthless—" He bit off his words. In her current state of mind, she would never believe her clansman had attempted so cowardly an attack. He dragged in a deep breath and tried to clear his mind. "I know ye have an aversion to Campbells. But just because I've regained my memory doesn't change the fact I'm still the same man I was yesterday."

"Alas, I'm certain that's true." She sounded on the edge of tears, and instinctively he reached out to her. She'd had a shock. He could understand that. But before he could comfort her, she batted his hand away as if he were nothing but an irritant. "How amusing it must have been to ye, that I never questioned yer loss of memory."

"Questioned it?" God damn it, did she really think so little of him? "Isolde, I had no idea I was William Campbell until I saw Hugh."

"And how quickly ye recalled everything, once ye did." Derision dripped from every word, and he stared at her, speechless, as for the first time he realized how that must have seemed to her.

He didn't understand how it had happened himself, much less enough to try and explain it to her. But when Hugh had approached him, when he'd said his name, the fog in his mind had vanished, like early morning mist in the mountains.

He hadn't simply recognized his cousin. All his missing memories had flooded back, settling in his mind, and a great weight had lifted from his chest at the knowledge of who he was.

But it wasn't just the fact he now knew he was William Campbell, the laird of Creagdoun. It was the realization that the woman he was pledged to wed wasn't a faceless MacDonald of the isle who wanted him as little as he wanted her.

No, by God. He had washed up on Sgur Beach, and all his preconceptions had been left deep in the sea. He'd known nothing of his past or his future duty. Yet Isolde, the wild MacDonald lass to whom he was betrothed, had bewitched him from the moment he'd first gazed into her eyes, as though their destinies had always been entwined.

He wasn't one for thinking such outlandish thoughts, and he'd rip out his tongue rather than voice such a belief to anyone. But he couldn't dislodge the notion from his mind that the reason Isolde had found him, when neither of them knew of the prior connection between them, was proof that they were meant to be together.

And not just because her grandmother and his father had forged a contract ten years ago. Contracts were drawn up all the time. But what were the chances he and Isolde could be given time to learn to know each other without the shadow of that damn contract hanging over their heads?

This marriage was meant to be. And once Isolde was over the shock of discovering who he was, he was certain she would see it that way, too. All he needed to do was be patient.

"Didn't ye always say my memories would return when I least expected them to?"

"That was before I knew ye had come to Eigg under false pretenses."

She was determined to believe the worst of him, and despite his vow to be patient, it grated. "Why would I use such subterfuge? We're pledged to wed regardless. I'd never try and win yer favor through such low tactics."

"We are *not* betrothed." Her denial quivered in the fraught air between them. "An understanding is not the same as a binding contract."

He sucked in a breath between his teeth before he said something he'd regret. He knew this was a shock for her. Hell, recovering his memories in one fell blow had shaken him, too.

But she was being damned unreasonable, and blaming him for things he'd had no hand in.

"Ten years ago, Lady Helga herself visited Dunstrunage Castle to negotiate this alliance. And ye know that's true, since ye found that out the other night. And let me tell ye this." Caution hovered. He should really keep his mouth shut, but her stubbornness irked. "I wasn't happy at having my future dictated to me. But it was more than an understanding, Isolde. It's a binding contract. Lady Helga made sure of it."

She licked her lips, a nervous gesture, and he instantly regretted his harsh words. But then she straightened her spine and shook her head, as if that might help clear her mind.

"Aye. I cannot deny that. And I'm still . . . I still cannot quite fathom my grandmother's actions. But now we've met, don't ye see? We can make our own choices, Njor—William." She swallowed as if the unfamiliar name unnerved her, and despite everything, a warm glow ignited deep inside at hearing her speak his God-given name. "If we're both against this marriage, they cannot force us."

He raked his gaze over her. She clutched her shawl about her and gave the impression of an aloof noblewoman with ice in her veins.

But he knew better. Unbidden, the vision of her in his bed last night invaded his mind, of how her glorious hair had spread across the pillows and how she'd gasped in pleasure as he'd all but made her his.

His body responded to the vivid recollection. So violently, a groan lodged in his throat. A damning thought thudded in his mind. If he'd known last night they were betrothed, would he have stopped when he had?

Stealthily, he shifted his weight from one foot to the other, but it made no difference. He was as hard as a damn rock, and the fact she appeared so adamant in wanting to terminate their betrothal added fuel to the fire scorching his blood.

He stepped closer to her, and she backed up against the door of the armory. His grin felt feral as he braced his fists on the door, either side of her face, entrapping her. They didn't touch, but they didn't need to. The flame that had sparked between them from the first time he'd looked into her eyes smoldered as hot as ever.

And then he spoke. "Who says I'm against this marriage?"

༺⚛༻

ISOLDE'S GRIP ON her shawl tightened as Njord—*William, how would she ever remember to call him that?*—loomed ominously over her, imprisoning her.

Why had she been so foolish as to trap herself against the door? Now, instead of stalking off with a shred of dignity intact, the warmth from his body, which had nothing to do with the lantern he grasped in one fist, swirled around her like a sensual caress and she was once again falling under his mesmeric gaze.

No. She would not be fooled again by his honeyed words and—

Her tangled thoughts collided as his words finally penetrated. "Ye still want to go through with this marriage? Despite knowing how I feel about it?"

Lord help her. How *did* she feel about it? Part of her wanted to grab her claymore and challenge him. To show him she was not simply a prize that could be taken without her consent.

Except she had already fought him, the Campbell she'd despised for the last ten years, and he hadn't laughed at her or refused her challenge.

No. He'd bested her.

It hadn't upset her that Njord's skill had defeated her. But it burned like the pit of hell to know William Campbell's had.

And as for the other part of her . . . *no*. There was no other part. She couldn't trust anything that had happened between them this last week. It had all been a façade, nothing but a mockery, and she refused to torture herself by even thinking of it.

"Aye." His voice dropped to a sensual rumble, and she tried, in vain, to ignore the desire that rippled through her at the sound. "Why wouldn't I? Ye're a beautiful woman, Isolde. And I'm committed to making ye mine."

Heat flooded her face as disjointed echoes from the previous night flashed through her mind. Shame burned through her at all the things she'd whispered to him in the darkness.

Had he been silently laughing at her gullibility?

Something deep inside her breast shriveled at the notion.

"So ye wish to wed me merely to satisfy yer lust." As soon as the words were out, she wanted to snatch them back. Because despite how much she had wanted him before she learned the truth, surely there was more between them than that.

"There are worse reasons to wed."

He sounded so damn nonchalant. Even if he'd been hiding who he really was, had all the conversation and laughter they'd shared these last few days meant so little to him? Did it all truly amount to nothing more than a tumble in the hay?

"Maybe so," she retorted. "But I cannot think of one."

He tilted his head, and his gaze dropped to her mouth. How could a single look cause her heart to race so despicably?

"Ye cannot tell me ye don't feel this connection between us. If not for my name, ye wouldn't be so hostile to the prospect of wedding me."

"But ye are yer name, and I cannot trust a word ye say."

A cloud passed over his face, or maybe it was simply a flicker of flame from the lantern he held. Either way, it made her heart ache, and she would never forgive him for it.

"When we are wed," he said, and there was hardness in his voice she'd never heard before, "ye'll learn to trust me again, Isolde. I promise ye."

Panic gripped her vitals. But it was more than panic, and she knew it. But she didn't want to acknowledge the illicit thread of anticipation that sparked her reason. To know a tiny part of her wanted to go through with this marriage was a betrayal she couldn't stomach.

"I'll not wed ye." She wanted to sound commanding. Instead, her denial was like a breathless invitation to call the banns without haste. "I've told ye how I cannot leave the Isle."

"I know ye love yer isle. There's no reason why ye can't visit yer kin whenever ye wish."

Had he listened to anything she'd said this last week? A forlorn voice of reason whispered through the back of her mind. No, he likely hadn't. Because his sole aim had been to lower her defenses, so that she'd agree to be his bride without any argument.

"How noble of ye." Bitterness threaded through the words. Aye, she had thought him so noble. But that was before she'd learned of his bloodline and his deception. Just because he came from noble stock didn't mean he possessed honor. "'Tis not the same and ye know it."

"We can't stay on the Isle." He spoke to her as though she were a child, devoid of understanding, and that wounded her more than if he'd shouted and behaved like an ill-bred oaf. "I must return to my castle, Creagdoun. 'Tis in sore need of a fine mistress, Isolde. I know in time ye'll look on it as yer home, as I do."

A great vise compressed her chest, squeezing the air from her lungs, and a dark sliver of panic wound about her heart. She didn't want to be the mistress of an unknown castle, no matter how grand it was.

She wanted—she needed—to stay on her beloved isle, where the essence of her foremothers permeated every rock and grain of sand.

Where she knew who she was and where she could call upon the strength of her ancestors whenever she was in need.

How could she survive in a Campbell castle, far from everything she had ever known?

"Creagdoun will never be my home. All ye want is a woman to run yer castle and bear yer bairns."

Instead of rising to her bait, which would have given her at least a small measure of satisfaction, he tilted his head, as though her remark intrigued him. Damn him to hell. The lantern enhanced his aristocratic cheekbones and strong jaw, and his beautiful mouth evoked treacherous stirrings between her thighs. "Don't ye want bairns, Isolde?"

This was not the conversation she wished to have with him. Why had she even started it? She should have known better than to think he'd take offense at her blunt comment, the way she imagined most Campbells would take offense. Because he wasn't like the Campbells of her imagination.

He wasn't like any other man she'd met, or imagined, and until his identity had been revealed, she'd been fascinated by that aspect of his character.

But not now. Because how could she know if this was yet another masquerade?

He was so close to her his warm breath brushed her face like an ethereal caress. His gaze roved over her, and she couldn't draw breath, but it had nothing to do with apprehension concerning her future.

Was he going to kiss her? Did he think he could seduce her into submission?

*Do I want him to?*

Somehow, that was the worst betrayal of all.

"William Campbell."

Her grandmother's commanding voice cut through the lust-filled air like a frigid slap, and she gasped, but William Campbell didn't swing about with guilt dripping from him. No, he leisurely pushed himself from the wall before turning to face the small contingent before them.

Patric was there, along with Amma's personal guard, and half a dozen warriors. Her sisters, too, and various servants brought up the rear, along with Hugh Campbell and the rest of his men.

If only she could sink through the door behind her and disappear, but since there was no option but to face them all, she straightened her spine and tugged her shawl more securely about herself.

"Lady Helga." William bowed, and she was disgusted that she noticed how elegant it was. "My deepest apologies for my hasty departure. I had to speak with Lady Isolde."

"Indeed." There was a touch of frost in Amma's voice which Isolde hadn't expected. Wasn't she happy that Njord had turned out to be the very man she had underhandedly pledged Isolde to? "There is much to speak of. We shall return to the castle and proceed forthwith."

With that, Lady Helga beckoned for Isolde to join her, and after glancing at William's implacable face, she obeyed her grandmother.

Her sisters immediately came to her side, linking their arms through hers as though they feared she might stumble if they released her.

"Is this not the most romantic thing?" Roisin whispered, so only she and Freyja could hear. "To think, the man ye care for is none other than the man ye're destined to wed."

Isolde bit her tongue before she said something to upset her sister, but Frey was not so concerned with such niceties. "Romantic?" she whispered back. "That's not the word I would call this, and that's for sure."

"What do ye mean?" Anxiety threaded through Roisin's voice. "Njord cares for Izzie, I know it."

"He's not Njord." Her hiss sounded harsh, but she couldn't help it and didn't regret it, even when Roisin flinched at her tone. "His name is William Campbell."

"I'm vexed I didn't press him further when he first awoke." Frey exhaled a frustrated sigh. "I should have, but I believed his tale. It seems the only one not taken in was Colban."

But it wasn't just Colban MacDonald who had seen through the subterfuge.

Even her grandmother had been skeptical of how he'd washed up on the beach. The irony of how Amma had tried to keep her away from Njord—*William, damn it*—wasn't lost on her.

"Well, I think ye are both wrong."

Sometimes Roisin could be so stubborn. Although how Isolde wished that this time her youngest sister was right.

## Chapter Thirteen

At Lady Helga's command, William and Hugh followed her to a chamber which, had it belonged to a man, would bear all the hallmarks of a war chamber. She sat behind a great desk, with Isolde and her sisters flanking her, and Patric and another three warriors positioned themselves at strategic points.

It appeared Isolde wasn't the only one who doubted him, and he drew in a deep breath. Of all the ways he'd imagined regaining his memories, and the subsequent reaction, it had never occurred to him Isolde would reject him so utterly simply because of his name.

He needed more time to speak with her alone, to win her around. Unfortunately, his attempt to ease her concerns earlier, outside the armory, had been little short of disastrous. For all his noble thoughts of showing her patience, her vehement rejection of their alliance had prickled his pride.

His pride. Aye, to be sure that's all it was. Except he had the feeling it was more than his damn pride she'd wounded by her harsh words.

"So ye are the Baron of Dunstrunage's son." Lady Helga's face was impassive as she held his gaze. "Tell me plainly, William Campbell. Did ye set out to deceive us this last week?"

"No, my lady. I swear on the honor of my forefathers I told only the truth as I knew it."

Lady Helga glanced at Isolde, who didn't look in the least impressed by his pledge, before returning her attention to him. "'Tis a strange coincidence. But I have learned the Isles conceal more wisdom than they ever reveal to us."

He had no idea what she was talking about, but since she appeared to believe him, he was willing to agree with whatever she said if it meant his betrothal with Isolde remained unbroken.

"I've only been here a week, but even I can see their beauty."

"'Tis more than skin deep, William Campbell," Lady Helga said, "but I understand yer sentiments. It is hard indeed for any daughter of Sgur to make her life elsewhere."

Warning spiked through his blood. Was she going to break the betrothal she had gone to such lengths to procure ten years ago?

Before leaving Skye, he'd have welcomed it. Celebrated his freedom. But now he'd met his future bride, and no one—not even Isolde's revered grandmother—would take her from him.

"Aye, my lady. But I shall do all within my power to make Lady Isolde happy in her new home."

Isolde, standing beside her grandmother's chair, shot him a glare, and he admired her restraint. Considering how she'd reacted on discovering who he was, had he said such a thing to her when they were alone, he could well imagine her tart response.

But once they were wed, once he had made her truly his, she'd come around. How could she not?

"I believe ye will." Lady Helga stood. "We shall convene in the morning and make arrangements for a spring wedding."

Hell, no. He wasn't waiting that long for his bride.

"My lady," he said, bowing his head in deference before once again catching Lady Helga's steady gaze. "When I leave the Isle of Eigg, I shall take my bride with me."

Isolde's sharp intake of outrage echoed around the silent chamber, and their gazes clashed. Her cheeks were flushed with anger and her beautiful green eyes sparkled with affront, and it wouldn't have surprised him if she'd pulled her dagger from her skirts and launched it in his direction.

Thankfully, she resisted the temptation.

"Ye're mad if ye think I'll wed ye within a month."

He wasn't waiting a month for the banns to be called, either. He had a would-be assassin among his men and needed to flush him out as swiftly as possible. Not to mention Creagdoun was in serious need of attention to bring it up to the standards a noble-born bride would expect.

But since they were both reasons enough to postpone their marriage instead of wedding in haste, he pushed them to the back of his mind.

"Alas, I cannot stay on Eigg for another month. We shall wed at the week's end before leaving for the mainland." With the Earl of Argyll's blessing for this alliance, he was certain any irregularities could be easily overcome.

Shock etched Isolde's face, and he braced himself for her denial, but before she could respond, Lady Helga spoke.

"The marriage contract must be ratified first with all that entails. In the morning, William Campbell."

He knew when to retreat, and bowed once again before he and Hugh left the chamber.

"We didn't know ye were missing until we reached Oban." Hugh's voice was low as they returned to the great hall, where his men stood beside the fire. "The storm was so bad, we couldn't search for ye until it broke. I'll be honest, man. I didn't think to find ye alive."

"I know every man who was on that ship, Hugh. Who the hell would want me dead?"

Hugh shook his head. "Christ knows. Best to keep yer counsel between us, until we discover the traitor."

He swept his gaze over his men. "Where's Alasdair?"

"The earl summoned him as we were boarding. Ye know Alasdair."

Aye, he did. Alasdair would drop anything if the earl called him to his side. Not that he blamed him. They were all beholden to the Earl of Argyll, one way or another.

He greeted his men, a hard knot forming in his chest as he looked at each one with new eyes. Which one had tried to kill him?

"William." Robert Fletcher gave him a nod. "Glad we found ye, man."

"Get that down ye." Malcolm MacNeil handed him a tankard of ale.

"Good health," David Cunningham said, and William took a long swig of the ale as the rest of his men gathered around.

Some were childhood friends. A couple, like Hugh, were close relatives. But he'd been alongside all of them at different times during the last three years in skirmishes against the cursed MacGregors and had always trusted they had each other's backs.

He no longer had that luxury.

His men spoke of the violence of the storm and the shock of discovering he'd vanished when they'd docked at Oban. He grunted, nodded, and drank, mindful of the wisdom of Hugh's caution.

Best to let the would-be murderer think he didn't recall that vicious smash to his head.

"Lady Isolde is quite the beauty," David remarked, and William fought to keep the scowl from his face at the familiar tone in the other man's voice. "Hardly the wild Norse heathen we'd been led to believe."

"That's my bride ye're speaking of." He'd not stand for any man disrespecting Isolde.

"Aye, and ye have my congratulations." David smashed his tankard against William's, apparently oblivious to the threat behind William's words.

"A noble mistress for Creagdoun," Malcolm remarked. "What the hell was John MacDonald talking about? Lady Isolde doesn't look like a woman who wishes she were a man with a sword in her hand."

"Watch it." There was a thread of amusement in Robert's voice as he gave Malcolm a friendly punch on the arm. "There's only one sword Lady Isolde will handle from now, and it doesn't belong in an armory."

"Enough." William's voice was harsh, and the laughter among his men died instantly. With difficulty, he released his death grip on the tankard before he splintered the damn thing. He wasn't usually averse to bawdy talk. But it was entirely different, he discovered, when it involved Isolde.

Fortunately, there was no more time for talk. Supper was served, and Lady Helga had invited his men to join them. But tonight, he wasn't sitting next to Isolde, and she avoided looking his way, whereas he could scarcely keep his eyes off her.

It was obvious there would be no surreptitious visit to the solar this night, and he shifted on the uncomfortable bench, but it didn't help relieve his throbbing cock.

The sooner they were wed the better. And then he could claim his bride.

※

THE FOLLOWING MORNING after breakfast, Patric sought Isolde out, and they went into the courtyard for privacy. She shivered and tugged her shawl more securely about herself but couldn't stop her mind from snagging on the fact William had not been at the table with the rest of his men.

Was he making good on his threat for them to wed without having the banns read? Did he really expect her to participate in such an irregular ceremony?

"Isolde." Patric's voice was low, and she dragged her attention back to the present. She hadn't heard a word he'd said to her.

"I'm sorry." She sighed. "What did ye say?"

"I'll accompany ye to Creagdoun. I've no doubt Lady Helga will allow it."

Mute, she stared at him, this loyal warrior to her father who had been such a steadfast mentor and, aye, a friend to her over the last ten years. She'd been so incensed at how William had hoodwinked her that it hadn't occurred to her to consider who she might take with her in her new life. Because she was still wrapped up in the conviction that she'd remain on Eigg until her dying breath.

Having Patric tell her of his plans to accompany her was akin to being plunged into an icy loch.

How did she plan to escape this fate?

Her own grandmother had arranged it. Her bridegroom was more than eager to seal the alliance. And, much as she loathed to admit it, even here, on the Western Isles, the cursed Earl of Argyll was not a man to be crossed.

Spectral wisps of alarm spun through her breast, disorientating her, and she struggled against the overwhelming compunction to sink to the ground and bury her fingers in the mud.

That wouldn't help. Because this time it wasn't the strength of her foremothers she needed.

It was a miracle.

Patric grasped her arm, a concerned frown wreathing his face. Clearly, she hadn't hidden her feelings as well as she had imagined. And although she longed to rest her forehead against his shoulder and feel his kindly arms about her, she remained rigid as her future fragmented and reformed before her very eyes.

"I believe he's a good man." Patric's voice was rough, and she couldn't trust herself to speak. It was foolish, she knew it, yet his words felt like a small betrayal. "But know this. My loyalty lies with ye, and always will."

THE SEA WAS calm, and any other time Isolde would have enjoyed her solitary walk on the beach with Sjor, but her mind would not still, and no wonder. At least her grandmother had granted permission for her to be present at the meeting this morning, but only after extracting a promise that she wouldn't interfere with the negotiations.

Negotiations that would affect the rest of *her* life.

She huffed out a breath and glared at the misty horizon, but she could delay returning to the castle no longer. As much as she didn't want this cursed meeting to go ahead, it would be far worse if she were excluded altogether due to her tardiness.

As she entered the great hall, she pulled off her gloves and then stopped dead as she saw Roisin standing beside the hearth, entrapped by Hugh Campbell.

Protectiveness and a hot wave of anger rushed through her, and she marched over to them. How dare he accost her sister in their own home? Roisin was far too shy to tell a stranger, and a man at that, to back off, or even leave herself for fear of being considered rude.

Luckily, Isolde had no such difficulties when it came to putting obnoxious individuals in their place.

As she drew closer, she heard Hugh speaking. "I should be honored to see that, my lady."

Honor be damned. It was a foreign concept for all Campbells. Before he could upset her sister any further, she came to her side and hooked her arm through hers.

"There ye are," she said, as if she'd been looking for her. "Where's Grear?"

"She's here." Roisin shot her a bemused glance before indicating where their maid stood, just behind Roisin. "Why do ye want me?"

She didn't, but could hardly admit that while Hugh Campbell still stood there, apparently oblivious to the fact he was blatantly overstepping his welcome. She gave him a tight smile, and belatedly he turned his attention to her and offered her a swift bow.

"Lady Isolde," he said. He glanced at Roisin, and then the obvious appeared to strike him as he took a hasty step back and took his leave.

She expelled an exasperated breath before turning to her sister. "Are ye all right?"

"Aye." Roisin sounded decidedly *not* all right. "Hugh is most charming, Izzie."

"He's a Campbell," she hissed. "So be wary. And don't be afraid to tell him to stop bothering ye, either."

"He wasn't bothering me. I was telling him about my illustrated histories of the Tuatha De Danann."

Momentarily speechless, she stared at Roisin. Her sister rarely spoke to anyone she didn't know well, and as for sharing anything about her precious work with someone outside the family, well. It was unheard of.

Obviously, Hugh possessed the same charm as his cousin, and look where that had got them.

"Just . . ." she hesitated, biting back the warning that hovered on her tongue. Just be careful? The way she had been so careful with Njord before she'd discovered who he really was? "Just remember who he is, that's all."

"I will," her sister promised. "Don't worry about me."

*That* would only happen when Hugh Campbell left Eigg. Except he'd only leave when William did. And unless the elusive miracle she hoped for appeared, when William sailed, she'd also be leaving her beloved Isle.

And she'd be leaving her sisters.

It seemed like a lifetime ago when she'd so foolishly wished that she'd give anything if only he decided not to board the ship and sail away from her. But the fates had heard and granted her wish, in the twisted way wishes were always granted.

He wasn't sailing away from her. And the price she had to pay would scar her heart forever.

Her stomach churned, and she gripped the edges of her shawl as Roisin and Grear left the hall. For ten years the shadow of this impending marriage had hung over her. But until now, she hadn't allowed herself to think of everything she'd lose.

The Isle was her strength. But her sisters were her blood. Would she ever see them again if she wed William?

William, damn him, was waiting for her outside her grandmother's chamber. How dare he look so dashing? If only she'd had the good sense to tidy up her windswept appearance before this meeting. Not that she cared what he thought of her anymore. That had long passed.

What a pity she could see through her own lies so easily.

"Good morn, my lady." He appeared uncommonly pleased with himself, and it wasn't hard to guess why. Clearly, his early visit to the kirk had not thrown any obstacles in his committed path of undertaking an irregular ceremony at the end of the week.

"That depends on a satisfactory resolution to the negotiations," she shot back, irked that he was so damn *cheerful* about everything.

"Rest assured, ye'll have no cause to be dissatisfied, Isolde." His voice dropped to an intimate whisper which caused contemptible desire to ripple through her, momentarily paralyzing her good sense. "Tis not yer fortune I want in my bed."

Instantly, the vision of them clasped together in the box bed the other night thundered through her mind, and to her intense irritation, her cheeks heated. She refused to recall all the foolish things she'd said to him when she'd imagined him so noble, since she couldn't take any of it back, and the last thing she was going to do was wilt in front of him.

"I cannot fathom why ye want an unwilling bride in yer bed."

"I don't." His grin was utterly infuriating. "And I won't, either."

How ignoble of him to throw that in her face. Even worse, she feared he wasn't wrong, and it stung her pride. Aye, that was all. Simply her pride. "Then what do ye call this?"

He sighed, and for a fleeting moment it wasn't William Campbell who stood before her but Njord, a man without a past, and sorrow pierced through her for the loss of something that had never truly been real.

"I don't know, Isolde. Can ye honestly tell me ye feel nothing for me anymore?"

How she wished she could tell him she felt nothing but contempt for him. But despite how he'd tricked her, she still wanted him. It was demeaning, but that didn't make it untrue.

"I feel a great many things about ye. And every one of them vexes me greatly."

"I'll take that above indifference any day."

She gave an impatient sigh. "Can ye not be serious for more than a moment?"

"I'm serious. We're talking about the rest of our lives here."

"Aye." She pounced on that comment. "And ye know how I can't leave my isle."

"I know ye love yer isle." He seemed to be picking his words with care, and for some reason it irked her more than if he'd simply dismissed her comment as being irrelevant. William Campbell wasn't supposed to be thoughtful or mindful of her feelings. She wanted to hate him, but no matter how hard she tried, she couldn't. "I hope one day ye might love Creagdoun, Isolde. 'Tis my dearest wish ye'll be happy there as my bride."

He sounded so sincere. But Creagdoun was in the Highlands, far from her beloved isle and so different from every dream she'd woven around her stranger from the sea. Fear of an uncertain future caught in her throat, and before she could stop herself, she whispered, "I don't even know who ye are."

"Whatever else has changed between us, I'm still the same man whose bed ye shared the other night."

She didn't want to think about the other night. Because the other night she had believed they could have a future together, here on Eigg, when that had always been nothing but a foolish fantasy.

"Ye're wrong. For ye're not Njord, and ye never were."

Her barb hit home, and his smile faded, but no spark of triumph warmed her heart. Only a hollow sense of regret.

"That's right." There was no hint of amusement in his words, only a hard edge she'd never heard from him before. "I never was, Isolde, and I never claimed to be. But by God there's one thing I promise ye. When we are wed, I'll have ye screaming my true name when I make ye mine."

Her regret vaporized as a maelstrom of fury and, God damn it, lust blurred her reason. And only one word hammered through her mind.

*Bastard.*

# Chapter Fourteen

The meeting in her grandmother's chamber had been intolerably long. But not because of any unreasonable demands from William.

It was Amma.

Had the contract been for anything other than the capsizing of her own future, Isolde would have been utterly mesmerized by her grandmother's attention to every detail. Nothing had been left to chance, including the future security of both her sisters regarding their rights to Sgur Castle in the event of Lady Helga's death.

And this was the contract the Baron of Dunstrunage had agreed to.

William signed the contract with a flourish, and then Amma turned to her.

"Isolde, do ye agree to honor the contract and wed William Campbell, laird of Creagdoun?"

The silence in the chamber was like a thick fog, pressing into her mind. She stared at the clause on the parchment, at the words that would bind her to William Campbell and tear her away from everything she had ever known.

The words that went against everything her grandmother had taught her of the Deep Knowing.

For ten years she'd been so adamant that, if things came to a head, she'd simply refuse to go through with it. But now she was out of time. Now, she had to make the decision to either disgrace her beloved Amma and the honor of her foremothers by rejecting the contract—or accepting her fate and all that might entail.

She cast a surreptitious glance at William, who sat on the other side of the desk. She half expected him to appear smug that he was so close to achieving his objective. And how much easier that would make it to despise him.

But he didn't look self-satisfied or give the air of a man who knew he had won. There was a subtle sense of watchfulness about him, as though even now he wasn't certain she'd go through with it.

And if she didn't, what could he do about it?

Once again, she focused on the contract, but the words blurred, and her heart thundered in her chest. No one said a word. Despite how much Amma wanted this, in the end she was leaving it up to her to make the final decision.

A decision that would take her away from her isle and make her William's wife.

She didn't want to leave Eigg. The very notion of it gripped her stomach. And yet the prospect of wedding William—which should have disgusted her to the core of her being—sent tremors of treacherous anticipation spiraling through her.

It was wrong. She shouldn't still want him on any level, but she couldn't hide the truth from herself. Deep inside, in a place she hadn't even known existed until now, she still craved him.

She took a deep breath and signed the contract.

⁂

"'TIS DONE, THEN." There was a hushed note in Freyja's voice as Isolde and her sisters sat on their bed later that afternoon.

"And the wedding is set for the end of the week?" Roisin buried her face in her dog's fur, but it didn't disguise the catch in her voice.

"Aye. 'Tis scandalous." She wrapped her arms around her knees as Sjor, sitting on the bed beside her, gazed at her in mournful silence.

"And ye're set to sail that very morning." Freyja drew in a ragged breath. "Should we wish for another storm to delay yer departure?"

"It will only delay the inevitable." Aye, her fate was set now. But if William Campbell expected a meek little wife to do his bidding without question, he didn't know her at all.

But then, she didn't know him either, did she?

IT WAS THE morning of his wedding.

William turned to Hugh, the only one of his men he could now fully trust, and the only one who'd shared the solar with him these last five days while the rest of the crew spent their nights on the ship. Not that his men found that unusual. After all, none of them expected to be accommodated within the castle.

He hadn't passed on the message that Lady Helga had extended an invitation for them to all sleep in the relative comfort of the solar. The last thing he needed was to share a small chamber with a potential murderer.

Even though he'd had days for that knowledge to sink in, it still caused a shudder to inch along his spine whenever he thought of it. But for now, caution prevailed. There was no way of knowing who he could trust. Which was why, when he'd sent word to his father letting him know he was alive, he'd kept his counsel.

"Well?" He folded his arms and glowered at Hugh's prolonged silence.

Hugh ran a critical gaze from his boots to his head. "Ye'll do," he said.

William grunted at his cousin's sardonic praise. "'Tis all I have."

"Aye."

That's all Hugh said, but William knew exactly what he meant. If he'd done the expected thing, and merely made arrangements for

Isolde to travel to Creagdoun in the spring, on his wedding day he'd be wearing new boots instead of a pair warped by the sea, fresh linen, his own plaid, and his father's heirloom brooch.

But spring was months away. He couldn't wait that long until she became his bride.

"I'm glad, though," Hugh said before glowering, as though the words had fallen from him unbidden. Then he shrugged and focused on the wall. "That she pleases ye, after all."

"I'm fortunate," he agreed. Even Isolde's frosty attitude these last few days hadn't dampened his need for her. The woman had addled his senses, but once they were at Creagdoun, when they could begin their life together, she would soon thaw.

He had no doubt.

&

IT HAD BEEN decided between Lady Helga and Isolde that the wedding would take place in the great hall, rather than the kirk, and when he and Hugh entered, it had been transformed.

The castle's chaplain stood before the top table, which was draped in the colors of the MacDonalds of Sgur, and winter foliage and candles filled the hall. It seemed most of the inhabitants of Eigg wanted to witness the ceremony, as aside from Lady Helga's entourage and his men, the back of the hall was crammed with warriors, servants, and local villagers.

With Hugh by his side, he stood before the chaplain, and from the corner of the hall, a lone musician played the clarsach. The haunting notes filled the hall, and Willian sucked in a deep breath.

For ten years, the prospect of his marriage had crouched in the back of his mind like a poisoned toad. Something unavoidable that had to be endured for the good of his clan. He'd always expected it would happen in Argyll, under the watchful eye of the earl and surrounded by his family.

It seemed oddly fitting that none of his expectations of his wedding day had come to pass, since his bride was nothing like he'd once resigned himself to.

A ripple stirred through the crowd, and he glanced over his shoulder. And then he couldn't tear his gaze away, as his bride, surrounded by her sisters and Lady Helga, advanced towards him.

Isolde's forest green gown was threaded with gold, and jewels sparkled around her throat and wrists. But it wasn't the opulent silks and furs that rendered him immobile. It was her glorious hair that cascaded unbound over her shoulders and glimmered in mesmeric waves of red-gold curls in the glow from the candles.

She was a vision.

And soon, she would be his.

She came to his side, but whereas he couldn't drag his bewitched gaze from her, she didn't spare him even a fleeting glance. Her attention was fixed on the chaplain as though she didn't want to miss a word.

When he slid the ring on her finger, regret flickered through him. It was his bride's right—Isolde's right—to wear his beloved mother's ring. That had always been his intention, even before he'd met her. But for now, they had to make do with a ring from Lady Helga.

Finally, the service finished. And he couldn't recall a word of it. But that didn't matter, since the only thing of consequence was that Isolde was now his bride, and with so many witnesses, no one could ever doubt it.

As the hall erupted with activity, with servants rearranging the tables and benches to ready the wedding feast, he clasped her fingers and kissed her hand.

"My lady," he murmured, his gaze meshing with hers, and lust gripped his vitals so violently he barely managed to swallow his groan. It would be hours before he and Isolde were alone. Maybe he should've accepted Lady Helga's offer for them to remain in the castle for their wedding night and set sail in the morning.

But he wanted to begin their married life in Argyll. At Creagdoun, the castle he'd one day pass onto his son. And, irrational or not, he wanted that son conceived at Creagdoun as a testament of his right to the land.

"William Campbell," she responded. "It's not too late to change yer mind and remain on Eigg with me."

At least she now agreed they belonged together. It was an improvement on her previous stance. Unfortunately, her request was impossible for him to grant.

"My castle needs a mistress. And I can't leave my lands for too long." Because if he did, the cursed MacGregors would do all in their power to claim Creagdoun, and Clan Campbell could never allow such a significant stronghold to once again fall into their enemy's hands. "But all being well, we could make plans to visit the Isle in summer."

Unless Isolde was with child. He wouldn't risk her health, or the bairn's, by allowing it. Besides, surely she wouldn't wish to undertake an arduous journey unnecessarily.

He was so caught up in the enticing notion of her nurturing his bairn, it took him a moment to realize her serene expression had turned hostile. It was obvious the prospect of waiting so long before seeing her family again did not sit right with her.

The last thing he wanted was to upset his bride on their wedding day. Once again, he raised her hand and brushed another kiss across her fingers. "But Lady Helga and yer sisters are welcome to visit any time they wish, Isolde. Creagdoun is yer home now, as well as mine."

"How gracious." She accompanied her words with a smile so filled with ice, it could easily rival a frozen loch in midwinter. "I'll be sure to inform them of yer benevolence."

He could feel the eyes of everyone in the hall upon them. And, most likely, judging him. While he didn't care about the opinion of strangers, Isolde's rancor grated and threatened his good humor. Was she going to blame him for who he was *forever*?

"Do ye really wish to argue today of all days?"

She cast a swift glance around the hall and appeared to realize they were the center of attention. A shudder rippled through her, and he had to force himself not to pull her into his arms to comfort her. Although, she was now his bride in the eyes of God, so would it really cause a scandal if he did?

Before he got the chance to test his theory, she swung about to face him.

"No. This sacrifice will be for nothing if no one believes our alliance is true."

Stung by her choice of words, he whispered in her ear, so no one might overhear. "'Tis no sacrifice, Isolde. We are wed, not planning to be murdered by yer Pict queen ancestor."

"Don't mock things ye know nothing about."

"Then don't compare this to being sacrificed for the good of yer isle. I've no ill intentions to desecrate the memory of yer foremothers. Alliances are arranged all the time. Aren't ye at least relieved not to be tied to an old man who can barely leave his disease-ridden bed?"

Her eyes sparked green fire at him. "Ye paint a disgusting picture, William Campbell."

"Well?" He would not let her ignore his challenge.

She let out a vexed breath. "Aye. I understand what ye're saying. But that's not the way of the MacDonald women of Sgur. We don't wed for those kinds of alliances."

"Ye do now."

He regretted his retort the moment he uttered it and saw the stricken expression flash over her face. But it was gone in an instant, and she offered him a brittle smile instead.

"Aye. It seems we do."

He couldn't take his hasty words back, but he had to make her admit that what they had was worth something.

"Damn it, Isolde. Can't we at least try and make this work?"

From the corner of his eye, he saw her sisters approaching, doubtless to tell them that it was time for them to take their places at the high table so the wedding breakfast could begin.

"Very well." Her voice was so soft, he barely heard it above the noise of laughter and chatter that filled the hall. "I shall make the best of it, since I have little choice."

He should have been satisfied that she didn't intend to make their marriage a battlefield, but her choice of words irked him greatly. "Neither of us had a choice," he reminded her. "Do ye plan to throw that in my face every day?"

"No. 'Tis not *that* I blame ye for."

"Isolde—" Exasperated, he bit off his retort as her sisters arrived, and they settled themselves at the high table. Isolde sat by his side, as regal as a princess, with a serene smile on her face. Playing her part of the happy bride to perfection.

He didn't want her playing a part, God damn it.

Across the hall, he caught sight of his men, laughing and jesting as befit the occasion. None of them threw him hostile glances, and during the last few days he'd not felt any antagonism when in their company. Whoever had hit him on the head and thrown him overboard was a cursedly fine actor.

He was thankful Patric was accompanying Isolde. When William wasn't by her side, he knew he could rely on the other man to protect her with his life.

As the last dish was cleared from the table, he turned to Isolde. "My lady, we need to leave if we want to reach Creagdoun before sundown."

The journey to Creagdoun would take several hours but as long as they left Eigg by sunrise they'd reach the castle before daylight faded.

Her bottom lip trembled, just once, and the sight of it caused the lingering remnants of irritation to vanish. She was leaving everything she had ever known, and a sliver of guilt chewed through him at how hastily he'd arranged this wedding.

Yet he wouldn't change things, even if he could. The prospect of returning to Creagdoun without her by his side was unthinkable.

He took her hand as they rose from the table, his thumb grazing her knuckles in a gentle caress, a silent message of support. To remind her that, however they had arrived at this point, it was meant to be.

Her gaze clashed with his. He'd half expected her eyes to be filled with tears, or, more optimistically, understanding, but he should have known better.

Her eyes flashed with suppressed resentment, and sparks ignited in the charged air between them. She wasn't on the verge of weeping, no, not his Isolde, and anticipation scorched through him, obliterating his guilt in a blaze of untrammeled lust.

Once he'd imagined he wanted a gentle lass as his wife. But Creagdoun needed a strong woman as its mistress, one who would never back down from a challenge.

Once she made the castle her home, and accepted the reality of their alliance, she'd understand this was the only way it could be, for them both.

He just hoped it didn't take her too long.

## Chapter Fifteen

Isolde stood at the prow of the ship, her shawl wrapped tightly about her, as they approached the port of Oban. It had been an uneventful crossing, and although the relentless wind had turned her face numb with cold, it was nothing compared to the bitter chill creeping through her blood.

Enclosing her heart.

Before they'd left Sgur Castle, she'd had a few moments alone with her sisters and Amma. They had held each other tight, not speaking, but the sorrow had been a tangible thing woven around them like strands of gossamer.

"I'll visit in the spring," she reminded them. William had been agreeable to it, and by God she intended to hold him to his promise. "That's not so very long to wait, is it?"

Roisin shook her head, but her bottom lip trembled, and Frey gripped her hand in silent support. But it was when Amma cupped her face in a tender gesture that she nearly lost her composure.

"I'm proud of ye, lass."

The bittersweet memory would remain with her always.

She sucked in a jagged breath as the ship docked. William had tried to sequester her away in a corner of the ship, out of the frigid elements, so he'd told her, but mainly, she knew it was because a woman standing on the deck discomposed his men.

That was too bad. She would not sit quietly in a corner, out of sight, simply to appease Clan Campbell. This was her future now, and she'd face it squarely, and if William didn't like it, he had no one but himself to blame for going through with this farce.

She picked up the basket by her feet, where Sjor had spent the journey under great protest.

"Ye can stretch yer legs in a moment, my bonny wee lad," she whispered. Before they began the next leg of their journey to Creagdoun. But she knew it wasn't just the unfamiliarity of the ship that agitated him. He missed his littermates.

"Here." William appeared by her side and attempted to take the basket from her. She tightened her grip, and he expelled a loud sigh. "Are ye still being contrary, Isolde? I'm merely trying to help."

"I can manage to carry Sjor's basket," she said with as much dignity as she could, considering she dearly wanted to take issue with his *contrary* comment. "I'm not a fragile southern maiden who cannot undertake such a simple task."

"Just as well." He eyed her and despite everything, flickers of warmth raced over her skin. Curse her foolish feelings. "A sassenach lass would never suit me."

With that, he remained by her side until he'd safely deposited her on dry land before he returned to the ship to supervise the unloading of her trunks.

With a silent sigh of relief, she placed Sjor's basket on the ground. She'd rip out her tongue rather than ever admit it, but her darling lad was heavier than she'd anticipated, and it hadn't been easy maintaining her dignity as she'd disembarked while grasping onto the basket for dear life.

Emer, one of her grandmother's loyal serving women who was now her personal maid, hurried to her side. The voyage hadn't agreed with her, but thankfully she no longer looked as though she were about to throw up her breakfast.

Patric joined them, along with the dozen warriors he'd handpicked to accompany her to Creagdoun, and her heart squeezed in her chest when she spied her beloved claymore secured on his back.

How could she ever use it again, so far from the isle of her birth?

The port was busy, but even between the throngs of people going about their business, it was easy to spot William as he strode through the crowd towards her. Why did her breath catch in her throat every time she saw him? It was most annoying.

When he reached her side, he took her hand. "We'll rest here for a short time while we procure wagons and horses. There's a patch of grass yonder where Sjor can run."

Why was he so thoughtful? Surely not many men would be so mindful of her dog's needs. It made it harder to recall why she couldn't trust him.

And she couldn't afford to trust him. Not when she couldn't believe anything he said to her.

"He'll enjoy that," she acknowledged, especially since she knew how much he'd hate being secured in his basket in a bumpy wagon. But there was no help for it. He wasn't as young as he once was and couldn't possibly make the journey to Creagdoun under his own steam.

"William." Hugh hailed him as he approached. "There's a messenger from Dunstrunage. Yer father requests ye and yer bride visit before traveling to Creagdoun."

"If we detour to Dunstrunage, we'll never reach Creagdoun before sundown."

"I doubt the baron expects ye to continue yer journey today. He's sent horses and wagons for yer use."

William expelled an impatient breath before turning to her. "It seems we are delayed, my lady. Dunstrunage is less than an hour north from here, but even if we don't stay the night, I doubt we could leave the castle before dark."

"I should like to meet the baron." Aye, she'd very much like to meet the powerful Campbell who had agreed so readily with her grandmother's proposed alliance. "And it will be good to recover overnight from the crossing before another lengthy journey."

Concern flashed across his face. "Ye should've told me ye were feeling weary, Isolde."

Why would he leap to that conclusion? And why did his obvious care for her comfort still manage to touch her, when she knew how easily insincere, honeyed words could drip from his tongue?

"I'm perfectly well." Inadvertently, she glanced at Emer before returning her attention to William. "It simply makes sense to visit the baron, since we are so close."

He also glanced at Emer, and she saw understanding dawn.

"Aye." He sounded reluctant. "I know my father is eager to meet ye. He would have had us wed five years ago if he'd had his way."

"Then let us be thankful for small mercies."

He flashed her a grin. Evidently, her barb had entirely missed its mark. He leaned in close, so no one could overhear. "I wanted our first night together to be at Creagdoun. But Dunstrunage is my childhood home so I cannot be too disappointed."

Their wedding night. Heat scorched her as fractured images of the time she'd spent in his bed blazed through her mind. If only she'd remained in her own bedchamber that night, she wouldn't now be plagued by those cursed memories. Yet it seemed her treacherous body didn't care how William had manipulated her, and sparks of desire ignited between her thighs.

She drew in a steadying breath, but it didn't help calm her galloping pulse. "Alas," she whispered, "our wedding was so rushed ye didn't allow for a suitable date to be arranged. My monthly courses are upon me."

For an eternal moment, he appeared bemused. And then realization struck, and consternation wreathed his features. Indeed, he looked so mortified by her revelation she had the alarming urge to laugh.

Thankfully, she managed to keep her mirth contained and merely raised her eyebrows when he took a hasty step back.

"Apologies." He cast a furtive glance around, as though ensuring no one was close enough to hear their conversation, and although there was nothing funny about it, she had another mad desire to laugh. And then his gaze caught hers, and the laughter dried in her throat at the raw need that glowed in his eyes. "It appears we're destined to consummate our union at Creagdoun after all."

⧬

ISOLDE DIDN'T WANT to be impressed by anything connected to Clan Campbell, but the first sight of Dunstrunage Castle was, without doubt, breathtaking. Set on its own peninsula in the Firth of Lorn, the mighty towers of the castle were protected from any attack by land or sea by a formidable curtain wall.

As they went through the gatehouse, she stole a sideways glance at William, who had ridden by her side for the length of the journey. She'd always known, deep in her heart, he was of noble blood. And so he was. What a pity that blood was Campbell.

William had sent a messenger ahead of them, and a party greeted them in the courtyard. He helped her from her horse and held her hand as he led her to an older man who, judging by his bearing and uncanny likeness to William, could only be the baron.

"Sir," William said, bowing his head, before he introduced her. Bruce Campbell, Baron of Dunstrunage, smiled at her, clearly well satisfied by events, and she offered him a chilly smile in response.

"Lady Isolde," he said. "May I welcome ye to the family. How like yer mother ye are."

Startled by his greeting, which was nothing like she'd imagined, she glanced at William. But he appeared as taken aback as herself by his father's remark.

"Did ye know my mother, my lord?" she enquired, as she allowed him to take her hand and press a kiss against her knuckles.

"Aye." He released her hand. "A long time ago." He turned to a youth by his side, who looked to be seventeen or so. "My youngest son, James. And my daughter, Margaret." He smiled indulgently at the girl, who looked no more than twelve.

How remiss of her not to have known William had a younger brother and sister. But then, he had never mentioned them. Not even when he'd so wondrously regained his memories.

The reminder of how he'd tricked her smarted, and she hastily forced that memory to the back of her mind. She would not disgrace her foremothers by displaying bad manners to these Campbells.

After James and Margaret greeted her, the baron led them inside to the great hall. Surreptitiously, she admired the fine tapestries on the walls, and the grand stone-carved fireplace. It was obvious William's family not only possessed noble blood but also great wealth.

For the first time she wondered about Creagdoun. Sgur Castle was her home, and while she loved it with every particle of her being, there was no denying it was a constant battle to keep the roof from leaking, and their many tapestries, while exquisite, were over two hundred years old.

The tapestries displayed here, particularly one of a magnificent hunt incorporating the mythical unicorn, looked astonishingly new.

But then, it wasn't the wealth of the MacDonalds of Sgur the Campbells coveted. It was their land, and the gateway it gave to the Western Isles.

"We'll have dinner shortly," the baron said. "And ye will doubtless stay the night. It was a great relief, my lady," he added, glancing at her, "to discover my son hadn't perished in the storm."

"Indeed," she said, inclining her head. Did the baron know William had woven a tale of deception around her? Or not?

In the end, it scarcely mattered, since the outcome was exactly what he and her grandmother had plotted all those years ago.

Patric came to her, holding Sjor's basket. Warily, she eyed the large deerhound that stood beside the baron. The baron scratched the dog's head and nodded at her darling lad.

"He'll be safe, my lady, no fear of that."

Relieved, she released Sjor, and the two dogs sniffed each other with mutual curiosity.

"Sir," William said. "My bride needs time to refresh herself after the sea crossing. Might I take her to her chamber?"

"I'll take Lady Isolde." Margaret stepped forward, and the baron laughed.

"Aye, Margaret will do the honors as the lady of the castle." He gave her hair an affectionate ruffle, and the girl gave a long-suffering sigh.

It was clear that, when it came to his daughter, at least, the baron wasn't an ogre. Which was disconcerting, to say the least. During the last ten years, she'd built a picture of him in her mind, and being a caring father had not been on her list.

"This way, my lady." Margaret glanced over her shoulder at William. "'Tis yer old chamber, since that is the second-best in the castle."

Isolde followed Margaret up the spiral staircase, taking an odd comfort in how the stone steps were worn away through centuries of use. It reminded her of home.

Margaret opened a door and stood back to allow her to enter the chamber. William followed her, and Patric and Emer remained by the door.

"'Tis beautiful." Isolde tried not to stare at the sumptuous four poster bed, but it was impossible. She'd never seen such a beautiful thing before, although she'd heard many rumors of their splendor.

"It was our lady mother's bed." There was a reverential note in Margaret's voice as she traced her fingertips along one of the carved oak posts.

"Just so ye know," William said, giving her a smile that made her treacherous toes curl. "When this was my bedchamber, I had nothing as grand as this to sleep on."

"My lord father moved the bed in here when William claimed Creagdoun," Margaret said. "When we received the message earlier in the week that ye were arriving, I had the chamber aired and bed linen freshly washed. If there's anything ye need, my lady, please let me know."

"Ye're very kind." She smiled at Margaret, for how could she not? The girl was delightful and certainly not in league with her brother's deceptions.

*But what does she mean when William claimed Creagdoun?* Maybe she merely meant when William had inherited the castle from their father.

"Thank ye, Margaret," William said, and his sister beamed at him before leaving the chamber. Patric, after casting a critical eye around the chamber, nodded at her before ushering Emer away, and she and her husband were finally alone.

She gave him a sideways glance as he shut the door. *My husband.* How strange that fact hadn't crossed her mind before.

"Yer sister is most attentive."

"She takes her duties seriously." He came up behind her and wrapped his arms around her shoulders. His body was a wall of solid muscle against her back. How she longed to melt against him. But she'd melted beneath his charm before, and she doubted her pride would ever recover from it.

She dragged her scrambled thoughts to order. She would *not* let him see how easily he could shatter her defenses.

"Yer lady mother?" She left the question hanging, suddenly unsure if he'd wish to speak of her, when he hadn't mentioned her before. But then, he hadn't mentioned any of his family to her, and surely, now she was his wife, she had the right to know.

A great shudder ripped through his body, and she bit her lip, glad he wasn't facing her. She didn't need to see the pain in his eyes to know how deeply he'd loved her.

"She died in childbirth. I was thirteen. Margaret is the image of her. I think somehow that gives our father comfort."

"I'm so sorry." Her voice was soft. For such a natural event, childbirth could be so cruel. How many times had Freyja raged in the night when a new mother she'd cared for had succumbed, despite all her efforts?

He rested his jaw on the top of her head, a tender gesture, and she blinked back the unexpected prickling behind her eyes. She didn't want to feel sadness for him. He was her husband, and she would do her duty, but not because she wanted to.

Because she had no choice.

How bleak that future would be, when once she'd imagined so much more could be theirs.

"I must speak with my father." He sounded reluctant, and his arms tightened around her before he slowly released her. "I'll send Emer in, to tend to yer needs."

She turned and gave him a perfunctory smile, even though it foolishly hurt her heart. It wasn't Emer she wanted. It was her sisters.

But most of all, she wanted her imaginary Njord back.

## Chapter Sixteen

William found his father in the courtyard, talking with Hugh, David, and Malcolm. Several of the men had gone their own ways after they'd docked, and while he'd rather keep any possible enemy close, he could hardly demand they remain without explaining why. And as soon as he alerted his would-be murderer that he recalled those last moments on the ship, the slender advantage of using their ignorance against them would vanish.

Admittedly, it was a shit advantage, since he still had no clue who wanted him dead. But it was the only one he had.

At his approach, the men made their excuses and left the two of them alone.

"What the hell happened?" His father kept his voice low. "Ye fell overboard?" Skepticism dripped from every word.

"I don't know who hit me on the head and left me for dead. But if not for Lady Isolde and her kin, the assassin would've succeeded in their mission."

"Christ." His father exhaled a long breath. "Who the devil was on the ship with ye?"

"I've known every man for years." Frustration clawed through him again, the way it did every time he thought of what had happened. "Only Hugh knows the truth. Safer that way."

"Aye. I agree. It sickens me to think we have a traitor among us. It's good Lady Isolde has her own band of warriors to protect her." He drew in a deep breath, and William refrained from telling his father that Isolde was his responsibility and only he could protect her.

God damn it, he couldn't even trust the people closest to him. How could he ever entrust her safety to them when he wasn't around?

"Aye," he agreed, even though the word burned his throat. "Her men are loyal."

"I'll speak to the earl. He might know something."

It was possible. The earl's influence was like a spider's web across Argyll and beyond.

Then his father clasped his arm and gave a satisfied grin. "So ye are now wed. Well done, lad. She's a bonny lass, as I always knew she would be. When we've flushed out the traitor, we'll have a Campbell wedding in the chapel here, so there'll be no doubt about it."

"There's no doubt," he said. "Most of Eigg witnessed our marriage."

"Good. 'Tis the right thing to unite Campbell and MacDonald."

And that reminded him. "It was always the intention for Lady Isolde to wear my lady mother's ring. I should like to give that to her, with yer permission."

"From the day ye were born, it was yer mother's greatest wish that her ring should, in time, go to yer wife." His father gave a ragged sigh. "I'll find it for ye. And my wedding gift to ye both is the Brussels tapestry in the great hall."

Taken aback, he stared at his father. The tapestry was only a few years old and had cost a small fortune to commission from the artisans in Brussels. "That's very generous."

"Creagdoun is sound, but now ye have a wife, ye'll need to furnish it appropriately. Every woman appreciates a few luxuries, William. Never forget that."

He'd spent the last three years improving Creagdoun's fortifications and estates, and although he'd always known the inside of the castle needed attention, there had always been other tasks that had taken priority.

An oversight he intended to remedy as soon as possible. His bride deserved nothing less than the best.

"Lady Isolde will never have cause to regret our marriage."

"Make sure of it," his father said. "I gave Lady Helga my word I'd honor her granddaughter as though she were my own blood. She'll want for nothing."

It was good his father wanted only the best for Isolde. But she was *his* wife. And he was responsible for Isolde's happiness, not his father. What's more, the baron's remarks grated along his senses, as though his sire suspected William was incapable of keeping a noble-born wife in the manner to which she was due.

But there was something else, something that scraped along the edges of his affront, dulling its sting, as he recalled the odd greeting the baron had made upon meeting Isolde. How would his father know Isolde looked like her mother, unless he had met her?

"Sir, forgive me. But did ye know Lady Helga before she came to Dunstrunage ten years ago?"

At first, he didn't think his father was going to answer. The baron gazed into the distance, as though lost in the distant past, before expelling a deep breath and finally meeting his eyes.

"Aye." He sounded reluctant. "'Twas before I wed yer lady mother, God rest her soul. I met Lady Helga's daughter, Ingrid, one summer I spent on the Small Isles. But in the end, I couldn't remain on Eigg, and she refused to leave Sgur. But I never forgot her."

It was disconcerting to learn his father had once set his sights on Isolde's mother. If only he'd kept his mouth shut, but it was too late to regret his curiosity now. He didn't even know what to say, and instead gave a grunt which hopefully conveyed whatever his father wished it to.

Then his father grasped his shoulder. "Yet here we are, thirty years later, and Ingrid MacDonald of Sgur's daughter is my son's wife. And Clan Campbell has a strategic foothold in the Small Isles."

As William watched his father return to the castle, an uneasy question slithered through his mind. Had he wanted Ingrid MacDonald for herself, or for Sgur?

He knew it didn't matter. Marriages were rarely undertaken for reasons other than strategic gain. But for a few surreal moments, he thought he'd seen something more in his father's eyes when he'd spoken of Ingrid, rather than merely a politically advantageous alliance.

Either way, it didn't affect him. He hadn't wed Isolde because of her lands. She could have been the third daughter with nothing of value but her name, and he'd still have wanted her as his bride.

At least his memory loss had proved that to him, without a doubt. And once Isolde was truly his bride, she'd see it that way, too.

༺༻

IT WAS EARLY afternoon the following day when Isolde caught the first glimpse of Creagdoun. Between the trees, a loch glimmered, and the L-shaped castle stood not far from its banks. It was an imposing sight, although it lacked the elegant style of Dunstrunage, but that wasn't why a sense of dread gripped her heart.

It was because Creagdoun was so very far from the coast.

There wasn't even the faintest hint of sea in the breeze, and the sound of gulls had faded long ago. Her fingers tightened on the reins, and she took a few deep breaths to calm herself, but all that did was reinforce how far she was from everything she knew.

William, who'd scarcely left her side throughout the journey from Dunstrunage, caught her gaze and gave her a smile that caused the breath to catch in her throat. The crisp winter air made his stormy blue-gray eyes glitter, but there was nothing cold about them. Heat lurked deep in those enigmatic depths, and a responding curl of flame licked through her blood.

Last night, he hadn't shared that magnificent bed with her. He'd respected what she'd told him and sprawled on a chair by the hearth. But how a foolish part of her had wanted to spend the night simply wrapped in his arms.

"What do ye think, my lady?"

It was obvious he was referring to her first sight of her new home. A week ago, she would've confided her fears to him. But a week ago, he had been Njord.

Now, he was her husband. And while she had to admit he still possessed traces of the honor she'd once thought were an inextricable part of Njord, she couldn't bring herself to share with William Campbell how daunting she found this new future. For the sake of her pride, it was best to let him believe all was well. "'Tis very grand."

"Aye." There was no mistaking the pride in his voice as they drew closer to the castle. And then a frown slashed his brow. "It will be, Isolde. I give ye my word. I'll make ye proud to be the lady of Creagdoun."

She cast him a sideways glance as they approached the gatehouse. What an odd thing to say. As though that truly mattered to him when surely all he cared about was the fact he'd achieved his objective in making her his bride.

*Is that really all he cares about?*

How comforting to believe his concern was genuine. But she'd trod that path before, until her eyes had been opened, and she wouldn't lose sight of the truth again.

As they rode across the forecourt, the castle's servants waited at the doors, and she kept a serene smile on her face, despite the unease that tangled in her stomach. From the time she was a small child, she'd learned the importance of how to run a great house, but she'd also always imagined that great house would be Sgur Castle, and the servants would be those she had known all her life.

She shouldn't have been so complacent. After all, her grandmother had given her fair warning, ten years ago, when she'd signed that alliance with the baron.

William helped her dismount, and his seneschal, Lamond, greeted them, before motioning forward several of the higher-ranking servants, who all seemed pleased to welcome her.

Finally, the ordeal was over, and William led her into the great hall, where several large tapestries covered the walls. She tried not to stare, but it was still a shock to see the substantial fire and smoke damage that disfigured the woven country scenes.

The baron's wedding gift, which William had told her about last night, was welcome, indeed. But why hadn't the tapestries been repaired before William had inherited the castle? It seemed the baron, despite his wealth, had neglected to maintain Creagdoun.

"After dinner, I'll show ye the rest of the castle." William took her hand, evidently unconcerned by such lack of etiquette, and led her across the hall. It was hard not to recall all the times they had held hands in the past, those secret, hidden, moments, when no one else was around to voice their disapproval.

And now they were wed, and William was the laird of a grand estate, no would dare remark upon his behavior towards his wife.

Despite her best intentions, a ragged sigh raked through her for those few precious days when anything had seemed possible. It seemed like a lifetime ago. Nothing more than a dream.

His hand tightened around hers, as though he'd heard her unwary thoughts, but he didn't say anything as they went up the stairs. Then he paused.

"We'll be sharing my bedchamber, Isolde. Just so ye know."

He made it sound like a challenge. Did he expect her to rise to it?

She wouldn't give him the satisfaction. And then couldn't help herself. "How can a castle such as Creagdoun lack a lady's chamber?"

"I didn't say it lacked the chamber. Just that ye would be sharing mine."

She squashed the flare of excitement that ignited at his arrogant assumption. It didn't matter that a week ago she would've welcomed the prospect of such a scandalous proposition, because a week ago she'd been utterly in thrall to Njord.

The despicable truth was the prospect still thrilled her. And it was that, more than his imperious command, that truly rankled.

"This is a political alliance, William, not a love match. Ye and I both know the terms of the contract state I'm to be afforded all rights due to my rank."

A muscle flexed in his jaw, as if her barb had found its mark. "And so ye will, make no mistake. The lady's chamber is currently not fit for yer use, which is why ye'll share mine."

Momentarily deflated by his retort, she fell silent as he continued along the passage. God, what was wrong with her? She didn't want to share his bedchamber. Why did it matter what the reason was for him suggesting it?

Yet it did. Because she'd assumed only nefarious purposes whereas it appeared there was a genuine explanation.

How mortifying.

He paused, his hand on an iron door ring, and gave her a sideways glance. Warning skittered through her at the blatantly predatory gleam in his eyes.

"In case ye're in any doubt," his voice dropped to a low rumble that, infuriatingly, caused heat to bloom between her thighs. "That's not the main reason why I want ye in my bed, Isolde. Ye're my bride, and I want ye by my side. Ye'll discover the merits of that, soon enough."

With that, he opened the door, as she silently seethed at his brazen promise. He presumed that she'd enjoy the marriage bed so thoroughly, she'd overlook propriety.

She'd never allow that to happen. It didn't matter how much a part of her still craved his touch. That was something she'd have to learn to live with. Aye, and hide it, too, until it finally faded to nothingness.

And another thing. She had to stop believing everything he said. Hadn't she learned that lesson the hard way?

She cast her glance around the good-sized antechamber, with two chairs set before the hearth and a great oak chest along one wall. Rushes and dried herbs were strewn across the floor, which gave the chamber a fresh scent, although without any rugs, or tapestries on the wall, even with the fire blazing there was a distinct chill in the air.

She suppressed a shiver, but she wasn't going to let him think she'd accept every word he uttered without proof. "Where is the lady's chamber? Perhaps ye have unrealistic expectations as to what I find acceptable."

"I'm not lying to ye, Isolde." There was a faint note of affront in his tone, but she didn't deign to answer since they both knew she had the perfect response. He expelled a harsh sigh and shook his head. "Very well, the lady's chamber is through there." He indicated a door on the far wall. "It backs onto the master chamber, but for an unfathomable reason the chambers don't possess a connecting door."

He released her hand and marched across the chamber, before flinging open the offending door. "Let me know yer opinion."

She inclined her head and joined him at the door. Good Lord. What had happened in there? The chamber was empty of furniture, the shutters on the windows were broken and let in the icy wind, and chunks of stone were scattered across the floor.

"It certainly needs some work," she conceded. Curse the man. He hadn't lied to her. But why was it in such a dreadful state? "Why is it uninhabitable?"

"I'll make it habitable. That doesn't mean I want ye sleeping in here."

Exasperated, she rounded on him. "That's not an answer, and ye well know it, William Campbell. How could the baron allow it to fall into such a state of disrepair in the first place?"

To be sure, his lady wife had died many years ago. But this chamber wasn't merely sadly neglected. It appeared maliciously damaged.

Instead of a cutting retort, which she expected, William frowned, as though her criticism made little sense. "Creagdoun has never belonged to my father. I assumed ye knew. The earl granted me the castle and land after I claimed it in battle three years ago."

All her preconceived notions shifted and, obscurely, she felt wrong-footed. "Well, how the devil was I supposed to know that? Ye've told me nothing of yer life, never mind about yer castle."

"If ye recall, I extended an invitation three years ago for ye to visit Creagdoun. Lady Helga declined on yer behalf. Did ye not receive the message, Isolde?"

Aye, she had. And the reminder did not improve her mood. "The message said nothing about ye having just been granted the castle."

"Would it have made any difference?"

Damn him. "No," she admitted.

"Right."

"But still," she persisted. "Ye could have told me once we were wed."

"To be fair, we are only just wed."

She heard the hint of laughter in his voice. She was so glad one of them found this discussion amusing. "Who owned Creagdoun before yer conquest?"

The humor drained from his eyes, and perversely she was sorry for it, but she couldn't live in ignorance.

"Torcall MacGregor. Ye know—I assume ye know—of the bad blood between Clans Campbell and MacGregor?"

"We heard how Clan MacGregor seized Campbell land in Argyll."

"Torcall MacGregor set his sights on Dunstrunage. A fatal error of judgement. The castle is a strategic stronghold and can never be allowed to fall into MacGregor hands. They were crushed, and for my service the earl granted me Creagdoun." He indicated they should return to the antechamber, and he led her to the other door. "That's when I discovered how much work it needed to bring it up to a standard fit for a bride. Although the castle itself is sound enough, and I've improved its fortifications."

He opened the door, and they went through to the master bedchamber. At least in here the chill wasn't as noticeable, as faded tapestries hung upon the wall and threadbare rugs covered the wooden floor. Had everything she'd seen so far belonged to the disposed MacGregor?

"'Tis not what ye're used to, I know." He folded his arms and cast a grim glare around the chamber. "My plan had been to improve the inside of the castle during the next few months, so it'd be fit for ye before we wed. But now ye're here, ye can pick whatever furnishings ye best like."

"I believe repairing the lady's chamber should be the priority, before commissioning pretty fripperies." Although without more tapestries to put on the wall, the lady's chamber—even when it was repaired—would be as cold as a tomb. But she could hardly back down now, especially when William's mouth twitched as though he found her remark amusing.

"The estate can well afford both," he said. "Now ye're here, I promise to see to the lady's chamber. And in the meantime, ye must tell me what luxuries Creagdoun lacks. I won't have a wife of mine going without her essential comforts."

She wasn't entirely certain whether he was mocking her or not. But since it appeared that she was obliged to share this chamber with him for the foreseeable future, she might as well make the best of it.

"I brought a rug from home. We can use it in here, for now, and these older ones can go in the antechamber."

"Agreed." He didn't even pause to think about it. "And we'll put the unicorn tapestry on the wall in here, until ye find something more appropriate to keep out the chill."

"I doubt the baron would approve of his gift being hidden away up here." She was surprised William even suggested it. The tapestry was a prestigious piece of art, something to be displayed in the great hall for guests to admire and secretly covet.

William shrugged. "Yer comfort is more important to me than displaying a Brussels tapestry in the great hall."

Why did he insist on saying things like that? It made it so hard to remember that his tongue was gilded with honey, and he'd say anything to get his own way. Yet even knowing that, warmth spread through her at his words.

After all, she was already his bride. He had nothing more to gain by uttering sweet lies.

She stifled a sigh and shook her head, but her thoughts remained as tangled as ever.

"Isolde." His calloused palms cradled her face, pulling her back to the present with a rush of awareness that spiked through her blood. Her breath caught in her throat, and it was hard not to let him see how desperately she wanted to wrap her arms around him. "Should I sleep on the chair again tonight?"

She swallowed, her mouth dry. How many men would be so thoughtful? It was something Njord would ask. Not William Campbell.

Yet here they were.

How easy it would be to tell him she needed another night before he shared their bed.

But she didn't need another night. And sooner or later, this union would need to be consummated.

Treacherous flickers of desire ignited, threatening every good sense she possessed. But there was no point lying to herself.

Even knowing how he had manipulated her, she still wanted him.

Her gaze meshed with his, and she couldn't have lied to him even if she'd wanted to. "No." Her voice was husky, and his eyes darkened in understanding, obliterating the stormy blue-gray of his irises. "There's no need to sleep on the chair this night."

# Chapter Seventeen

As promised, after dinner William showed Isolde around the rest of the castle. She'd been unnaturally silent, and he'd been forced to see Creagdoun through her eyes.

He was fiercely proud of Creagdoun. And the fact the earl himself had bestowed the castle and lands on him as a reward for how he'd fought in the bloodied battles to drive back the MacGregors. To be sure, the estate and village had been neglected for years, but he'd spent every hour God had sent working to make the land profitable.

He'd told Isolde the truth. It had always been his intention to start on the interior of the castle this year, since his father had made it plain that he and the earl wanted the alliance with Isolde of Sgur to be formalized by summer at the latest.

In fact, he'd been set to begin upon his return from Skye. But if only he'd set his mind to such matters a year ago. Because the stark truth was, Creagdoun was in no fit state to welcome a mistress with Isolde's noble heritage.

It was too late to regret that now. But he'd make it up to her, and she'd soon be mistress of a fine castle she could be proud of, too.

He left her in the solar with her serving woman, and while up until now he'd merely been appreciative of the light that streamed in through the windows, now he couldn't help but compare it to the comfortable solar at Sgur.

There was nothing he could do about that today, and as much as he didn't want to leave her for even an hour, he needed to be seen about his estate to quell any rumors that might've sprung up during his absence.

Rumors that would find their way back to Clan MacGregor, who would doubtless attempt to take advantage to try and reclaim Creagdoun.

Aye, they'd attempt anything. The black thoughts swirled in his mind as he marched into the courtyard on his way to the stables.

"William." Hugh's voice penetrated his dark suspicions, and he swung about. His cousin came to his side, a frown slashing his brow. "What is it, man?"

"Do ye think a MacGregor is behind the attack?" William kept his voice low, even though no one was close enough to overhear. "That they managed to bribe one of the men?"

"It sickens me to think that's possible."

"Aye. But what else can we think? None of the men were strangers, Hugh. Who the devil can we trust, if not the men we've known for years?"

"My brother knows some lowlifes. I'll see if I can get any information from him about suspected MacGregor spies. I won't tell him why."

Hugh didn't elaborate, but William understood. Douglas, Hugh's older brother, might have the ability to charm his way out of all the trouble he'd landed in over the years, but he was also a drunkard. They'd learned not to trust him with secrets when they'd been lads, since Douglas had a loose tongue when in his cups.

Robert Fletcher, one of the men he'd sailed with, met them at the stables. "William, are ye in any need of extra hands about the estate? I and a couple of the men could do with the work."

It wasn't an unusual request. The Fletchers had pledged their loyalty to Campbells long ago, and since becoming laird of Creagdoun, he'd often enlisted the services of Robert and some of the other men and was grateful for it.

But now, suspicion gnawed through his mind. Did Robert have an ulterior motive for staying at Creagdoun?

*Keep yer enemies close.*

It was ancient advice, but no less sage for that. Even if the prospect that it was Robert who was the traitor turned his guts.

He managed to keep his face impassive as he gripped Robert's shoulder. "That'd be grand. There's plenty to be done, now my bride is here."

But there was no way anyone was getting close to her. She'd remain within the castle walls, protected by him and the men she'd brought with her from Eigg, until he'd flushed out the traitor and justice had been served.

It took far longer than an hour to ensure his presence was noted about the estate and in the village, and it was already dark by the time he and Hugh returned to the castle. As always when he saw Creagdoun, gut-deep satisfaction gripped him at what he'd achieved through his own prowess in battle. But for the first time, his hard-won pride was a secondary consideration as anticipation pounded through his blood at the prospect of finally claiming his bride.

It wasn't until after supper, and Isolde had retired, that it struck him there was, in fact, one inconvenience in having them share a bedchamber.

He had nowhere to bathe. And while the prospect of bathing while Isolde washed his back was more than enticing, he had the feeling if he suggested such a thing to her, she might well push his head under the water until he all but drowned.

Besides, just before she'd left the hall, he'd heard her instruct the maids to ensure hot water was sent to the chamber for her own use.

He barely managed to swallow a groan, as the image of her sinking into a tub of scented water invaded his mind and he was halfway to the stairs before he realized what he was doing.

With a silent curse he swung about. He'd use the solar. Maybe a lukewarm bath would cool his ardor for long enough until his bride was ready for him.

※

WILLIAM SUCKED IN a deep breath as he stood outside the door to the bedchamber he now shared with his wife. There was nothing stopping him from simply entering. He knew she was alone. And waiting for him.

Why then did he hesitate?

But he knew why. It was because as soon as she'd discovered his heritage, Isolde hadn't wanted this marriage. And although he was confident that by the morning she'd be as invested as he was in their alliance, the truth was he didn't want to face her antagonism when he opened the door.

Not tonight, their belated wedding night.

But she'd wanted him well enough that night in Eigg. And that was the woman he wanted in his arms.

The woman he needed.

He rapped on the door before pushing it open. Isolde stood before the hearth in a simple shift, her hair tumbling over her shoulders in fiery waves, as the glow from the flames surrounded her in a halo of gold.

His mouth dried and blood thundered in his veins. She was a vision. And she was his.

He kicked the door shut and strode across the chamber to her. She pulled her shawl more securely across her breasts as he halted in front of her and drank in the sight of how her eyes glittered like emeralds in the firelight.

"I've dreamed of this." His voice was hushed, as though she might vanish if he spoke any louder. "Yet ye're more exquisite than I imagined."

She smiled and shook her head in mock disapproval. "There's no need for such flattery when ye've already caught me."

He wound one of her damp curls around his finger. Her hair was soft like silk, an irresistible caress against his skin. "'Tis not flattery when it's the truth."

"Well, tis not the first time ye've seen me in such a state of undress. Am I more exquisite now than I was before?"

"Aye. Because tonight I shall not be holding back."

The tip of her tongue moistened the seam of her lips, a fleeting gesture and one he found uncommonly fascinating. "Ye do know," she said at last, "that doesn't make sense at all."

He could scarcely recall what they'd been talking about. "When I look at ye, my brains addle. Don't condemn me for it, since I fear I'll never be able to look at ye with a clear head."

"That's a pity. I should like to know yer clear-headed thoughts, and that's a fact."

Too late, he realized discussing the state of his mind was likely the worst thing to talk about while she still harbored doubts about him. But tomorrow, after he'd proved how much she meant to him, she'd see the truth.

"Ye cannot expect such a thing while I hold my beautiful bride in my arms on our wedding night." He cupped her face, before threading his fingers through her hair and pulling her close. "Ye've bewitched me, and I've no wish to be released from yer spell."

"Tis not a bewitched husband I want, but one I can speak with plainly."

"Ye can say whatever ye wish to me."

"If only that was true."

Belatedly, he realized she wasn't merely jesting with him. She may have welcomed him into their bed tonight, but she was still irked.

"I'm grieved ye doubt it." More than she'd ever know. "But there's no reason why we can't find what we had on Eigg here at Creagdoun."

"What we had on Eigg wasn't real." There was a wistful note in her voice that tugged at his heart. "There's no going back. I know that."

"Then we'll find a new way forward. 'Tis better that way, surely? A fresh beginning to start our married life together."

"Ye could be right." She sounded reluctant, but at least she wasn't disagreeing with him. That had to be a good sign.

She tipped her head back, and her lips were a temptation he could not resist. His mouth captured hers, his tongue penetrating and exploring, and her small gasp of pleasure ignited his blood in a blaze of lust.

He pulled her shawl from her shoulders and dropped it to the floor, and memories of when he'd done this before flickered through his mind. But tonight, everything was different. Because tonight there was no risk to her reputation.

Panting, he pulled back to drink in his fill of her flushed cheeks and how her delectable breasts strained against the fabric of her shift. Except something caught his eye and he glanced at her feet, where Sjor regarded him with an unblinking stare.

"God damn." The oath slipped from him before he could prevent it. 'Twas just the dog, but for a heartbeat all he'd seen were a pair of black, glowing eyes. "Should Sjor be in here with us?"

Her lips twitched with evident mirth. "Will knowing Sjor is watching affect yer performance?"

"My performance is for yer benefit only. I fear loyal Sjor might attack my arse at a vital moment."

"That would be unfortunate, indeed." There was no mistaking the laughter in her voice. "A wedding night to remember, that's for certain."

"Aye. But I'd rather remember it for other reasons than a dog bite."

"I'm not against sending Sjor to the antechamber. But he'll be alone, and he's missing his littermates dreadfully."

Momentarily lost for words, he gazed into her eyes. Of all the things he'd imagined might occur on this belated wedding night, discussing how Isolde's dog was homesick hadn't even crossed his mind. He gave Sjor a doubtful sideways glance. The terrier still stared at him in apparent wounded affront.

A disbelieving laugh escaped. He was becoming as daft as Isolde was over her beloved dog. But the fact remained, allowing Sjor to stay in the bedchamber was a small price to pay for Isolde's peace of mind.

"Can ye extract a promise from him that he'll mind his business if we let him stay?"

"Sjor, bed." Isolde pointed to a pile of blankets in a corner by the hearth, and the dog obeyed without so much as a snuffle. She gave him another mocking smile. "Are ye satisfied now?"

"Not yet." It took every shred of willpower he possessed not to rip the shift from her body and take her where she stood, but somehow he managed to contain himself. "But before this night is done, we'll both be well satisfied, Isolde. Ye have my word."

With that, he unwound his plaid, a torturous maneuver, with Isolde watching his every move as though she had never witnessed anything so intriguing before. With a silent sigh of relief, he dropped it onto a nearby stool before kicking off his boots. But when he began to unlace his shirt, she stepped closer and unlaced him herself.

"'Tis only fair." She glanced up at him through her lashes, and the breath damn near stalled in his chest. "Ye didn't give me the chance to strip ye the last time we were together."

With Isolde's fingers brushing against his naked chest, and a delightful frown of concentration on her brow as she loosened the ties, he could scarcely recall the last time they'd been together. In truth, he could barely remember his own name. Which all things considered, should have been a worry.

But he didn't even care.

A frustrated growl tore his throat, and he ripped his shirt over his head before hooking his fingers into the neckline of her shift and tugging her forward. "Now we are wed, ye can strip me every night if it pleases ye."

Her hands flattened against his chest, and his heart thundered so loud it was hard to think straight. But then, what was there to think about tonight, save claiming his bride?

He trailed kisses along her throat, and she tipped her head back with a soft sigh. The elusive scent of lavender filled his senses, and he worked the ribbons on her shift loose before sliding the material over her shoulders.

Slowly, he eased her shift along her arms and sucked in a harsh breath when it slithered to the floor, leaving her naked before him. The firelight danced over her lush body, shadows concealing as much as the golden glow revealed, and his cock throbbed for release.

*Not yet.*

Tenderly, he kissed her, threading his fingers through her hair, holding her still for his exploration. Her tongue pushed against his, and need thudded through his blood, pushing his control to its limits.

His fingers traced along her back and over the swell of her backside. He gripped her cheeks and she groaned, the sound filling his mouth like a forbidden caress. When a shudder rippled through her, he wrapped one arm around her, holding her close. Her breasts pressed against his chest, her nipples erect and driving him out of his mind.

His control slipped and his kisses became more urgent, but she didn't pull back. She wound her arms about him, and his fingers stroked her damp folds, dipping inside her and teasing her sensitized clit.

Her nails clawed his shoulders, and her gasps grew ragged, urging him on. Not that he could have stopped. Not when Isolde clung to him, mindless with desire, and he caressed her with his fingertip as her release spilled through her in endless shudders of pleasure.

He held her close as she sagged against him, but raw lust pounded through him, demanding satisfaction. He swept her into his arms and took her to their bed, and fragmented memories of the time he'd carried her to the box bed at Sgur hammered through his mind.

But tonight, everything was different. Because tonight nothing would hold him back, and he'd finally make her his.

She lay on the bed, her glorious hair spread across the pillows, and with a primitive growl of need he spread her thighs and loomed over her. His bride.

*Mo chridhe.*

He pushed into her, and her sharp gasp caused him to still. "Isolde?" His husky voice filled the chamber, as lust and want pounded through his veins.

"Don't stop, William," she whispered, and wrapped her legs around his thighs.

His name on her lips was more potent than he'd ever imagined, and the last tattered remnants of his control fled.

Christ, she was so tight around him, an exquisite sheath of flame and silk. He thrust into her, and nothing mattered but this moment, this woman, and when she shattered around him, he followed her over the precipice.

# Chapter Eighteen

Isolde stirred, an unfamiliar weight wrapped around her, and still half asleep she snuggled closer to the solid warmth pressed against her back. It was comforting, and felt oddly right, and she gave a small smile, luxuriating in the blissful languor that bathed her mind.

A gentle, unhurried breeze caressed her hair. For a few pleasurable moments she sank into the rhythmic sensation of utter peace. Such a strange dream. If only she could stay here. And as soon as the wish floated through her, a discordant note hummed along the edges of her senses.

No, it wasn't a breeze that teased her hair.

*Breathing.*

Her eyes sprung open. Dark shadows swathed the chamber, relieved by a subdued, flickering glow from the hearth. William's arm was securely around her, holding her as close in sleep as it had last night.

Heat suffused her as memories of last night danced through her mind. She had imagined nothing could be as wonderful as those stolen hours in the solar at Sgur. How could anything be as perfect as that, when Njord didn't even exist?

Yet William had managed the impossible. Her foolish pledge to remain aloof during the necessity of their consummation had turned to ashes the instant he had entered the chamber, and instead of ice, fire had triumphed.

Worse, she couldn't even summon the energy to berate herself for the betrayal. For all she could think of was how she longed to lose herself in his arms once again.

Her breath stalled in her throat as his fingertips stroked her naked waist. Exquisite tremors raced across her sensitized skin, and she pressed her thighs together, but to no avail. Dampness bloomed, warm and irresistible, a potent reminder of how readily her body had surrendered to William.

That didn't mean she was enslaved to her lust. She had done her duty last night, and there was no reason to tarry in his bed. She'd rise and start the day. Now she was mistress of his castle, there was plenty to occupy her, and she would never give him reason to doubt her ability.

But instead of following through on her noble decision, desire licked through her as unmistakable evidence of his arousal thickened against the curve of her bottom. Her heart thundered in her breast, and it was increasingly difficult to remain absolutely still when all she wanted was to twist around and have him take her once again.

No. She would not surrender. It was humiliating enough that he knew how easily he could make her forget all her grand principles with nothing more than a touch, without him also guessing how she craved the deeper connection that had once glimmered between them.

Except it never had existed, outside of her mind. Why was it so hard to remember that?

He shifted, his muscles flexing around her, before his mouth found the back of her neck. Despite her best intentions, desire rippled through her as he teased kisses along her shoulder, the overnight roughness of his beard grazing her flesh in a tantalizing caress.

"Good morn, bride of mine." His throaty greeting was as potent as his touch, and she barely managed a breathy sigh in response. "I trust married life is living up to yer expectations."

Lust simmered in every word, but there was a thread of amusement too, and it was far too much effort to follow through on her earlier resolve to leave the bed—and him.

"Thankfully, I had few expectations." She turned her head and couldn't help smiling when he pushed himself up on his elbow and grinned down at her. His black hair was disheveled, and the shifting shadows across his face made him as devilish as she imagined a barbarous pirate might look.

"'Tis lucky I had a great many, then." His hand cupped her breast, and she gasped as his thumb circled her nipple. "And I have every intention of fulfilling them all."

His mouth captured hers, and his kiss was hard and possessive, and need surged through her like a tempest. She attempted to roll onto her back, but he had her trapped beneath him, and as though to reinforce how utterly she was in his power, he shifted his leg over her thigh, pushing her more securely into the mattress.

He broke their kiss, and she panted in his face. "What are ye doing?"

"Ye'll see." His husky response caused shivers to race through her as he straightened before pushing a pillow beneath her hips and rolling back onto his knees. It was obvious he was examining her bottom, and illicit thrills singed her tender cleft. "Ye have a delectable arse, my lady."

"'Tis fortunate ye find it so, since it's the only one I possess."

He snorted with laughter. "I'm relieved to hear it."

She craned her neck and aye, there he was, admiring her behind as though he'd like to devour it. The image should have been alarming, and yet she found it inexplicably riveting. "I trust ye'll allow me the same consideration to admire yer backside, William Campbell."

"Any time ye wish, but ye'll not find it half as alluring as the sight that's filling my vision right now."

She doubted that, but she wasn't going to tell him so. "Ye have a way with honeyed words, and that's a fact."

As she knew to her cost when he'd seduced her with pretty compliments on Eigg. But she wouldn't think of that now, in this twilight haven, when she could pretend the outside world didn't exist.

"Honey?" He gave a rumble of laughter that was far more intoxicating than it had any right to be. "'Tis the first time anyone has accused me of that."

How odd. She had so often condemned his honeyed tongue that it was a surprise to recall that until now she'd kept the condemnation inside her head.

Not that William appeared to consider it a reproach, despite his remark, and she couldn't resist teasing him further.

"Are ye certain? It comes so naturally to ye."

He grasped a length of her hair and pulled it back from her cheek, his knuckles grazing a sensual path across her shoulders. Then he leaned over her, his breath a seductive whisper against her ear.

"Ye're insulting me again, aren't ye?"

"Can it be an insult, if ye cannot tell?"

"Ah, so they're words of endearment, is that what ye're saying?"

She could scarcely recall what she was saying, when his fingers traced a seductive path along her body and his unyielding erection pressed along the curve of her bottom. It was most distracting, and illicit thrills raced through her when he slid his hand beneath her and teased her sensitized clit.

"Ye're putting words in my mouth," she managed to gasp, as his fingers worked their wicked magic, and his primal growl caused every sane thought to flee her mind.

"Tis not my words I intend filling ye with."

His promise scorched through her, and she sucked in a ragged breath as he pushed into her. How different it felt, being taken from behind, almost as though it was her first time again. He stretched her flesh that was still tender from last night, filling her more completely than she could ever imagine was possible, and a choked breath caught in her throat.

Last night she'd thought William had shown her everything he could do to her body. How wrong she'd been. This primitive joining was like nothing she had imagined, and involuntarily, she clenched around him.

"Christ, Isolde." His tortured groan against her ear ignited a thousand white-hot sparks. He rocked into her, and she clutched the sheet as desire spiraled through her. And when he pumped his hot seed inside her, she splintered into a thousand rainbow-bright shards.

※

WILLIAM HELD ISOLDE'S hand as they entered the great hall to break their fast. He could scarcely drag his gaze from his beautiful bride, and any illusions that once he'd had her she'd no longer occupy his every thought irrevocably shattered.

He wanted her more than ever.

Even now, after the enjoyable night and early morning bed sport they'd shared, his cock thickened as though it had been weeks since he'd lain with her. His predicament wasn't eased when she glanced at him and bestowed a knowing smile his way.

They took their places at the high table, and he sat beside her, trying to ignore the discomfort between his legs. There were at least a dozen essential tasks he needed to attend to this morning, but to hell with that. They could wait until after dinner.

He was devoting this morning to his wife.

"Ye're looking well pleased with yerself, William," Isolde said under her breath, and he almost choked on his ale. "I cannot think why that might be."

"I'm looking at the reason right now." He grinned when she shook her head in mock disgust, and aye, he had to confess, relief washed through him, too. This was his Isolde from the isle. Not the one who had spat venom in his face when he'd recalled his real name and wed him under duress.

He'd always known she'd come around, once he'd made her his.

Well pleased by events, he once again took her hand and pressed a kiss on her knuckles. How refreshing it was to be master of his own castle, and able to show her how highly he regarded her whenever he wished.

"Hmm." For once, Isolde appeared at a loss for words, and he had the urge to grin at her again like a besotted fool. And while the prospect of his bride being speechless at his compliment was gratifying, he'd rather not display to the entire hall just how in thrall to his new wife he was.

As he rubbed his thumb against her fingers, his gaze snagged on the ring she wore. It was a magnificent piece of jewelry, but it wasn't the one he wanted her to wear as the symbol of their union.

Despite how they were wed in the eyes of God and the people of Eigg, his father still wanted a second ceremony at Dunstrunage, so that all the clans in the Highlands could be left in no doubt of the validity of their marriage. Although he didn't feel the need for it, it was a small price to pay to ease his father's concerns. And it would be the perfect occasion to present Isolde with his lady mother's precious ring.

When breakfast was finished, and they rose to leave the table, he wound his arm about her waist. She shot him a scandalized glance but didn't follow up with a scathing retort, which was merely more evidence that she had settled into their new life.

"This morning," he said, "I'm showing ye the hidden side of Creagdoun."

"Ah. I wondered if the castle had any secret passages. 'Tis always a concern when one's ancestors didn't live there."

"Aye." He understood her meaning. And her concerns. "We searched the castle thoroughly, and ye may rest assured Creagdoun is secure."

"I've never doubted it."

He led her back upstairs, and as they reached their antechamber she gave him an exasperated look. "Really, William Campbell?"

"My motives are pure, I promise ye." Then he couldn't resist and gave her a lingering kiss. It was a mistake, and he swallowed a frustrated groan. "Being with ye addles my brains, and that's a fact."

"Ye're meant to be showing me the hidden passages in the castle. I can't be left in ignorance of such things."

"I've no intention of leaving ye in ignorance." He wasn't certain if she was serious or not, but she didn't seem very amused. They went through to the master's chamber, and he took her to the corner nearest the door where a chest stood. "Stand back," he told her, before shifting the chest aside and rolling up the faded rug that covered the trapdoor. "See? I had no nefarious purpose for bringing ye into our bedchamber."

She stepped closer, frowning as she stared at the trapdoor set in the floor. "Where does it lead?"

"I'll show ye." He pulled open the trapdoor before taking a lantern and holding it over the hole where the steep steps leading downward looked suddenly ominous. "'Tis a bit tricky. The main thing is ye know of it. It leads to—"

"Tricky," she scoffed, peering into the gloom. "Ye didn't see the secret places in Sgur Castle, and I can assure ye, they were far trickier than this."

"Maybe so, but I've no wish for ye to fall and break yer neck."

She laughed at that. "I can't tell if ye're serious about my lack of balance or merely jesting. But just so we're clear, ye'd better not be serious."

He had been serious, although not for the reason she'd stated, but it was likely wiser to keep his counsel on that. "I'll go first. If ye slip, I'll save ye."

"I won't slip."

He eyed her before stepping into the stairwell. She flapped her hand at him in a shooing motion, and with reluctance he went down a few steps to give her room to follow him.

He led her down the spiral staircase until they reached the ground floor, where a passage led between the inner and outer walls of the castle. "Along here," he said, "we're behind the wall in the great hall."

"Spyholes." She went onto her toes to get a better look. "Have ye ever spied on yer guests, William?"

"Not yet. Never felt the need to."

"At least we know where not to hang the fine new tapestry the baron gave us. Once we have appropriate tapestries for yer bedchamber, that is."

"True." He glanced through one of the spyholes. Malcolm MacNeil, Robert Fletcher, and David Cunningham appeared deep in conversation as they strolled across the hall, and once again the suffocating knowledge wrapped around his chest that one of his men had betrayed him. And he was no closer to discovering who.

༺༻

IT WAS ALMOST dinner time before he finished showing Isolde all the secret places he'd discovered in the castle.

"I'll have the tapestry and yer rug taken to our bedchamber," he told her as they made their way back to the great hall.

"No need. I can deal with that."

Of course she could. He'd need to get used to having a wife who was responsible for the comfort of the castle. It was a heartening prospect, and he smiled at her. Married life was grand indeed.

"Although after we've eaten," she added, "the first thing I plan on doing is exploring the local countryside."

The hell she was. Grisly images of her being attacked by whoever had tried to kill him flashed through his mind, and he suppressed a shudder. "No. Ye'll stay within Creagdoun and attend to yer duties."

"I've no intention of neglecting my duties." There was an unmistakable edge of frost in her voice, and he sighed. She'd misunderstood him.

"I know that, Isolde. I'm not accusing ye of not." He dropped his voice, so no one would overhear. "But until the man who attacked me is found, I can't risk yer safety."

"Oh." Skepticism dripped from that one word, and he frowned at her, uncomprehending. "So this mysterious attacker is to be the reason for my confinement, is he?"

"Confinement?" Had he heard her right? "Now ye're the one jesting, surely."

"How long will it take before ye find this murdering fiend?"

Heat crawled over his scalp, and it wasn't a pleasant sensation. She sounded as disparaging as when he'd caught her by the armory on Eigg, after Hugh had arrived. "It's my priority, I assure ye."

"I'm sure it is."

Except the scathing note in her voice conveyed the opposite.

He pulled her to a halt at the entrance to the hall and backed her against the wall. "Do ye still doubt my word, Isolde?"

"Does it matter? Ye got what ye wanted. A MacDonald bride."

He'd got what he wanted? He could scarcely believe she'd thrown such an accusation at him. Except deep inside he acknowledged the truth of her words.

He'd got exactly what he wanted.

"Ye're wrong," he said, aggravated that she still held onto her ill-conceived beliefs that he'd lied to her on Eigg. "I never wanted a MacDonald bride until I met ye."

Confusion flashed over her face. "Honeyed words again."

She didn't sound so sure of herself, though, and he pounced on it. "Why would I put on such a charade when we were destined to wed regardless? When ye've worked that one out, let me know."

"It's a puzzle." She sounded reluctant to admit it.

He should leave it, since it appeared she was finally coming around to seeing how foolish her conviction was, but he couldn't keep his mouth shut. "No, it isn't."

Slowly, he straightened, and his arms dropped to his sides. She tugged her shawl tighter about her shoulders before casting an inscrutable look his way.

"Maybe." Not that she sounded convinced, but the fact she'd even admitted the possibility that she was wrong was, he acknowledged, progress.

He cast her a sideways glance as they made their way into the hall. He'd been so sure everything would fall into place once Isolde was his bride. That she'd return, unquestioningly, to the trusting lass he'd lost his head over when he'd simply been her stranger from the sea.

The last thing he'd expected was that he'd still need to prove himself worthy of her. It seemed there was a lot more to married life than he'd blithely presumed.

# Chapter Nineteen

They had been wed for two weeks, and after they finished breakfast, and William held her hand as she rose from her chair, Isolde had to admit he was a most attentive husband. And not just in the bedchamber.

As always when she thought of their bedchamber, she recalled their bed sport and warmth suffused her. He smiled, as though he could read her mind, and while she fervently hoped he couldn't, she smiled back.

After their confrontation, she'd been forced to face the accusation she'd flung at him, and with every day that passed, it became harder to believe he had lied to her during the days they'd shared on Eigg.

But if that was the case, it meant William's life truly was in danger. And that was something she didn't want to contemplate.

"The earl is seeing me today," he reminded her as they made their way to the solar. He'd mentioned last night at supper he had received a summons from the Earl of Argyll, and she inclined her head in response. The invitation didn't include her, but as William had told her last night, the visit wasn't for social purposes.

"Will ye be back later?" She hoped so, although she also hoped her eagerness didn't show in her voice. It was all very well enjoying the delights of the marital bed, but she still wasn't comfortable with him knowing just how much she'd miss him if he didn't return this night.

He leaned in close, so his lips brushed her ear. How could such a featherlight touch cause such havoc to her senses?

"Queen Mary herself couldn't keep me away from ye for a single night, mo chridhe."

She didn't much care for the queen, but as always, his endearment melted her heart.

"That's good to know."

He opened the door to the solar, and as she entered the chamber a suffocating vice squeezed inside her breast. Every morning, William brought her here, where she would start on the tasks of overseeing the castle's daily requirements. During the last few days, she'd had the new tapestry and her rug moved into the master bedchamber and supervised the unpacking of the trunks of goods she had brought with her from Sgur.

Superficially at least, the castle was starting to feel a little more familiar.

She had also inspected the larders and checked the winter stocks, and this morning she planned on evaluating the kitchen gardens.

None of her duties were the cause of why that relentless curl of panic simmered just below the surface. It was because William had still not relented on the order that he'd issued the day after they had arrived at Creagdoun, that she was not permitted to set foot outside the castle walls.

It still stung. Even if he thought he was doing it to keep her safe.

"William." She spun around and took his hands. Surely, she could make him see sense. There hadn't been a hint of danger since he'd brought her to Creagdoun. "I should like to ride today. My men can accompany me, so there will be no risk."

"No." His voice was hard and brooked no argument, and all her soft, kindly thoughts of him evaporated like steam from a boiling pot.

"No?" Her voice was sharp, and she dropped his hands as though they were burning logs. "Is that it? No discussion?"

"There's nothing to discuss, Isolde." He shut the door, before returning to her. "Until the danger is passed, I cannot allow ye to wander the countryside. Anything could happen to ye."

"I didn't ask to go alone." God only knew how she kept her voice so calm, when resentment churned within her breast. She had never needed to ask permission from her grandmother when she wanted to escape Sgur Castle. She had been her own mistress, and responsible for her own actions. Yet now she was wed, she was treated like a serf. "Ye know Patric would never allow me to go anywhere unaccompanied."

"I'll speak to Patric and ensure he's aware ye're not to go riding. I can't protect ye if ye're not within the castle's walls."

She sucked in a sharp breath, affronted to the core of her being. "Patric is not yer man. Ye can't issue orders to him."

"Patric answers to me. Ye will not go riding, Isolde."

Speechless, she glared at him. Could he have made it any plainer just how little he valued her opinion? But she would not be defeated so easily.

"Ye forget yerself. The wedding contract plainly states Patric and the men remain within my jurisdiction."

"Aye. And ye forget that while ye retain all yer worldly goods and attendants, ye're my wife, and as such the final word rests with me."

Pain squeezed her heart. She didn't want to face it, but the truth was stark. William's highhanded behavior hurt. But then, he was a Campbell. What else could she expect?

Just because the truth had become blurred since they had wed didn't mean anything had changed. He was not Njord, even though he so very often reminded her of that illusory warrior. But she wouldn't let him see how easily he could wound her.

"And what if ye never find this so-called assassin?" She coated each word with the contempt they deserved. Even if, deep inside, she now questioned her conviction that his loss of memory had been nothing but a masquerade. "Will ye keep me a prisoner within yer castle forever?"

"A prisoner?" Finally, something she'd said appeared to have struck a nerve. "Ye're not a prisoner. Ye're my wife."

"Aye. And I fail to see a difference in the two states."

He expelled a patently irritated breath. "Ye're impossible to reason with when ye're in such a mood. I trust when I return, ye'll be more amenable."

With that, he gave a stiff bow before leaving the solar.

She gripped her fingers together and glowered after his retreating back. Damn the arrogance of the man. She was *not* in a mood. How dare he suggest she was, simply because she craved a sliver of freedom?

A moment to escape the shadow of the castle, so she could merely *be*?

But no. He could not even allow her that small consideration. Instead, he expected her to be happy to be tethered to a crumbling castle, far from everything she had ever known. Maybe he had never lied to her, but in his heart he was, and had always been, William. Not Njord.

She sucked in a jagged breath and attempted to compose herself before she started her day. But it didn't matter how she tried to push William from her mind, his imperious words haunted her.

*"Ye're my wife and as such the final word rests with me."*

After dinner, she escaped to the courtyard with Sjor, who enjoyed exploring every nook and cranny he could find. Not that it was much of an escape, since Emer trailed in her wake and several of the men she'd brought with her from Sgur stood guard.

How different married life would've been, had she remained on Eigg.

She pulled her shawl more securely about herself and glanced at the gray clouds that hid all signs of the sun. She was used to gray skies, damp mist, and the bitter chill of winter. But she wasn't used to being confined. And how she missed the tang of salt in the air and the sound of the sea in her ears.

Anxiety swirled low in her stomach, and she took a deep, calming breath. It didn't help. She fought the overpowering urge to sink to her knees and dig her fingers into the earth, because it wouldn't ease her panic or quiet her mind.

All it would do was make the servants and everyone else in the castle think she was mad.

The earth here at Creagdoun couldn't help to ground her. Her foremothers had lived and died on Eigg, and that was where the source of her strength resided, and always would.

"My lady." The low voice behind her caused her to swing about. Patric gave her a half smile, but she saw the sympathy in his eyes, and she hated that he knew how lost she felt.

Almost as much as she hated how he had lately started to address her as *my lady*.

"Patric." At least she didn't sound as if she were falling apart, which was a relief. And then she noticed what he held. Her claymore. And another wave of panic swept through her at the prospect of trying to use the sword when she knew, in her heart, how dismally she'd fail. Her skill, after all, was tired to the land of her birth.

He held out her claymore. "I've been slack. Ye'll be losing yer edge."

She didn't take the sword from him. "Not today."

"Aye, today. There's a perfect spot yonder."

When she shook her head, he stepped closer, and his voice dropped to a coaxing whisper. "Come, lass. Ye must keep up yer skills."

His kindly tone, the one he'd used with her since she was a child, was almost her undoing. He reminded her so much of home, and everything she'd left behind.

She cleared her throat. It would never do to show any weakness when she was surrounded by those who had long ago pledged their loyalty to Clan Campbell. She carried the honor of Clan MacDonald on her shoulders, and she would not disgrace her kin.

Once again, he offered her the sword, and with reluctance, she took it. Its familiar weight was bittersweet, but the fear that she no longer deserved her father's claymore remained.

Patric led her to an area beyond the stables where a well had been dug long ago, and turned to face her. All the training she'd undergone during the last ten years fled, and she stared at him, mute, as he raised his sword.

"Isolde." His voice was calm but with a thread of steel, and slowly she raised her claymore.

Patric's sword slashed through the air. It wasn't unduly unexpected or fierce. Yet instead of instinctively deflecting the blow, the blade clashed against hers, the impact quivering through her fingers and, unforgivably, her beloved weapon clattered to the ground.

Mortification seared through her, made worse as she belatedly realized a crowd of William's servants had gathered in obvious shock at seeing their new mistress wielding a sword. *Abysmally.*

She'd brought dishonor upon the MacDonalds of Sgur, and proved, beyond doubt, that any skill she'd once possessed had deserted her when she had deserted her beloved Isle.

Patric picked up the claymore but didn't hand it back to her. Somehow, that small non-gesture underscored the depths into which she had fallen.

"Come." He gave a brusque nod, and she fell into step beside him as they headed to the armory. She waited in silence while he secured the claymore, and when he returned to her side, she released a heavy sigh.

"I've brought shame upon all I love."

He grunted. "'Tis one poor performance. Ye needn't think I'll allow ye to forego yer training just because ye're now a married woman."

She tugged her shawl tighter about her shoulders, even though she wasn't cold. Not with the abject humiliation burning through her blood. "Being wed has nothing to do with it. 'Tis because I'm no longer a part of Eigg."

Patric was silent for so long, she thought he'd decided the discussion was over. Thank God. Because she certainly didn't want to discuss her tangled thoughts with anyone. But then he gave her a contemplative look and her heart sank. He hadn't given up on the subject at all.

"Yer skill is yer own, my lady. Never let anyone tell ye otherwise."

Bizarrely, she recalled when William had bested her in their sword fight. She'd told him it was the blood of her foremothers in the earth beneath her feet that gave her the skill with the sword.

He hadn't agreed. And his words echoed in her mind.

*"Maybe 'tis the blood of yer foremothers in yer veins. But I cannot see how the land has anything to do with it."*

William hadn't understood. But she'd thought Patric would.

"It scarcely matters," she said. And then, before she could stop herself, her hurt spilled out. "Do ye really think the mistress of Creagdoun will be permitted to wield a sword? I'm not even permitted to go beyond the castle walls."

As soon as the words were out, she regretted them. Even though she was still upset with William, it felt disloyal to say such a thing to Patric. If only her sisters were here so she could share her distress with them.

"I'll be blunt," Patric said, and she shot him an aggrieved glance. Obviously, he didn't agree with her. And when had he ever been anything but blunt? "William Campbell is a fair man, for all he's not a MacDonald. He wants to keep ye safe, and for that I cannot fault him."

When things were put that *bluntly*, of course no one could fault him.

"Safe from the elusive traitor who attacked him on his ship?" She managed to inject a trace of scorn in her voice, even though a shadow of alarm stirred. Because she was no longer certain that was a fabrication, was she?

"I don't claim to know what happened on his ship," Patric said, which, considering how he was defending William, was surprising. She'd expected him to declare he believed every damn word that had ever come out of William's mouth. She narrowed her eyes and glared ahead so Patric wouldn't see the gathering confusion in her expression. "All I know is he's an honorable man who wouldn't resort to lying about such a thing simply to gain an advantage with ye."

"'Tis gratifying ye can be so sure about such a thing."

"Did he ever tell ye about Colban?"

Startled by the turn in the conversation, she swung about to face him. "Tell me what?"

"Aye. I thought not."

"He told me he acted in self-defense when he punched Colban, and I believed him." She still believed him. But that had nothing to do with what they were talking about, did it?

"I saw none of that. But I was on the beach, and I did see Colban prepared to run Campbell through when he turned his back. Colban only retreated when I made myself known."

Shock spiked through her. "Colban attacked William when his back was turned?"

She could scarcely believe a man, a MacDonald, that she'd known all her life could be capable of such a dishonorable action. But she'd never doubt Patric's word.

More to the point, why hadn't William told her the truth when she'd asked him?

"Aye. I assumed he'd inform Lady Helga, but he didn't. Ye may draw yer own conclusions from that, lass."

Because he hadn't wanted to cause any trouble. But it was more than that. If the only reason he'd washed up on the beach was to ensnare her in some tangled net of his own making, then surely it made sense he'd try and enlist her sympathy by telling her how Colban had attacked him.

Especially when he had an impeccable witness in Patric.

The fact that he hadn't simply reinforced her original impression of him.

As a man of honor.

Her grandmother had told her she needed to learn to keep perspective in all matters to be a fair judge of the truth, but when it came to William, she'd allowed her wounded pride to blind her. The last shreds of doubt that he'd lied to her about losing his memories died, and she released a soft groan. "I misjudged him, Patric."

"Ye're not the first to misjudge a man. And ye had fair reason." Then he paused, a dark frown slashing his brow. "My loyalty is to ye, my lady, and always will be. Never doubt that. But William Campbell and I are of one mind when it comes to yer safety."

She knew Patric would defend her with his life. And now the last doubts had faded about William, she understood why he'd commanded her to stay within the castle walls, even if the prospect still caused a tight knot to lodge in her chest.

But her distress at being confined was nothing compared to this. Because now she was convinced that he'd never lied to her, another fear that she'd managed to suppress over the last few days clawed through her heart.

Someone had tried to murder William on his ship. And he was still in danger.

## Chapter Twenty

After leaving Isolde, William gathered half a dozen of his men to accompany him to visit the earl, but as Creagdoun vanished into the early morning mist behind them, his mind was only half on the task.

All he could see in his mind was the contempt on Isolde's face as she'd accused him of keeping her a prisoner.

His bride. A prisoner. How could she even think that?

After the harsh words they'd exchanged on the day he'd shown her Creagdoun's secret passages, he'd believed they had come to a new understanding. Or, rather, that she'd accepted she'd been wrong to distrust him.

Yet she'd flung *assassin* at him like an accusation. As though she still refused to see the truth.

God damn it, all he wanted was to keep her safe. Her petulance was a small price to pay for his peace of mind.

Except peace was the last thing he felt when her condemnation rang in his head like a clarion.

A wife was not meant to question her lord's every word. Yet even as that fact crawled into his mind, he knew its folly. If Isolde was the kind of woman to obey everything he said without argument, was it likely he'd find her so irresistibly fascinating?

The rebuttal echoed in his mind, when all he should be concentrating on was what information the earl had for him. But he couldn't even discuss that with any of his men, because he couldn't damn well trust his men, and as far as they were concerned, he'd lost his footing in the storm and tumbled overboard.

Involuntarily, his fingers tightened on the reins. It irked him more than it should that his injury was attributed to a moment's clumsiness rather than the truth. But there was no help for it.

He hoped to God the earl had good news for him.

It was late morning before they arrived at the manor where the earl had lately been staying since surrendering Castle Campbell to the queen, and were shown into the great hall, where he waited, standing before the fire.

"My lord," he said as the earl greeted him, and from the corner of his eye he saw Hugh and Alasdair with a group of the earl's men. He hadn't known Hugh would be here. His cousin had left Creagdoun a few days ago, as another crisis had arisen at his father's stronghold that he'd needed to deal with.

"I'm told ye wed the MacDonald lass while ye were lost at sea." The earl eyed him, and William wasn't sure whether his comment was a rebuke or not. "That bash on yer head as ye fell overboard obviously knocked some sense into ye. Congratulations, William. Good work."

He gave a grim smile and hoped the earl couldn't tell how his remark had rubbed him the wrong way. Not the implication that he'd fallen overboard. That was a strategic maneuver when there was no telling how many ears might overhear them.

No. It was the *good work* comment. As if he'd somehow manipulated Isolde into an early wedding.

*Didn't ye, though?*

The earl thrust a tankard of ale at him, and he took a long swallow as good-natured jibes and congratulations from the earl's men were aimed his way. But he couldn't easily dismiss the lingering accusation in his mind.

Aye, he'd rushed her. He would admit to that. But whether they had wed at Sgur or waited until the summer and married in Argyll, the end result was the same.

She was his bride. And he would never regret ensuring she had returned to Creagdoun with him.

"William. Alasdair. Follow me." The earl glanced at Hugh, who had fallen into step beside William. "Not ye, Hugh."

What in hellfire was that about? William frowned at his cousin, who offered him a tight smile and shrugged his shoulders. It was plain the earl wished to speak of the traitor in their midst, so why exclude Hugh, who had been on the damn ship with him?

Since he could hardly question the earl on it, especially in public, he strode after the other man who led them into his private chamber.

Alasdair closed the door behind them, and the earl narrowed his gaze at William.

"Yer father told me what happened. Do ye have any new information for me?"

"I've spoken to each man who was on the ship who returned with me to Creagdoun, but none of them gave me any reason to suspect they were the one we're looking for." Frustrated, he expelled a harsh breath. "It turns my guts to think a man who tried to kill me can look me in the eyes and feign relief that I'm alive."

"Who didn't return to Creagdoun with ye?"

William gave the earl their names.

"I doubt it's any of them," the earl said. "But I'll take no chances. I recently received word from a reliable source that Torcall MacGregor's son, Alan, didn't die alongside his father three years ago. He's alive, William, and it would seem he's out for vengeance."

William expelled a harsh breath. "He's the one who forced one of my men to try and kill me."

"Either that, or Alan MacGregor and the unknown man are working together." Alasdair sounded grim. "Ye cannot always give men the benefit of the doubt, William."

He'd rather think one of his men was being forced against his will than that he was acting on pure greed or spite. But still, he had to concede Alasdair had a good point.

"The MacGregors are planning something big," the earl said. "And those still loyal to Torcall MacGregor are now backing the son. They want Creagdoun back, and how better to gain an advantage than by murdering the rightful laird?"

He'd suspected as much, although the fact Alan was alive certainly complicated things. "They won't succeed."

"None of the clans will support their claim," Alasdair said. "With or without Alan MacGregor."

That reminded William that he had yet to speak to the earl about their visit to Skye. Even though he knew Hugh had already informed the earl, it was still his responsibility to confirm it.

"We have the support of Clan MacDonald of Sleat. John MacDonald is no friend of the MacGregors."

"Aye. That's good. And now ye are wed to Isolde MacDonald of Sgur, we have another foothold in the Small Isles which will serve us well. When I have more information on what the MacGregors are hatching, I'll send word."

His alliance with Isolde was advantageous. It was a fact, and he didn't know why having the earl point it out so baldly rankled.

"I don't need to remind either of ye that everything we've discussed is not to be shared outside this chamber." Then the earl caught his eye. "That includes Hugh, William."

WILLIAM WAS STILL reeling from the earl's command when they returned to the great hall where dinner was served. He trusted Hugh with his life, God damn it, and if the earl thought his cousin had anything to do with what had happened on the ship, his brains were addled.

Hugh was the only other man who'd been on the ship, besides Alasdair, who knew the truth. God's blood, he was the one who'd suggested they keep the truth to themselves, so as not to alert the would-be murderer.

He didn't have the chance to speak with Hugh until they left the earl and were heading back to Creagdoun.

"What was that about?" William kept his voice low so no one might overhear.

Hugh shrugged, but he clenched his jaw, belying the casual gesture. "I believe he's running out of patience with Douglas."

"Since when are ye yer brother's keeper?"

"Since the day I was born." Hugh gave him a sideways glance, and William shook his head. Thank God his younger brother, James, had never given him half the headaches that Hugh had put up with from his elder sibling. "Did the earl have any useful information?"

Aye, he'd delivered the blow that Alan MacGregor was still alive. Yet he'd been specifically ordered to say nothing to Hugh. It burned, but he couldn't disobey.

"He'll let me know if he discovers anything." It wasn't exactly a lie. Yet it was one, by omission. And the way Hugh gave a brusque nod and said nothing more merely confirmed that his cousin understood what William hadn't said. Unfortunately, there was nothing he could do about it. "Did ye have the chance to speak with Douglas?"

"Not yet. I'm hoping to hear from him later this week. I'll send word if he shows his face."

They rode in silence for a while before Hugh drew close once again. "How's married life treating ye, William? I trust Lady Isolde is well."

"Aye. She's well." Once again, he saw the disdain that had glowed in her eyes just before he'd left her. An odd tightening sensation assailed his chest. Had he been too harsh? He didn't want her to feel she was a prisoner. Maybe he hadn't explained his reasons to her well enough.

Except surely she understood his reasoning. How couldn't she?

"Send my regards to yer lady wife," Hugh said, and William clasped his cousin's arm in farewell before Hugh headed to his father's stronghold.

As William watched his cousin ride off, an uneasy sliver of doubt raised its ugly head.

No. He wouldn't contemplate it. The earl could think whatever he liked, but he, William, knew in the depths of his soul that Hugh would never betray him.

⁂

WHEN ISOLDE RETURNED to the castle after her enlightening conversation with Patric, a restless energy consumed her. To be sure, a brisk walk along the beach would cure that malady, but even if she could leave the castle walls, there were no beaches closer than a day's ride away.

She drew in a deep breath. Of course, there was always something that needed attention, but she wanted to do something other than the usual daily chores of running a grand castle. Something that would show William her commitment to their new life together. Besides, she had already completed the duties she'd set herself for the day before she'd disgraced herself with her father's claymore.

No. She wasn't going to dwell on that, and she forced the humiliating memory to the back of her mind. There was something of far more importance she needed to focus on.

She'd misjudged William, and the knowledge of how she'd disdained him gnawed through her. He'd never deserved her harsh words. All he had done was his duty, and she wanted to do something to make it up to him. As she and Emer entered the antechamber, she paused before going into the bedchamber she shared with William, and her gaze snagged on the door that led to the lady's chamber.

Aye. There was something she could do. He'd told her she had free rein to do whatever she wished to make the castle more comfortable. So far, she hadn't taken him up on it, because a part of her simply couldn't see Creagdoun as her home.

But it was her home, and even if she could never feel it was a part of her soul the way Sgur was, William loved Creagdoun. All her life, she had been trained to be the mistress of a grand estate. And, as his wife, it was her duty to ensure the interior of the castle befit his status.

It wasn't his fault Creagdoun wasn't Sgur. And maybe by bringing the castle up to the standard William deserved, she might find a way to ground herself in this new life.

Restoring the lady's chamber offered an intriguing challenge before she set her mind to enhancing the great hall.

She turned to Emer. "It's time I looked to improving the castle. We should start on the lady's chamber."

Emer didn't look convinced. "'Tis a right mess in there, milady. 'Tis in need of a mason to repair that damage."

Isolde's enthusiasm wavered since Emer wasn't wrong. But she'd made up her mind and wouldn't be dissuaded.

"Indeed. And I shall ensure the finest stonemason is found. But first, I must evaluate exactly what needs to be done."

With obvious reluctance, Emer accompanied her. As Isolde opened the door and surveyed the chamber, her heart sank. She'd forgotten just how damaged it was.

She pulled her shawl more securely around her shoulders and tried to stop shivering. "The window and shutters need repair first of all," she remarked, and Emer hastily agreed. "And, of course, a mason to repair the stonework."

She crossed the floor and examined one of the dust-coated tapestries that hung upon the wall. Surprisingly, it appeared in reasonable condition, and she turned to Emer.

"Find a couple of maids, Emer. I do believe a good beating will work wonders on these tapestries."

Emer nodded and departed, and Isolde returned her attention to the chamber. She'd speak to the steward about finding a mason. Now she'd had time to look closer, the damage appeared more superficial than she'd first feared.

Sjor barked, and she smiled at him indulgently as he nosed along the far wall.

"What is it?" She went over to him and ran her gaze over the large tapestry. It was in poor condition, but it was the wall upon which it hung that caught her attention. She lifted the edge of the tapestry and gazed at the wooden wall panels. Had the entire chamber once had such beautiful coverings? It was a shame to hide it. She'd make a feature of this wall.

Sjor had finished sniffing and was now scratching madly at the wood. "No," she admonished him, crouching down and wrapping her arm about him. "Don't ruin the panel, Sjor."

She frowned. There was a faint draft, and it wasn't coming from the broken shutters. Intrigued, she pressed her fingers against the edge of the panel.

There was no mistake. There was definitely a draft. She patted Sjor as excitement surged through her. "Have ye found me a secret chamber, my bonny lad?"

He barked in clear agreement, and she laughed. "Do ye think William knows of it?"

She had a feeling he didn't. Why would he have explored this chamber for such a thing when he'd never used it? Besides, if he *did* know about it, he would've told her of it.

It didn't take long to find the concealed latch, and she warily eased open the panel. A wooden door was set into the stone wall, secured by two sturdy bolts.

"Tis most intriguing," she said to Sgur. "Do ye think this passage leads to the master's chamber?"

It was a romantic idea to be sure, and one Roisin would find irresistible. But why put a connecting passage on the wall farthest away from its neighboring chamber? It likely led somewhere quite different. Maybe, years ago, the lady of Creagdoun had smuggled her lovers into her chamber by this route.

The bolts proved a challenge, but she wouldn't let such a minor detail deter her, and finally she pushed the door open. A musty smell swirled out, and she covered her nose with her hand as she peered into the darkness. The passage ran to her left, towards the outer wall of the castle, and in the distance was a faint glimmer of light. Doubtless the source of the draft.

With Sjor at her heels, she went back to the antechamber and lit a lantern before returning to the secret passage. She placed the lantern on the ground and hauled a broken chunk of stone across the floor and wedged it so the door couldn't accidentally slam shut, entombing her.

She suppressed a shudder at the thought, but the prospect of discovering where this mysterious passage would lead her was too exciting to abandon over a fear of becoming trapped within Creagdoun's walls.

"Come," she said to Sjor as she entered the narrow space.

The lantern illuminated the passage where the uneven stone steps led downwards, away from the small source of light she'd seen when she'd first opened the door. She could only imagine it came from an arrow slit in the outer wall, to allow air into the passageway.

She glanced over her shoulder. The shaft of light from the lady's chamber seemed very far away. And still the passage led downwards. Surely, she must be on the ground by now. Was there a concealed door that opened directly into the great hall that William knew nothing about?

The atmosphere turned dank and oppressive, and apprehension twisted through her, not helped by the way Sjor stuck by her ankles as though he, too, no longer found the adventure exciting.

"We can't go back now," she told him, even though she knew she was merely trying to persuade herself. But instead of the sound of her voice reassuring her, it echoed eerily along the passage and sent shivers along her spine.

Maybe they should return. Yet she was mistress of Creagdoun, and ought to know about the secrets it held. She lifted the lantern higher as the passage grew narrower, and the ceiling was uncomfortably close to the top of her head.

They were no longer within the boundary of the castle walls. She was sure of it. This underground tunnel had been constructed as an escape in times of siege.

Except that also meant it was a point of entry if enemies knew of it.

Her stomach churned with sudden nerves, and her determination to explore no longer seemed like such a clever plan. But she couldn't stop now. The safety of Creagdoun might depend upon her discovering a vulnerability in their defenses.

The tunnel sloped upwards, which could only mean they had breached the castle's line of sight. Finally, in the distance, she saw a glimmer of light. Her mouth dried, and she gripped the lantern tighter. If only she'd had the foresight to bring her claymore.

Except she could no longer wield her beloved weapon.

As she drew closer to the dim light, her heart hammered in her chest, making it hard to draw breath. But the light didn't grow bigger as she'd feared, and with a ragged sigh she gazed at the sturdy wooden door before her, with a small, barred window at the top which was the source of the illumination.

It was set into a stone-built wall, and not only did two bolts secure the door against the outside world, but it also possessed a thick iron bar across it.

Her heart slowed as she noticed how wild grasses wound around the bolts and bars. It was obvious the door hadn't been used in years, and she went onto her toes to peer through the window.

Tangled branches and vines partially obscured her vision, but beyond that she could see trees. She frowned and craned her neck to get a better look, but it seemed the passage led directly into the forest behind the castle.

She released a relieved breath that she hadn't uncovered a nefarious plot against William and glanced at Sjor. "That's enough adventuring for ye in one day. Come on. Let's get back."

Thankfully, Emer had not yet returned with the maids when she reached the chamber, and she hastily pushed the stone aside and closed the door and panel before straightening the tapestry. It wouldn't do for servants to know of this passageway before their laird did.

The security of Creagdoun wasn't compromised. But she'd tell William of her discovery as soon as he returned to the castle.

## Chapter Twenty-One

It was dark by the time William arrived at Creagdoun, and as a stable lad took his horse, he drew in a deep breath and headed to the castle. By rights, the only thing in his head should have been the question of who the traitor in his midst was. But all he could think of was that his own wife still believed he'd deceived her.

It was more than that, though. He'd been so certain that once they were wed, she'd no longer doubt him. What the hell did she expect him to do to prove how wrong she was?

As he entered the great hall, Isolde came to greet him with a welcoming smile on her face. Warmth flooded through him, thickening his cock, and he swallowed a groan. Would she always affect him this way?

Half of him hoped so. The other half just wanted her to trust him, the way she had when she'd called him Njord.

"Ye must be famished." She dusted his shoulders of nonexistent snow before patting his chest. Bemused, he gazed at her. Where was the angry woman he'd left this morn? Not that he was complaining. Women were a mystery, but none were so unfathomable as Isolde MacDonald. "I'll have supper served directly."

As she turned away, he grabbed her wrist and swung her back. She raised her eyebrows in enquiry, but there was the faintest trace of a smile, too, as though she held a secret close.

His heart smashed against his chest as a possibility for her change in attitude hit him. Could it be possible to know this early that she had conceived his child? He wasn't sure it was, but then again, Isolde was from the Isle of Eigg and had never made a secret of how she followed the ways of her ancient foremothers. And those ancient foremothers might well have passed down such knowledge through their daughters' lineage.

"Ye have something to tell me?" He kept his voice low, scarcely daring to believe his suspicion was right. But he could imagine no other reason why she was being so attentive.

She blinked, as if his perception had taken her aback. "I do," she whispered. "But not here, William. I'm not certain ye'll want it to be common knowledge yet."

He wanted to shout it from the tallest tower. But if she wanted to wait, that was fine by him too. Tenderly, he cradled her face, even though she was now giving him a decidedly wary look. "Whenever ye're ready. 'Tis early days, after all."

"Early days?" There was an edge in her voice that, bizarrely, reminded him of their conversation this morning. "What are ye talking about?"

His fingers froze against her cheek. It was glaringly plain they weren't speaking of the same thing, but he had to be sure. "Ye're not with child, then?"

Her face heated, and while he was silently charmed by the blush that suffused her cheeks, he wasn't fooled into thinking she'd appreciate him remarking on it. Her next words confirmed it.

"Certainly not." She kept her voice as low as his, but there was no mistaking her affront. God in heaven, what was there to be affronted about? "Are ye mad? We've been wed scarcely a fortnight. Even if such a thing were possible, it'd be far too early to know anything for sure."

He didn't appreciate being called mad, but at least no one was close enough to overhear. Unfortunately, he could feel plenty of curious glances arrowed their way, and he'd be damned if he'd give them any more entertainment by responding to Isolde's insult.

He unpeeled his fingers from her face and gave her a grim smile. "It may be too early to tell, but ye cannot deny it's certainly possible. I don't know why ye appear so offended by the idea."

So much for not responding.

"I'm not offended." She gave an oddly furtive glance about the hall, as though suddenly aware of their surroundings and how they were the center of attention. Her blush deepened and she didn't meet his eyes, instead staring with deadly intent at his chest. He wasn't sure why he found it all so fascinating. "I simply forgot ye're a Campbell and expect yer wife to be nothing more than a broodmare."

He recoiled as if she'd smacked him across the face. And was flung back to the first time they'd kissed, on their walk to Kildonnan village, when she'd confided how a future of bearing countless bairns filled her with dread.

Her distress had touched him, and what's more, the prospect of her bearing another man's child had silently enraged him. But she wasn't with another man. She was with *him*.

There were a great many things he wanted to say to her. But all he could manage was one outraged word. "*Broodmare?*"

She cast another surreptitious glance about the hall before reluctantly catching his glare. "Ye caught me off guard."

Was that her idea of an apology for slighting his honor?

Now wasn't the time, and it sure as hell wasn't the place, but he couldn't let it go. "Do ye still really think so little of me, Isolde?"

"No. I don't. I . . ." Her voice trailed away, and she bit her lip. "Must we discuss this here, William? 'Tis most mortifying."

Somewhat mollified by her response, he gave a brusque nod, and they continued to where servants were waiting with their supper. But he still couldn't keep his mouth shut.

He bent his head, so his lips brushed her ear. "I've no wish for a dozen bairns if that isn't what ye want. But I need a son, Isolde. And truth be told, a daughter, too." Aye, a daughter he would dote upon, with her mother's incomparable green eyes and fiery temper. "Tell me that doesn't make ye feel like a broodmare."

She shot him a frankly startled glance, and despite the scandalous nature of their conversation, he had the bizarre urge to laugh.

"No." She sounded as though the word all but choked her. "I've no, uh, objections to such a reasonable request."

"Good."

As they sat down and everyone else took their place at the table, she leaned close. "If ye must know," she whispered, "I'm willing to give ye four bairns, Just not one a year, like so many men expect. But then, ye're not like most men, William Campbell, and that's a fact."

He choked on his ale. God in heaven, would this woman ever cease to astonish him? He had no idea how she expected to arrange such a thing as to how many children they would have or how often she might birth them, but right now that was of no significance.

All that mattered was she was looking at him with warmth in her remarkable eyes and a softly mocking smile on her lips.

Damn, it was good to be home.

AFTER SUPPER, DESPITE wanting nothing more than to carry his bride to their bedchamber, he had his usual daily meeting with Lamond, his seneschal. When they returned to the hall and Lamond took his leave, William wasn't best pleased when Robert Fletcher and Malcolm MacNeil approached him.

"I trust all's well with the earl," Malcolm said.

"Aye." He wasn't in the mood for idle talk, even if the subject hadn't been about the earl. He wanted to seek out his bride.

"William." There was a concerned expression on Robert's face that caused him to draw in a long breath and push his impatience aside. It was obvious the man had something of importance to share. "'Tis not my business, I know, but I can't help but be wary. Lady Isolde and her man, Patric, were seen sword fighting earlier this day. We thought ye should be aware." He glanced at Malcolm for confirmation, who, with some reluctance, nodded.

Irritation flared through him, and before he could stop himself, he said, "Are ye spying on my wife now, Robert?"

Robert reeled back as though William had struck him. "'Tis no secret. Half the castle saw what happened."

In which case, half the castle had witnessed Isolde's skill with the sword. "And yer problem is?"

"The problem is Lady Isolde only narrowly escaped dire injury," Malcolm said.

Incredulous, he shot dark glares between both men. "What?"

"The weight was too great for her. 'Twas a damn claymore. Who gives a noble-born lady a claymore?" A frown slashed Malcolm's brow as though he took it as a personal insult.

"The timing seemed suspect, with ye gone from Creagdoun," Robert added. "As though Patric knew ye'd never grant permission for him to engage Lady Isolde in such a dangerous pastime."

He conceded the sight of Isolde fighting Patric must have been alarming, since neither man was aware of her prowess nor had seen her expertise on Eigg.

And yet . . .

That wasn't what they were saying, was it?

*The weight was too great for her.* What in hellfire was Malcolm suggesting?

Before his attack, he would have demanded clarification and corrected their assumptions. But now he had to watch every word he uttered, even if Isolde's actions had nothing to do with what had happened to him.

"Leave it with me," he said, instead, knowing full well how both men would interpret his words. Let them. They'd soon discover his wife's skill with the sword with their own eyes. But for now, he needed to hear Isolde's side of the story.

He found her in their antechamber with her serving woman, who took one look at him and made herself scarce. Isolde gave him a smile, and he strode across the chamber and pulled her into his arms.

She sank against him, her arms winding around his back, and her elusive scent of lavender teased his senses, causing him to all but forget what he needed to ask her.

"Now we're alone, can ye tell me what news the earl has for ye?"

The earl had sworn him to silence. But Isolde was his bride, and outside the purview of such edicts the earl might issue. Besides, if not for her, he'd be dead.

"It appears Torcall MacGregor's son is still alive."

She drew in a sharp breath, clearly instantly grasping the situation. "And he wants Creagdoun back."

"Don't be afraid." Hell, he should have held his tongue, pretended all was well. The last thing he wanted was to alarm her. "Now we know who the enemy is, the earl's network will soon hunt him down."

"I'm not afraid for myself. Promise me ye'll take care, William."

Despite knowing how real the danger was with Alan MacGregor after his blood, Isolde's concern on his behalf caused heat to encase his chest. It seemed she finally believed he'd told her the truth about being smashed over the head on his ship. "I will. And ye must do the same, Isolde."

"I don't have a choice, seeing as I can't even leave the castle." Her smile was brittle, but it was also clear she was trying to be reasonable. While he'd like to know what had changed her attitude since they'd last spoken about it this morning, he didn't want to rouse her ire, and besides, there was something else he wanted to talk about.

"I hear ye and Patric practiced yer swordplay earlier."

Her arms slackened about him, but he held her close, and she couldn't escape. "Aye." She sounded reluctant, and his senses went on alert. Was there truth in what Robert and Malcolm had said? "It didn't go well."

"How do ye mean? Ye're a fine swordswoman." The word tripped up his tongue, but he wasn't certain what else to call her when the term was so apt.

She drew in a ragged breath. "I was, on Eigg. But here..." Her voice trailed away, and a shudder rippled through her. "My skills have deserted me, just as I feared."

He recalled a conversation they'd had on Eigg when she'd said a similar thing to him. He'd thought it far-fetched then and hadn't changed his mind. "Ye're a little rusty. That's all. If I'm not mistaken, it's been more than two weeks since ye last picked up yer claymore."

"I'm not rusty." There was an edge in her voice, and she flattened her hands against his chest, although she didn't attempt to push him. "I told ye what would happen as soon as I left my isle, but ye wouldn't believe me."

"A skill doesn't desert ye simply because ye live elsewhere."

"'Tis the skill of my foremothers, and their blood is the heartbeat of the isle that gives me my strength. How can I channel their power when I'm so far from home?"

Her words stung, but it was the pain in her voice that stabbed through him like, God damn it, the blade of her beloved claymore itself. Yet she was wrong, and not just about her skill with the sword.

"This is yer home now." Why couldn't she see that? But she didn't, and instinctively he braced himself for the scathing response she'd undoubtedly fire his way.

"I know that, William. Truly, I'm not blaming ye for any of this. But 'tis just the way things are, and I must reconcile myself to it."

He hadn't expected her to agree with him. Or absolve him from blame for her current situation. By rights, he should be glad she'd finally accepted her new life, yet all he felt was oddly deflated.

Because he didn't want her to reconcile with anything, least of all the fact she was the mistress of Creagdoun—and his wife. He wanted her to embrace it. To embrace her life with *him*.

"It won't always be this way." His voice was gruff. "Once we've caught Alan MacGregor and his followers, ye'll have the freedom ye crave. I don't keep ye within the castle walls on a whim, Isolde."

Her smile was unexpected, a glimmer of sunlight in the growing gloom of the chamber, and it fairly took his breath away. Would he ever understand how his bride's mind worked?

## Chapter Twenty-Two

Isolde stirred in the bed she shared with William, but something didn't feel right. She opened her eyes and in the glow from the fire realized she was alone in the chamber.

She let out a sigh and pulled the sheepskin covers tightly about her, but it wasn't the same as having William's body to warm her. While he often rose before her, he never left the bed without waking her with searing kisses and an early morning tumble, and disquiet flickered through her.

Was something amiss? But surely, if so, he would have awakened her. And if trouble brewed, he certainly wouldn't have taken the time to stoke the fire before he left, to ease the chill in the air for when she finally left the bed.

She rolled onto her side and gazed at the space beside her. With all they had discussed yesterday, she'd forgotten to tell him about the passageway she'd found, but that oversight faded to the back of her mind with what was now truly gnawing at her.

She'd been so hurt by his perceived betrayal when they had wed, she'd grimly clung onto her longstanding vow to not become a broodmare for a Campbell.

There were ways to prevent conception. She and her sisters had been taught the old ways by Amma, whose knowledge had been passed down from mother to daughter for generations, along with the Deep Knowing.

She hadn't even felt guilty about keeping it from William, since she'd been so convinced he'd trapped her by deceit.

But he hadn't.

Naturally, he wanted a son. What man didn't? And when he'd shared his expectations, his surprisingly reasonable hopes had shaken her, and remorse had burned through her.

It still did.

She released a ragged breath and pressed her fist against her breast. She hadn't lied when she'd told him she wanted four bairns. Indeed, now she was certain of William's honor, the prospect of bearing his children was entrancing. And 'twas an easy enough thing to stop taking the ancient preparations that ensured her womb was cleansed of his seed.

Unease shivered through her as the ancient words echoed in her mind.

*The bloodline of the Isle must prevail beyond quietus.*

For as long as she could remember, the meaning had been clear to her. Her bloodline could not leave the Isle. And if she wasn't meant to leave her beloved isle, it surely followed that if she did, her bloodline would end.

Did that mean she would be unable to have a child who wasn't of the Isle?

*No.*

She shoved the dark thoughts into the furthest corner of her mind as tendrils of fear tightened in her chest. Just as there were ways to prevent, there were ways to enhance the chances of conceiving. And she'd try every one of them, if it ensured she could give William the son he hoped for.

But what if the power of the Isle was too strong to overcome?

*✣*

IT WAS STILL dark when Isolde found William outside the stables with several of his men, including Hugh, and as she approached them an ominous foreboding crawled through her. He swung about, as though he knew she was there, and in the light from his lantern she saw his smile of greeting, but it couldn't disguise the concern in his eyes.

"What is it?" she said, unheeding of his men.

"Hugh arrived earlier with a message from the earl. 'Tis nothing to worry about."

She grasped his arm and tugged him away so they couldn't be overheard. "Tell me the truth," she whispered. "Ye cannot leave me wondering, William. 'Tis far worse not to know."

He cradled her face, and his thumb tenderly stroked her cheek. It was a gesture of comfort, and yet a thread of fear tightened deep in her gut.

"The earl's received word that Torcall MacGregor's followers are planning to attack. We're going to head them off at Glen Clach. There'll be a full contingent here to protect the castle, but I'm taking the men who were on the ship with me. It's the only way I know ye'll be safe from whoever attacked me."

Her stomach pitched, and she threaded her fingers through his where he still cupped her face. *Don't go.* The words echoed around her head, but of course she couldn't say them aloud. Her William was a warrior. He would never turn his back on his duty.

And neither would she. "I'll be fine," she told him. "And so will Creagdoun. Yer castle will not fall on my watch, William."

She'd meant to reassure him. Instead, consternation flashed over his face, and he grasped her arm. "We'll crush them. They won't get within half a day's ride of the castle. But even so, promise me ye won't put yerself in any danger, Isolde. I mean it."

She pressed her hand against his heart. Pride in her husband, and fear of what he was about to face entwined; a tangled web that all but consumed her. But she would never let him see her fear. It would serve no purpose but a distraction when he needed to focus on victory.

"I won't put myself in danger. But ye must promise me, too, William. Watch yer back."

His sudden smile all but stole the breath from her lungs. "Ye'll not get rid of me this easily, mo chridhe. We'll return before nightfall."

"I shall hold ye to that." She smiled back at him, even when all she wanted to do was wrap her arms around him and never let him go.

He turned to his men. "Gather yer things. We must leave before sunrise."

His men marched off, all but Hugh, who appeared ill at ease as he stood by his horse. Wiliam took her hand and pressed a kiss against her knuckles, and she forgot about Hugh. Forgot about everything but how easily she might never see William again, and her façade cracked.

"William," she said, hating the tremor in her voice but, still holding her hand, he pressed a finger against her lips.

"All the clans are with us," he whispered. "The rebels are as good as dead already, Isolde. The earl's spies came through for him, and we know the MacGregors' plans."

She nodded and brutally pulled herself together. Now was not the time for such indulgences. "God be with ye."

His gaze caught hers, and in the light from the lantern his stormy eyes held a mystical golden glow. Then he kissed her, a hard, possessive kiss, one that burned a promise of return, before he joined Hugh, and the rest of his men emerged from the shadows.

As they rode out of the courtyard, Patric came to stand by her side. Together, they watched as twilight swallowed up the warriors, and she drew in a deep breath as the portcullis dropped.

"The men are in position," Patric said. "Although I doubt the battle will last long, let alone reach Creagdoun. The Campbells are too powerful, and many of the other clans have sworn fealty to the earl. Any MacGregor who escapes with his life today should count himself fortunate."

"Aye." She knew Patric was right. She'd always known of the influence the Campbells held across Argyll and the Isles, too. The odds for victory were as good as they could ever be.

But this was different. It was personal. Because William was a Campbell, and it took only one arrow, or one well-aimed thrust of a sword by the enemy to end a life.

Instinctively, her fingers curled around her precious dagger concealed in her skirts. She wasn't sure why she still carried it with her, when it was glaringly obvious her skills had deserted her. Yet she couldn't bear the idea of leaving it in her bedchamber, if for no other reason than it reminded her of Sgur.

Reminded her of how her foremothers had once been an integral part of her.

There was no time to regret that now. It was done, and, if she was honest, would she really rather be on Eigg, without William, than here in Argyll as his wife?

She released a ragged breath as she faced the truth.

No. Even though it went against everything she'd been taught since she was a child about the Deep Knowing and her fierce Pict queen foremother, there was no other place she'd rather be than by William's side.

If only she had told him that before he'd left Creagdoun. Suppose she never got the chance to tell him now?

She swung about, heart thudding in her breast. She couldn't think that, nor imagine everything that might go wrong in the battle, or she'd go mad. Her task was to ensure the castle and its inhabitants prevailed.

Thank God for the well within Creagdoun's walls. At least they wouldn't die of thirst or poisoning, should the worst happen and the castle was besieged.

It wouldn't come to that. But it was always wise to be prepared.

DAWN HAD BROKEN, and William stretched in the saddle as anticipation thrummed through his blood. As much as he hated to leave Isolde, he relished the upcoming battle to secure, once and for all, his right to Creagdoun.

The right for Isolde and their unborn children.

God, he couldn't think of that right now. It brought to mind his beautiful wife, hair unbound, welcoming him in her arms, and he couldn't afford to be distracted.

But inevitably, the image scorched into his brain, along with every other memory he held of her, from the first time he'd seen her when he didn't even recall his own name.

It began to drizzle, and the clouds hung low over the mountains with fog creeping lower into the glens. Not a great day for a battle. If the weather didn't clear, they'd barely be able to see each other, let alone their enemy.

He frowned as an elusive glimmer of an idea took form. Before he could fully grasp it, Hugh came to his side.

"Let's hope this shakes out the traitor," he said under his breath, and William grunted in agreement. At least he was certain the man wasn't at Creagdoun, putting Isolde in danger.

The path narrowed, and his company slowed to take account of the treacherous terrain. From behind him, Robert Fletcher spoke.

"Damned MacGregors. They should have all gone to Eire with the rest of the redshanks."

"My brother tells me there's a faction still loyal to old Torcall MacGregor," David Cunningham said. "I wager they're the ones causing trouble for the earl."

Would David say that if he was working for the MacGregors? It seemed unlikely. But his comment reminded him of the previous day's conversation with Hugh, and he glanced at his cousin. "Still no news of Douglas's whereabouts?"

"He's with the earl already. He sent word with the messenger that arrived in the early hours. It seems we just missed his arrival yesterday."

"I haven't seen Douglas in years," Robert remarked. "What's he been up to?"

"Don't ask me." Hugh hunched his shoulders against the wind, or maybe it was simply against the aggravation that was his elder brother. "I'm not his confidant."

They emerged from the pass and traveled through yet another village, but as they left the last cottage in their wake, Malcolm MacNeil let out a loud curse. William glanced over his shoulder to see the other man dismount and inspect his horse.

"He's thrown a shoe," Malcolm said. "We passed a farrier in the village. I'll get him reshod and join ye at the earl's."

William gave a sharp nod. "Don't delay."

Malcolm gripped the bridle and turned his horse around and soon became nothing but a shadow in the mist.

The earl and his men, including Hugh's brother, Douglas, were waiting for them in the courtyard when they arrived at the manor, and William made his way over to the other man.

"My lord," he said, his voice low, and after giving him a shrewd look, the earl led him out of earshot of the rest of the company.

"What's on yer mind?"

"It's possible the traitor has passed on our plans to confront the MacGregors at Glen Clah to his network."

"Aye."

William drew in a deep breath as realization struck him. "That was the plan?"

The earl glanced at their contingent before catching his gaze once again. "I trust my own network, William, but it's always best to be on guard. The information seemed too convenient."

"A trap." Aye, that was the elusive feeling he'd had on the ride here. "Damn those bastards."

"Keep yer counsel. By the time it's clear we're avoiding the glen, it'll be too late for the informer to warn the MacGregors."

They returned to the men and set off, and within an hour were in sight of the glen. The earl raised his arm, his hand in a fist, and they drew to a halt.

"We'll not be confronting the rebels in the glen," the earl said, as he turned to face them. "They're expecting us, I have no doubt. We'll hunt them down in the mountains, where I wager they are lying in wait to ambush us."

The earl gave his orders, and William and the men got in position. There was always the danger a scout had spotted them and warned the MacGregors, but that couldn't be helped. God willing, they'd settle this once and for all this day.

The rain grew heavier, and the wind was bitter as William navigated his way up the treacherous slope. Their horses had been left at the foothills so as not to alert any hiding enemy of their approach, and he tightened his grip on his claymore as the elusive scent of impending battle thundered through his blood.

From the corner of his eye, he saw his clansmen stealthily making their way to strategic positions where an enemy would have a clear view of the glen below.

A movement ahead caught his focus, and he raised his arm in warning. Several of the men responded in kind.

His gut feeling had been right. The earl's informant had intended to lead them into a trap.

Archers were poised to cut them down as soon as they'd entered the glen. It would not even have been a fair fight.

One archer swung about, dropped his bow, and grabbed his sword, but William gave him no quarter. More men leaped up from their hiding places, their strategy in tatters, and the clash of steel filled the air.

The mountain was a treacherous quagmire, and as another man

lunged at William, it took all his skill to remain upright and not slide into the mud that sucked at his boots. Rain stung his eyes and mist twisted around the trees like skeletal fingers as he evaded the rebel's sword before plunging his own blade deep in the man's gut.

In the end, the battle was little more than a bloodied skirmish. When the rebels saw their fallen comrades, they fled, and William sucked in a great breath, scanning the men, searching for any of his own who had been slain.

Hugh came up to him and grasped his shoulder. "Are ye all right, man?"

"Aye. Ye?"

Hugh confirmed he was uninjured as David Cunningham and Douglas approached.

"Let's hope this has shown old Torcall's followers they're backing a lost cause." David wiped his sword on one of the fallen.

"Did we lose any of our men?" William glanced over the rest of the men as the earl made his way over.

"Robert's injured, but nothing mortal," David said.

"All the dead yonder are accounted for." The earl nodded in the direction he had come from. "None of our own, thank God. We'll take their bodies and leave them in the glen for their kin to collect."

William grasped the arms of the nearest body, and Douglas grabbed the legs. As they edged down the mountain, he took a silent inventory of every man he saw. But someone was missing. As he dropped the body in the glen, next to the others, he hailed Hugh.

"Have ye seen Malcolm MacNeil?"

"Malcolm MacNeil of Barra?" Douglas said before his brother could respond. "What in hellfire are ye talking about, William? Malcolm died of the bloody flux nearly three years ago."

William swung about and stared at Douglas as a paralyzing, black fear crawled through his gut. "What?"

"Aye, right in front of my eyes. 'Twas shortly after a skirmish with

Gregor MacGregor before he took off with his kinsmen to Eire."

"Then who the devil is the man using his name?" Hugh turned from his brother and grasped William's arm. "That's why he took off before we met with the earl. He knew Douglas would see through his masquerade."

"Isolde." Cold terror gripped William's vitals as a horrifying vision of her welcoming the man into the castle unfolded in graphic detail in his mind. "Alan MacGregor's returned to Creagdoun to take it from within."

"What?" Shock thudded through Hugh's voice. "Alan MacGregor is still alive? How can ye be so sure?"

He didn't have time to explain how he knew. Every moment he delayed increased the danger descending upon Isolde. He swung about and ignored the earl who hailed him as he mounted his horse and took off as though every demon in hell was at his heels.

But they weren't at his heels. They were closing in on Isolde. How long ago had MacGregor left their company? Long enough to have arrived at Creagdoun already?

The castle wasn't undefended. And Isolde had Patric by her side. But none of them would suspect the man they knew as Malcolm MacNeil was the traitor in their midst. The man who, there surely was no doubt, had tried to murder him on the ship.

He'd assured Isolde she was safe within Creagdoun. Safe away from her isle. Had pledged to protect her from his enemies. Nausea rolled through him, and he sent a desperate prayer to God.

*Don't let me be too late.*

# Chapter Twenty-Three

It was midafternoon, and still no word had arrived from William. Isolde paced the courtyard, breathing in deep as she waited for Sjor to finish his business. The weather was dull and damp, and she shivered as they returned to the hall. Even though William had promised to be back before nightfall, it was very possible he'd decide to stay at the earl's manor. She just hoped he'd send a messenger to let her know all was well.

*Please God, let all be well.*

"I'll fetch ye a dry shawl, milady," Emer said, and she dragged herself from her wretched thoughts and smiled at her maid, who looked frozen to the bone.

"No, 'tis all right. I'll go myself. See if ye can find something warm for us to drink."

Emer nodded and made her way to the kitchen, and Isolde went upstairs. As she entered the antechamber, she pulled off her shawl and draped it over a chair near the hearth before going into the bedchamber and wrapping a dry shawl about her shoulders.

Her glance caught on the unicorn tapestry that covered the wall. It was too grand for a bedchamber, and that was a fact, but she did love how welcoming it made the chamber. And along with the fine rug she'd brought with her from Sgur before the hearth, the chill in the air was scarcely noticeable.

It was, indeed, her favorite corner of Creagdoun. But it'd mean nothing to her if William did not return.

Why did she keep thinking that? She'd learned, throughout her girlhood, how to conduct herself and order her household through any contingency. But how different it was in reality, to put her personal feelings aside when this marriage was so much more than a mere political alliance.

Had she told William that? She had the terrible feeling she hadn't. All she'd ever said to him was how she despised his deception, when he hadn't deceived her at all.

But surely, he knew she believed his word now? How could he not realize how she really felt about him? In her heart, he was her Njord, and despite everything that had happened between them, that had never changed, even when she'd wanted to hate him.

A name was everything. She knew that. But in a secret corner of her soul, it didn't make any difference whether she called him by the ancient Norse name, or his God given one.

It didn't change the man he had always been.

She drew in a ragged breath in an attempt to compose herself. She couldn't hide up here, when the servants needed to see her about the castle doing her duties. It wasn't her place to indulge in secret fears. It was her responsibility to ensure she maintained a façade that all was well.

When William returned, he would have no cause to reproach her behavior. Because of course he would return. The odds were stacked too heavily against the MacGregors for any other outcome to be considered.

She clung onto that irrefutable fact, and as she left the bedchamber, Sjor darted across the floor and barked at the door that led to the lady's chamber.

"Come," she called, but for once her faithful lad ignored her. She sighed and followed him before dropping into a crouch and scratching him behind his ears. "Is it a mouse ye hear?"

Shaking her head, she opened the door. "Go on, then. Flush it out, lad."

Sjor raced inside, and she squinted into the gloom before lighting a lantern and following him. Far from chasing an unfortunate rodent, he was scratching frantically at the tapestry that covered the secret passageway.

"Hey," she admonished him, but again he ignored her which was . . . odd. She went over to him and lifted the tapestry.

Nothing was amiss. The panel was in place. What had she expected?

She glanced at Sjor, who gazed up at her expectantly. Unease twisted through her stomach, and she slowly ran a finger along the panel. There was nothing to see here. Why then could she not simply leave?

Sjor whined, and she shook her head in exasperation. "What are ye playing at? There's nothing here. Look."

She released the clasp and pushed open the panel.

The concealed wooden door was open.

Stupefied, she stared into the darkness beyond, while her mind scrabbled to make sense of it. She'd locked the door the other day. She was certain of it.

Her stomach pitched and ice spiked her blood as the truth clawed through her.

Someone had opened it.

There could only be one explanation. It was whoever Alan MacGregor had working for him within William's circle of men.

She needed to relock the door, find Patric, tell him of this passageway and—

Another thought struck. Dear God. Had they opened the gate at the far end of the passage?

Of course they had. Damn it. She spun about. Patric. She needed to find him.

"Sjor." She glanced over her shoulder, just in time to see her dog disappear into the tunnel. "*Sjor*. Come."

An eerie silence was the only response. She gripped the lantern tighter, indecision shredding through her. But only for a moment. She would never leave her beloved Sjor, although God help her, she'd give him a damn good talking to when she got ahold of him.

She stepped into the tunnel and hissed his name once again. This time he responded with an excited bark. Curse him. She strained her eyes, but the only light ahead came from the same obscured arrow slit as last time.

Could it be possible she was overreacting? That somehow the hidden door had swung open of its own accord?

*The door has two bolts. And I secured them.*

She sped up, even though the path was treacherous and seemed even longer than before. But finally, she saw the door ahead.

It was shut. She very nearly collapsed with relief.

"Sjor, ye wicked creature, come here."

Sjor whined and scratched at the door. With an impatient sigh, she marched up to him. And stopped dead.

The wild grass had been ripped asunder. The iron bar was propped against the wall, the two bolts drawn back, and the door, far from being shut, was opened a crack.

Ice prickled across her skin and her heart thundered in her ears. She peered through the barred window, but no hostile warriors gathered among the mist-shrouded trees. A small mercy, yet a mighty one. She placed the lantern on the floor and grasped the iron ring, intending to secure the door, but Sjor squeezed through the gap, and she momentarily froze in terror.

*Move.*

With another quick glance through the window to ensure no danger lurked, she edged out of the gap. The tangled vines and branches that had obscured this entrance for who knew how many years had been torn aside, the final proof that she'd stumbled upon a plot to infiltrate the castle by covert means.

Sjor was some distance ahead of her by an ancient rowan tree. Had the sacred tree been planted here deliberately, one hundred years ago or more, by the hidden entrance to the castle, to protect its inhabitants from evil? Or was it pure coincidence?

Either way, its presence was surely a good sign that she would prevail, and she stealthily made her way over to her dog who was most certainly *not* going to receive his nightly treat of sliced apple.

She picked him up, and he swiped a wet tongue across her chin. Before she could reprimand him for being a very bad dog indeed, she heard the distinct sound of someone approaching.

Sjor stiffened in her arms, and she pressed her finger across his muzzle. Was it one of her own men out there? Or the unknown enemy? Since there was no way of telling, she pressed her back against the tree and glanced at the entrance to the secret passage.

From this angle, the door looked as though it was still closed. No one would assume otherwise. But if she moved from the protection of the tree, how likely was it she'd make it back to the safety of the passage before she was seen?

If only she dared to peer around the trunk, to see how far away the intruder was. She gnawed her lip as indecision gripped her. But suppose she did, and he was standing *right there*?

"So, this is the place," an unfamiliar male voice said, and fear shivered through her as she tried to disappear into the tree itself. There was more than one man out there. How many?

God help her. She hoped they remained where they were and didn't plan on entering the passageway. They'd need to walk right by her if so.

"Aye. It leads right into the heart of the castle. They won't stand a chance."

She knew that voice. Who was it? But the answer wouldn't come to her petrified mind.

"I'll wait at the meeting point for our men."

The sound of them retreating filled the air until all she could hear was the pound of her heart echoing around her head. Agonized moments passed, each one seeming to last a year or more, until she could bear it no longer.

She had to secure the passageway before the attackers returned. And ensure the castle was safe.

Cautiously she stepped away from the tree, clutching Sjor tightly as she quickly scanned the area. No one was there. She'd—

Sjor let out a low growl, his body vibrating with fury as, from behind the very tree where she'd been hiding, emerged Malcolm MacNeil.

"Lady Isolde." He bowed his head, an incongruous show of respect, considering it was his voice she'd recognized but failed to place just moments ago.

"Malcolm MacNeil." She had no idea how she managed to sound so calm, when inside she was a churning mess of panic. Here, then, was the man who had betrayed William so despicably. And she had unwittingly walked right into his trap.

He smiled, but it didn't reach his eyes. "My name is Alan MacGregor, my lady, the true-born master of Creagdoun. I've come to reclaim what is mine by blood."

Alan MacGregor? So, he hadn't coerced one of William's loyal men, after all. A cold comfort. "Torcall MacGregor's son."

"Aye. I've no wish to harm ye. I know ye had little say in yer choice of husband."

Maybe she should agree with him. But his remark rankled, and before she could think better of it, she retorted, "Ye're wrong. William Campbell is the only man I'd ever choose for my husband."

His benign expression hardened, and her stomach churned with nerves. Truly, she should have held her tongue, but what did it matter? MacGregor meant her harm, despite whatever insincere words he uttered.

"That's a pity," he said. "For I intend to wed ye myself, once Creagdoun is secured."

His threat hammered through her mind, but it was the implication behind it that caused her heart to squeeze painfully in her chest. No. No, he didn't mean that William . . . she couldn't finish the thought. Wouldn't allow herself to finish what he implied, and without meaning to, her grip tightened around Sjor.

His growl became louder, and MacGregor cast him a cold glance. "Put the dog down, my lady, and tell it to retreat. Or I'll deal with it myself."

His meaning was more than plain, and slowly she placed Sjor on the ground, as far from the man as possible.

"Back." Her voice was harsh, harsher than she had ever spoken to her darling lad before, but she couldn't risk him attacking MacGregor. Thank God, Sjor no longer displayed his unusual streak of disobedience, and stood his ground.

"Good." He took a step closer to her, and it took all her self-control not to back away from him. But she wouldn't let him see how badly he unnerved her. She was no longer on Eigg, but she was still descended from her fierce Pict foremothers who had once ruled that isle.

Defiantly, she pulled her dagger from its concealed sheath within her skirts, even though she no longer possessed the skill to wield it. Simply holding the familiar weight in her hand gave her a sliver of comfort.

MacGregor paused, and then he laughed, a mocking sound that slashed through her like a mortal blade. "Ye're a fiery lass, and I don't disapprove. Ye'll warm my bed well enough and bear me many sons who'll learn to despise the name of Campbell as I do."

"Stay back." She angled the dagger at him, and although he didn't come any closer, his amusement was despairingly plain to see.

"I've witnessed yer incompetence with a blade. 'Tis a sad thing to behold, my lady. But rest assured, when we are wed, ye'll not be permitted to indulge in such fancies."

She waved the dagger at him even though she knew the folly of angering him further. Yet a thread of fury burned through her, and she could not remain silent. "I am already wed, and I'll defend Creagdoun against ye until the last breath leaves my body."

His face twisted into a cruel grin. "Ye're no longer wed, my lady. Did I not tell ye? The Campbells and their allies rode straight into our trap and were slaughtered like pigs. I killed William Campbell myself. There's no mistake. My men are on their way, and we will take Creagdoun."

MacGregor's callous taunt sucked the air from her lungs, and a burning pain seared her from the inside out. She would not believe it. Her Willliam wasn't dead. As if to reinforce its impossibility, his face swam before her eyes, his black hair whipping across his face in the wind, and his carefree laugh filled her head.

*Mo chridhe.*

My heart. Yet she had never told him, not even when he'd whispered that precious endearment to her and she'd held it close, treasuring it, thinking she had all the time in the world to tell him—one day—how very dearly she loved him.

One day . . .

That day had never come.

"Come now, lay down yer wee knife, there's a good lass."

His mocking voice scraped along her nerves like gravel across an open wound. A wound that would never heal, now she had lost the only man she could ever love. Her fingers tightened around the hilt, and the ancient runes that had been carved into the wood so long ago scorched her palm. Reminding her of who she was.

Where she had come from.

And where she was destined to go.

MacGregor swaggered closer and grabbed her shawl, hauling her to him. "Mind yer blade, lass, I don't want ye to injure yerself."

*I love ye, William.*

Time slowed; and as the sound of Sjor's frenzied barking faded, primal power surged through her, a power that came from the core of her being and the years of training she had dedicated to the memory of her formidable foremothers.

William had always believed in her. She would not prove him wrong.

As MacGregor's leering face loomed over her, she swung her head forward, connecting squarely against his nose. At his roar of pain, she thrust the dagger upwards, all but severing his ear, then twisted free from her shawl that he still grasped in his fist.

"Ye pox-ridden MacDonald whore," he spat. Blood splattered his face and murder gleamed in his eyes, but she hadn't finished yet. Her only hope of surviving was if she could escape him and secure the castle.

If only she had her claymore and could avenge William in the way he deserved.

Her husband. *My love.*

She hiked up her skirts and kicked MacGregor between his legs with all her might.

He collapsed to the ground like a felled tree, and reality once again crashed down around her. There was no time to weep for what she had lost. William had loved Creagdoun, and she would protect it in his memory with everything she had.

"Sjor." Her voice was hoarse as she turned and ran to the entrance that led directly to the castle. With Sjor at her heels, she squeezed through the gap before pulling the door shut, securing the bolts, and heaving the iron bar in place.

Panting, she peered through the window. MacGregor was on his knees, pushing himself forward, and for one heart-stopping moment, his gaze caught hers.

Her death would not be swift, should he catch her.

She turned and raced through the passageway, her erratic breath filling the enclosed space with eerie echoes. By the time she reached the lady's chamber and bolted the door, her chest was tight and ached so deeply she wondered how she could even breathe through the rock lodged inside her heart.

As she stumbled into the antechamber, Emer emerged from the master's chamber, looking distraught.

"Milady," she gasped. "I've been searching for ye." Her eyes widened as she took in her disheveled appearance. "God help us all, what's happened to ye?"

There was no time to explain. "I must find Patric."

She rushed from the chamber and found him in the great hall, along with several of the men that had accompanied them from Eigg. As soon as he saw her, he strode over, a harsh expression on his face.

"Emer was concerned," he began, but she brushed his words aside.

"Malcolm MacNeil is Alan MacGregor. He's not to enter the castle, Patric. He's the one who betrayed William, the one—" Her voice cracked, and she hitched in a sharp breath, desperately grasping at her jagged thoughts. Now was not the time to fall apart. "I fear the MacGregors may attack Creagdoun. We must be ready for them."

Patric didn't waste time asking her how she could possibly know such a thing. He merely gave a single nod.

"Aye, my lady." He turned on his heel and the men followed his lead.

Sjor sat at her feet, and she sank to her knees, pressing her throbbing brow against his head. If he hadn't led her outside, she wouldn't have discovered the identity of Alan MacGregor, and one way or another, he would've gained entry to Creagdoun and taken it down from within.

Her faithful dog had done his part. Now she would do hers.

For William.

## Chapter Twenty-Four

Twilight hovered on the horizon as William finally emerged from the thick of the forest and Creagdoun came into view. Despite his desperate prayers, he hadn't caught up with MacGregor. And as much as he hoped the man had simply disappeared into the mountains, in his heart he knew better.

As far as MacGregor was aware, William and the rest of the men had fallen in Glen Clah. He'd be expecting his own men to arrive so they could take the castle. And although that plan had been thwarted, it didn't mean MacGregor hadn't managed to breach Creagdoun's defenses.

He wouldn't need to breach them. Because everyone within the castle believed MacGregor was simply Malcolm MacNeil, and the gatehouse wouldn't be secured against him. The bastard would just ride in, unchallenged.

And take Isolde hostage. His only hope was that MacGregor's plan was not to draw any attention to himself until his men arrived, and only then capture Creagdoun's mistress. If so, she was still safe, until MacGregor realized his cause was lost.

There was no telling what that knowledge would make him do, and William's gut clenched as a thousand horrifying scenarios flooded his mind. He had to get to Isolde. Had to protect her. But how the hell could he do that, without alerting MacGregor that his strategy had failed?

He bore left, along the path beside the loch that led to the gatehouse. But his horse reared as a furtive shadow among the trees up ahead caught his eye. He pulled up short, primal warning spiking through him, and from the cover of the trees Alan MacGregor emerged.

William leaped from his horse, drawing his sword as he advanced on the other man. MacGregor pulled back his lips in a mockery of a smile and tossed a woolen and bloodied shawl at his feet.

Isolde's shawl. His heart slammed inside his chest, squeezing the air from his lungs.

*Isolde's blood.*

Wildly, he glanced around, his grip tightening on the hilt, but there was no sign of her. Was she hidden in the undergrowth, injured?

*Worse?*

"Isolde." He didn't recognize his voice, but even the rasping sound against his throat couldn't stop his mind from seeing graphic, ravaged images of Isolde, his beautiful bride, lying crumpled on the sodden ground while the blood seeped from her body.

God, the blood. He couldn't look at her shawl again, and not just because he needed to keep his focus on MacGregor, who'd drawn his sword and was inching closer.

It was because the blood-soaked shawl was stark evidence of how she'd already suffered at the hands of Alan MacGregor, because he, her own husband, had failed to keep her safe.

Why didn't she answer? The reason crouched in the darkest corners of his mind, but he wouldn't go there. Couldn't. Instead, he glared at MacGregor. "Where is she?"

"Yonder," the bastard said, which could mean anything and nothing. "She won't come running to ye, Campbell, no matter how ye shout her name. But know this. I enjoyed her well enough before the end."

Nausea surged through him, burning his throat, and for a horrifying moment, all he could see was an endless abyss of impenetrable blackness. A high-pitched buzzing filled his ears, threatening to take him under, just as the sea had once taken him under.

But this time there was no Isolde to drag him from the depths.

There was no Isolde.

*Isolde.*

Her name echoed through his head, and he sucked in a harsh breath, forcing the crucifying fog aside, and for an elusive moment he saw her smile in his mind's eye.

*Don't leave me, mo chridhe.*

But she did not reply.

MacGregor still stood before him, and the image of Isolde shattered like glass inside William's mind. The deadly shards embedded into his flesh and tore through his chest before ripping his heart into a thousand bloodied chunks.

He would avenge her honor, her life, and God help him, he didn't care if it cost him everything.

Their swords clashed, and a cold ferocity whipped through him as MacGregor retreated beneath his attack. There would be no prisoner taken this eve.

The other man grasped his hilt with both hands, and blood trickled from his mangled ear although William had no recollection of how that had happened.

"Creagdoun is mine," MacGregor panted. "I don't know how ye escaped, but my men will be here shortly, and the castle restored to its rightful bloodline."

William slashed, and blood bloomed along MacGregor's biceps. "Ye forfeited that right when ye attacked Dunstrunage three years ago. Yer men aren't coming to yer aid, MacGregor. They're lying dead in the glen. Did ye really think Campbells would fall for yer trickery?"

MacGregor stumbled on a root as he retreated, but finally the smirk on his face had gone. He lunged, missed, and William plunged his sword through the man's gut.

MacGregor collapsed, wheezing, blood oozing from his mouth. Malevolence filled his eyes as he caught William's glare. "'Tis almost worth dying, knowing I was the one who took yer woman from ye."

William thrust his sword once more, and this time it found its fatal mark. MacGregor fell back, lifeless, in a malignant pool of his own blood.

He staggered back, and the icy façade that had sustained him during the last few moments dissolved like snow before a forest fire.

Isolde. He had to find her.

*Whatever was left of her.*

With a tormented mixture of tenderness and reluctance he picked up her ruined shawl. It wasn't an omen. She might have escaped. He clung onto that slender thread of hope as he yelled her name until his throat was raw, frantically combing every inch of the undergrowth as the darkness in his heart spread across the land.

But there was no sign of where she had fallen, nor splatters of blood. What had MacGregor done with her?

Despair raked through him. He sank to his knees, his fist clenched around the shawl as he pressed the bloodied wool against his chest. Blindly, he stared at the mighty silhouette of Creagdoun as it loomed against the orange-streaked sky.

How fiercely proud he had been of calling the castle his own. How gratifying it had felt, to install Isolde there as its mistress, and how many grand plans he'd made to ensure Creagdoun, and his Campbell lineage, would prevail.

A dull ache seeped through his chest, corroding all it touched, engulfing him with a despairing inevitability.

What did any of it matter if Isolde wasn't here to share it with him?

Once, he'd wanted nothing more than to know who he was so his wild MacDonald woman could call him by his God given name.

But now he'd give anything to hear her call him Njord. Because when he had been no more than her stranger from the sea, he'd had everything.

If only he'd been able to see it.

Now she was gone, and he would never hear her voice again, never hear her laughter. Never have the chance to tell her the only reason he'd coaxed her into wedlock was because he couldn't face the thought of life without her by his side.

Instead, he'd let her believe it was because they were already betrothed, that a contract had been signed. That it was their destiny to unite their clans.

All those reasons were true, but none of them was the truth.

He'd rushed their wedding because he'd fallen for her from the moment he'd first seen her.

And his determination to get his way, no matter the cost, had destroyed her as surely as if he'd plunged her own claymore through her heart.

"William." The word slashed through the gathering gloom, but he didn't turn around. He heard the horses, knew the men who had fought by his side in the glen had arrived. But what did it matter?

He had arrived too late to save Isolde, and the men weren't needed for there was no danger facing Creagdoun.

Alasdair came to his side and gripped his shoulder. "Ye found MacGregor."

It wasn't a question.

"William, man, what is it?" There was an urgent note in Hugh's voice, as though he suspected the worst. "What did MacGregor tell ye before ye put an end to his misbegotten existence?"

He couldn't speak but instinctively gripped Isolde's shawl tighter as if, somehow, that possessed the power to bring her back.

"Lady Isolde?" Alasdair sounded uncertain as both he and Hugh stared at the shawl. "No, William. MacGregor was playing with ye. How could he have done anything to her, when she was safe within the castle?"

Aye, she should have been safe within the castle. Reluctantly, he glanced up at the dark shadow of Creagdoun, as doubt stirred deep in his soul. Isolde was stubborn, but she wasn't ignorant of danger. There was no reason why she would've been outside the castle walls. How then, had MacGregor accosted her?

The shawl was proof that he had. But maybe she'd escaped. He'd cling onto that slender hope. And if it turned out to be a false hope, he'd bring the dogs back here and search all night until he found her.

In silence they returned to the horses, and as they approached the gatehouse it was a grim satisfaction to note the portcullis was lowered and that doubtless archers were stationed at every arrow slit. MacGregor wouldn't have found an easy conquest here, had his plan to ambush them at Glen Clah succeeded.

Once the gate was raised, they rode through into the courtyard, where dozens of torches blazed, and the castle inhabitants gathered, their cheers of victory and relief echoing off the stone walls.

A hollow victory. But that was his own guilt-ridden burden to bear. As he dismounted, the crowd parted, and his heart slammed against his ribs as Isolde walked—no, *ran*—towards him.

"Ye're alive." She stopped short in front of him, not touching, just gazing at him as though he were an apparition. The air lodged in his throat, burning, and he couldn't move a muscle as his paralyzed mind took in the fact that *she was here*. "William, I thought ye were dead."

"No." His voice croaked, as if it had been a thousand years since he'd last used it. God, it seemed like it had been a thousand years since he'd last seen her, but he couldn't reach out and pull her into his arms, in case she was merely an illusion of his fractured mind and would vanish if he tried to touch her. His fingers clenched on the shawl that he'd brought with him. Somehow, it felt more real than the woman standing before him.

She gave a short laugh. "Aye, I can see that, William Campbell. Ye frightened me half to death, and that's a fact. Ye know, I suppose, Alan

MacGregor has been masquerading as Malcolm MacNeil?"

"MacGregor's dead." His gaze roved over her face, where bruising and streaks of blood marred her skin, but she didn't appear to be mortally injured. He released a ragged breath, but it did nothing to relieve the smoldering rock wedged within his chest. "He claimed to have—"

But he couldn't say the words. Because that reality could too easily have proved to be true. And just because it hadn't happened today didn't mean it couldn't another day.

He wouldn't always be able to defend her against his enemies. And every time he left Creagdoun, the fear of losing her would consume him.

Isolde glanced at the shawl in his hands and the question thundered through his mind.

How had MacGregor been in possession of it?

"Serve supper," he heard Isolde tell the servants. "The laird and I will have ours in our chambers."

There was a flurry of activity, and as the courtyard emptied, she cast him an anxious look. "Come, William," she said, almost as though she were speaking to a child. "Ye must be famished. We shall eat alone in the comfort of our chamber so we might speak more easily."

She held out her arm, indicating he should follow her, but she didn't touch him. Not that he blamed her. If not for him, she'd be safe on her beloved isle, where no one would dare raise their hand against her, let alone subject her to the obscenities MacGregor had intended for her.

Only rare good luck had saved her from such degradations. How could he live with himself if he forced her to endure a life where every day might be her last—because of his name?

As they went up the stairs and along the passage to their chambers, the fear that had gripped him from the moment he'd discovered the identity of the traitor in their midst, the fear that had scorched his reason when he'd found MacGregor on the forest's edge, now sank deep into his bones, polluting every particle of his being.

There was only one way to ensure she didn't live every day of her life under the mantle of dread, and he recoiled, rejecting it outright. He wouldn't do it. Couldn't.

But the answer was clear, regardless.

If he wanted to set her free from the bleak future that thudded through his mind, he had to send her back to her isle.

# Chapter Twenty-Five

Isolde closed the door behind them after they entered their bedchamber. She drew in a deep breath as she watched William walk to the hearth, where he paused and stared into the flames as though they were the most fascinating things he'd ever seen.

She wasn't sure what was wrong. When he'd ridden into the courtyard, she'd been so relieved she had forgotten she was the mistress of a grand castle with expectations as to how she should behave. All that had filled her head was that MacGregor had lied about killing Willliam and winning the battle.

William was alive. He was safe.

All she'd wanted was to wrap her arms around him, feel his heartbeat next to hers, hear him laugh in that way he did whenever she inadvertently amused him.

But he hadn't smiled at her loss of dignity or even seemed very happy to see her. And instead of hugging him close and breathing in his unique scent of soap and fresh woodlands, she'd come to an awkward halt before him.

He still clutched the shawl MacGregor had torn from her. She could only guess what he'd imagined when he'd found it. But why wouldn't he speak to her?

Well, they would get nowhere like this. She went up to him and gently touched his shoulder. He turned on his heel to face her, and her hand dropped back to her side. "What is it, William?"

He inhaled a shuddering breath. "I thought I'd lost ye."

Warmth and, aye, relief curled through her heart at his confession. "I'm sorry for that. I thought it prudent to get away from MacGregor as quickly as I could, but alas, it meant I left my shawl behind."

He didn't laugh at her absurd comment. He didn't even crack the smallest smile. "How in hellfire did MacGregor come upon ye, Isolde? He didn't breach the castle. Tell me ye didn't leave the safety of the walls after I left."

"Of course I didn't—" She snapped her mouth shut as she realized that she had, indeed, left the walls of the castle. But it wasn't as though she'd done it to deliberately annoy him. "I mean, aye, I did, but not the way ye—"

"Christ's bones, Isolde, ye knew the danger. How could ye be so foolish as to wander the countryside when ye knew my enemies were determined to bring me down?"

Stung by his accusation, she reminded herself he was only saying such things because MacGregor had obviously told him the same tale he'd told her. And this was William's way of dealing with it.

"I did not wander the countryside. There's—"

He thrust the bloodied shawl at her. "D'ye have any idea what went through my head when I saw this? I trawled through the undergrowth searching for ye, imagining the worst of things. Believing he'd done unspeakable things to ye before—" He swallowed and tossed the shawl onto the rug as though he could no longer bear to touch it. "All that blood. I couldn't believe ye'd survive whatever injury he'd inflicted upon ye."

Somewhere in the back of her mind it was gratifying to know how deeply he cared about her wellbeing, but as relieved as she was at knowing he was safe and home again, she didn't relish being accused of reckless behavior she hadn't committed.

"It wasn't my blood." Before he could launch into another ill-placed accusation, she added, "William, ye must listen to me. There's another hidden passageway that leads from the lady's chamber to out beyond Creagdoun's walls. Right to the forest's edge. I discovered it just the other day but didn't have the chance to tell ye about it."

He stared at her as though she had just spoken in tongues. She tried again. "'Twas secured when I first found it. But after ye left this morn, someone had opened the door that led into the chamber. I swear, I didn't mean to investigate. I intended to find Patric, but Sjor ran into the passage, and I couldn't leave him."

William's jaw flexed, but before he could respond, servants arrived with their supper. Instead of the usual light meal, she'd directed the cook to ensure a hearty stew was provided for the returning men. But her husband barely gave the meal a second glance.

As soon as the door shut behind the servants, he spoke. "Ye should have left him."

For the first time, anger sparked. "I would never leave him if I thought him in danger."

"He wouldn't be in danger, Isolde. MacGregor wouldn't care about a dog that's beneath his notice and could easily escape him. But ye—ye're a prize he'd never imagine would fall so easily into his clutches. I cannot believe ye were so foolish."

"Foolish, was I? 'Twas only by following Sjor I discovered Mac-Gregor's intention was to invade the castle through the secret passageway. To be sure, 'twas doomed to failure since ye thwarted his plan at Glen Clah, but I didn't know that at the time."

"He captured ye." The words burst from him, an accusation, yet the tortured expression on his face caused her anger against him to die. Deep inside, she acknowledged he was right. MacGregor had no use for Sjor, and her darling lad had only gone to attack when MacGregor had threatened her.

Even so, she still would never have left him at the edge of the forest and shut the hidden door against him. William hadn't been there. He couldn't understand.

"But I escaped," she told him. "He didn't hurt me, William. I bolted the door against him and put Creagdoun on alert for attack. Thank God, ye had already quelled the rebels, but at least ye know yer castle was well defended in yer absence."

"The castle." He appeared to choke on the words before swinging about and marching to the door where he paused, his hand on the iron ring. "I'd weather the loss of Creagdoun but—" He snapped his jaw shut before half turning to face her. "Ye were right. Ye should never have left Eigg. This marriage was a mistake, but I'll be sure to rectify it. Ye'll return to the isle as soon as it can be arranged."

His words hit her like a punch to the gut, and she stared at him, speechless, as his meaning thundered through her mind in an endless refrain. He wanted to send her back to Eigg? No. She wouldn't believe it.

"It wasn't a mistake." Her voice was hoarse. "Ye don't mean that."

"Don't ye understand? I won't always be here to protect ye."

"Ye weren't here today," she shot back before she could stop herself. "And I'm still alive, aren't I?"

His jaw tightened as though she'd hit a nerve. "Aye, but what of another day? I'm giving ye what ye always wanted, Isolde. Why must ye always be so contrary?"

*Contrary?*

"Ye're not giving me anything. Things have changed, William. Ye must see—"

"I do see." Anger throbbed through each word, and there was a wild gleam in his eyes that dried her protests in her throat. "Nothing's changed. And there's nothing left to discuss."

With that, he pulled open the door and left her alone.

She released a ragged breath and sank to the floor beside the hearth. Sjor came up to her and she wrapped her arms around him, the way she longed to wrap them around William. But it seemed he no longer wanted her.

Yet she was certain that wasn't true. The way he'd looked at her from the moment they'd entered their bedchamber. The things he'd said.

And the things he'd left unsaid.

His anger was directed against MacGregor, not her. But what difference did it make if he refused to open his eyes and see the last thing she wanted was to return to the isle of her birth?

&

WILLIAM PULLED THE door shut behind him, and the sound of the wood slamming against the jamb was a death knell that echoed through his head.

Besides the reddish bruise on Isolde's forehead, she was unharmed. Thank God. He squeezed his eyes shut, but his heart thundered in his chest, all the same. As though just to remind him how easily he could have lost her.

As if he'd ever forget that.

He ached to take her into his arms. To bury himself inside her welcoming heat and reassure them both that all was well. But he feared if he did, he'd never be able to let her go.

*"Ye weren't here today."*

Her accusation would haunt him until the day he died. He had no defense. He'd promised to protect her when he'd forced her to leave her isle, and he had broken his pledge within a month.

How many times had he assured her she would be safe within the walls of Creagdoun? And yet within weeks, she'd found a hidden passage he'd been ignorant of, that his enemies had intended to use to take the castle from within.

He picked up a lantern and, with damning reluctance, made his way to the lady's chamber. During the three years he'd been laird of Creagdoun, he'd barely been inside, despite his grand declarations to Isolde on how he'd always intended to make it fit for use.

But he should've done his duty as soon as he'd taken possession and ensured every nook and cranny of the castle had been examined for hidden vulnerabilities. Instead, he'd considered the lady's chamber scarcely worth considering, especially when so many other secret places had been found.

An error that had almost proved fatal.

If not for Isolde.

He entered the chamber and held the lantern high. A tapestry hung at a drunken angle, and when he drew closer, he frowned at the panel it partially concealed. There was no indication the panel was a false door, but he had to start somewhere.

Within moments, he found the latch and the panel slid back, revealing a recessed, bolted door, and guilt chewed through him. Even if he'd searched this chamber, without Isolde's information would it have occurred to him to give this panel more than a cursory glance?

She'd told him someone had opened the door this morning. They both knew who that was. And once again, it was his fault. If he hadn't told his men to gather their things before they'd left for Glen Clah, how would MacGregor have ensured the door was unbolted for his incursion?

Grimly, he drew back the bolts and stepped into the passage. It went on forever. There was no doubt that this was the primary hidden weapon of Creagdoun. The one known only to a chosen few, the secret passage that could lead the occupants safely away from the castle should it be in danger of falling, or, as MacGregor had intended, to capture it from within.

Finally, he reached a barred door, and he glared through the small window where, from the obscured light of the moon, he could see the dark shadows of the forest.

The place where he'd come upon MacGregor.

Where MacGregor had found Isolde and captured her. Pulled her shawl from her and—

"It wasn't my blood."

His tortured thoughts splintered, and he pressed his forehead against the bars across the window. The blood on the shawl wasn't hers. What the hell had happened? Had Patric followed her and fought MacGregor so Isolde could flee?

She had warned him, before he'd even recalled his own name, that her fighting skills would desert her once she left her isle. But he hadn't believed her, and even when she'd told him here, at Creagdoun, that she could no longer wield her beloved sword, he'd been skeptical.

God knows, he never wanted her in a position where she'd need to defend herself. It had never crossed his mind she would. Yet he'd taken a fierce pride in her prowess, nonetheless.

But now the full force of it hit him. Whatever had happened, she'd been unable to protect herself when she'd come under attack.

Isolde hadn't mentioned Patric. But how else could she have escaped MacGregor's clutches? It explained the blood, if Patric had wounded the other man in a fight.

His shoulders slumped. Thank God for Patric. Yet it should have been him who saved Isolde from his enemy, and he'd never forgive himself for putting her in danger's way because of his oversight.

*Because I brought her here.*

A scuffling sound behind him had him swinging about, heart pounding. She had followed him, and God help him, he hoped she had even though every time he looked at her it tore him inside out.

But the passageway was empty. Of course she hadn't followed him. She was likely already packing her trunks in readiness to leave for her beloved isle.

He lowered the lantern, and Sjor's dark eyes glinted.

William let out a sharp breath before dropping into a crouch. "What are ye doing? Ye never leave yer mistress' side."

He scratched the dog's neck, and Sjor gave his hand an appreciative lick. It was true. Sjor rarely left Isolde's side. But he'd run into the passageway, and she had followed him. If she hadn't, MacGregor would have entered the castle, and even without his men, he could still have inflicted severe injuries on Creagdoun's inhabitants before he was discovered.

"Good lad," he said, but the words sounded hollow in this dank tunnel. "Ye take care of her for me, ye hear?"

It was absurd, talking to a dog as if the creature could understand him. Yet Isolde spoke to him and of him as though he could, and when Sjor tilted his head and eyed him solemnly, William had the uncanny certainty he understood every word.

They returned to the chamber, and William bolted the door before sliding the panel back in place. Sjor dashed out of the chamber, but when he followed, Isolde wasn't there. The dog had disappeared, and the door to the master's chamber was firmly shut.

It was better this way. The truth was, if he saw her again, he didn't trust himself to go back on his word and demand she stay.

He scrubbed his hand over his face, but it didn't help ease the crippling weariness seeping into his bones and clouding his mind. What wouldn't he give to return to his beautiful bride, wash the grime of battle from his body, and fill his stomach with hot food.

But he was the laird of Creagdoun, and he needed to ensure his men were accommodated and the servants assured that all was well. When he entered the great hall, Hugh and Alasdair approached from where they'd been standing by the fire.

"Lady Isolde's hospitality is much appreciated," Hugh said.

"Aye, 'twas a good spread," Alasdair added.

William glanced at the tables, where several men still sat drinking ale, and the rich scent of the stew they'd lately consumed, which lingered in the air, caused his stomach to growl.

Of course, Isolde had already made the necessary arrangements to feed his men. She'd said as much when they'd returned. But he'd forgotten.

He grunted in response. It was too much effort to find appropriate words. Not that his friends appeared to notice, since Patric strode over and they turned their attention to him.

"Good work." Coming from Patric, it was high praise indeed.

This man had saved his life twice, and today he had saved Isolde's. And although Patric had known Isolde all her life, had given his pledge to her father to protect her, and would lay down his life for her, right now William was simply deeply, selfishly, grateful the man had rescued her so he didn't need to face the nightmarish horror of laying his bride to eternal rest.

He grasped Patric's arm. "Ye have my thanks. I owe ye everything."

"The castle was well prepared, and any stray MacGregor skulking nearby will have long since fled back to the safety of their clan. Even if ye had not subdued the rebels, Lady Isolde's discovery of MacGregor's plan gave us an edge."

"Aye." It was all true. But it wasn't what he meant. Even though he should keep his mouth shut, since Patric had acknowledged his thanks, and as warriors that was the end of the matter, he couldn't do it.

He had to ensure Patric knew how deeply he was in his debt. "And I thank ye for it. But for ensuring my lady remained unharmed when MacGregor attacked her, I swear to God, in my eyes ye are my blood kin."

A frown creased Patric's brow, and his eyes narrowed, an unexpected response. Had he inadvertently offended the older man?

"Ye're unaware," Patric stated, and from the corner of his eye, William saw Hugh and Alasdair exchange wary glances. Patric exhaled a long breath. "My lady had no help in eluding capture or securing the secret passage. She found me here, in the hall."

His gaze locked with Patric's as Isolde's words once again reverberated around his head.

*"It wasn't my blood."*

Her comment, made so casually, hadn't registered in his mind at the time. And later, in that secret passage when the words had haunted him, he'd assumed Patric was the one who'd drawn enemy blood.

But Patric hadn't left the castle. Isolde had faced MacGregor on her own.

And she had escaped him. *On her own.*

He had to get out of there. Clear his head. He swung on his heel and marched outside, and the frigid air was like being flung into an icy fog.

But it didn't clear his head. If anything, the images that plagued him of Isolde's possible fate, from the moment he'd found her shawl, grew sharper, driving out the shreds of sanity that reminded him *she was safe.*

Grimly, he trudged on, and only after he'd spoken to every man who stood guard over the castle, checked the horses, and ensured the armory was secured, did he make his way back to the hall.

It was late, and the hall was deserted. The glow from the banked fire sent shadows scuttling into dark corners and the silence as the inhabitants of the castle settled for the night sank into his bones.

During the last three years, he'd lost count of the times he'd returned to an empty hall after doing a late night round of Creagdoun. Always, the sense of peace and satisfaction had assailed him at the knowledge he was laird, and his people were well.

Tonight, he should be thankful MacGregor had failed and his castle was secure. And he was beyond grateful that Isolde was unharmed. But a deep ache consumed his chest, guilt and regret, and twisting through it all was the uneasy conviction that he was missing something fundamental.

He shook his head in a futile effort to dislodge the insidious certainty. Christ, what was he thinking? He wasn't missing anything. But by God, he would miss Isolde when she left Creagdoun, and the knowledge that soon she would be gone from his life burned like acid through his chest.

Through his heart.

He opened a leather pouch that hung from his belt and pulled out his mother's ring. There would be no gathering of the clans for a magnificent wedding at Dunstrunage castle now. No opportunity for him to give his bride his beloved lady mother's ring.

He closed his fist over the engraved band, and the gold dug into his palm. It had always been destined for his wife. But here, standing in the gloom of his great hall, it wasn't the symbolic joining of Campbell and MacDonald the ring would represent should Isolde wear it that filled his mind.

It was knowing the woman he loved would forever have a link to him, no matter how far apart they might be.

A small comfort. But it was something, and at least he'd know, when she was safely back in Sgur, she would never be in danger because of him again.

He went up the stairs and entered their antechamber, and despite his resolve to spend the rest of this cold, lonely night on a chair by the hearth, he went to the door of their bedchamber, like a cursed moth to an unattainable flame.

All he wanted was to hold her one more time, to breathe in her evocative scent, and pretend, for a few short hours, that she'd choose him over her beloved isle.

His hand was inches from the iron ring when the door was wrenched open, and Isolde stood there. Her hair cascaded over her shoulders like a molten river at sunset, an ethereal fantasy from his wretched imagination.

But she was no fantasy. She was his wife.

And he had to let her go.

## Chapter Twenty-Six

Isolde stifled a gasp as her gaze locked with William's. She'd been so sure he was still downstairs and had resolved to spend the rest of the night searching for him, if need be, until she found him and made him see reason.

But he was here, and hope sparked through her. It was plain he had intended to see her. There could be no other possibility as to why he stood outside their bedchamber.

Yet he didn't say a word.

"William," she said at last, when the silence stretched so taut between them it hurt her very ears. There were so many things she wanted—needed—to say to him, but they tangled in her mind until they made no sense at all. But she had to say something, to keep him here, since, unaccountably, he now appeared on the verge of retreating. "Have ye eaten?"

She barely kept from wincing at her inane question, but how much easier it was to speak of inconsequential things, rather than confront the fear that gnawed through her heart at the prospect of being banished from Creagdoun.

From William.

"I didn't mean to disturb ye." He sounded gruff, and a frown slashed his brow as though he found their encounter distasteful. But since she could think of no reason why he had been standing outside the door unless he'd intended to enter the bedchamber, she could only hope he'd had a change of heart about his intention to send her away.

"I should have waited until the morning."

She tugged her shawl tighter about her shoulders, but it wasn't an instinctive gesture against the chill in the air. It was the undercurrent of finality in his voice that caused a shiver along her spine.

"Well, ye're here now." The words were sharp, but she couldn't help herself. He hadn't changed his mind, and foolishly she wished she hadn't decided to go looking for him. Except that wouldn't have changed anything, since William had come looking for *her*. "What do ye have to say to me that cannot possibly wait until morning?"

He pressed his fist against his hip. In another man, the action might indicate impatience or suppressed rage at her retort, but that wasn't in William's nature, and the fanciful notion occurred to her that he was protecting something.

Aye, fanciful indeed. The despairing truth was, she didn't know her husband nearly as well as she had always imagined. Because the William in her heart would never demand she leave him.

"'Twas never my intention to put ye in danger." This time, there was no mistaking the thread of anger in his tone, and she threw her last remnant of caution to the wind. What did it matter what she said, when he was determined not to listen to her?

"Do ye think ye're the only man to put his wife in danger because of his name? Do ye imagine the MacDonalds of Sgur have no enemies of our own who would like nothing more than to see us dead? What a mighty opinion ye have of yerself, William Campbell."

He glared at her as though she had gone mad. Perhaps she had. But she wouldn't allow him to destroy their marriage under the pretext he was doing it for her. If he wanted to end their alliance, she refused to make it easy on him.

"This isn't a tournament, Isolde, to see which of us has more enemies. But I knew of the MacGregor threat, and I should've ensured it was stamped out before taking ye as my bride."

"Ye knew Creagdoun was compromised, and Alan MacGregor had

infiltrated yer men when ye insisted on our marriage, is that what ye're saying?" She knew it wasn't. He hadn't known any of that until this day, but his stubbornness was infuriating.

"Ye know I didn't." He appeared aggrieved by her accusation which, considering his own argument, proved her point, although he obviously couldn't see it. "But if I'd ensured the castle was fit for ye before forcing yer hand, if I'd had the lady's chamber restored, that cursed secret passage would've been discovered. But I couldn't wait. I couldn't risk losing ye simply because ye hated the very sound of my name."

A spark of guilt burned through her. It was true. She'd hated his name for ten long years and had made no secret of it once his identity had been revealed. But there was a difference between hating a name and hating the owner of it.

"Can ye blame me? I thought..." she hesitated. They'd had this conversation before. But had she ever told him she now believed he had always been truthful with her, during those blissful days in Eigg when nothing had mattered but being with her mysterious Njord?

"I know what ye thought. That I'd trick ye any way I could to make ye mine. I don't know how I can ever prove I never lied to ye, not with how things turned out."

The guilt twisted deeper, squeezing her heart. But it wasn't just guilt. And maybe it wasn't guilt at all. All she knew was if this was the last time she and William spoke, and she didn't tell him what he meant to her, she'd regret it for the rest of her life.

"Ye don't need to prove anything." Her voice was hoarse, and she swallowed, but it didn't help. "I know ye never lied to me. Not when I thought ye were Njord, and not now, when I know ye as William."

He gave a hollow laugh. "Ye'll never know how I wish we could return to the days when I was no one but yer Njord, the stranger from the sea."

Once, she had wished for that, too. But she knew better now.

"'Twas nothing more than a dream, William. Ye're needed here, I can see that. Creagdoun needs a strong laird, and she'll never have a finer one than ye."

"Or a finer mistress than ye."

Hope leaped in her breast, warmth suffusing her chilled flesh. He had seen the folly of his hasty words, and had changed his mind—

"It takes a battle to bring down a castle," he said. "But it only takes one stab of a dagger or sword to—" He sucked in a harsh breath, and a visible shudder racked him. "I took ye from yer isle, where ye were safe, and brought ye to Creagdoun and deadly danger. I was so certain ye'd grow to love the castle, but I was wrong. Ye'll never be happy here. Yer heart belongs in Eigg."

An eerie shiver skated along her arms. It wasn't anger driving him.

It was fear.

For her.

And if she couldn't reach him, that same fear would drive them apart forever.

She didn't quite have the nerve to reach out and pull him into her arms, but she took a step closer to him, and although he appeared to brace himself, at least he didn't back away.

"I once believed I could never be happy living anywhere but Eigg." Her voice was soft, but when he clenched his jaw and briefly squeezed his eyes shut, she hastily added, "But I was wrong. I can't claim to love Creagdoun the way ye do, but I'm certain, in time, I will."

"Creagdoun." There was a trace of bitterness in his voice as his stormy eyes locked with hers. "Don't ye see, Isolde? It's just a pile of rocks, and if it ever falls, it can be rebuilt. Aye, I do love the castle and my lands, and I'm proud to be laird, but it means nothing—nothing, do ye hear?—when compared to how I love ye. From the moment I awoke on yer Isle and looked into yer beautiful eyes, I was lost. I just didn't know it. Whether I'm Njord or William Campbell, my heart belongs to ye, and it always will. And that's why I must set ye free."

*He loves me.*

It should have been the happiest moment of her life, to know he felt the same as she. But it was because he loved her, he was sending her away. The way he had once been prepared to leave her on her isle to discover who he was, and despair entwined around the bittersweet joy that threatened to undo her.

She took another step closer to him, and this time grasped his hand.

"Do ye think I could ever leave Creagdoun, now I know how ye feel about me? William, I fell in love with my stranger from the sea before we even kissed, and that's never changed. The reason I was so angry when I thought ye had tricked me is because, even then, I couldn't stop loving ye. And God help me, I never will."

He cradled her cheek with his fist, such a gentle, despairing touch, she had the overwhelming desire to weep. Why did he still gaze at her as though the world were ending, when she'd just told him why she could never possibly leave him?

"Ye must return to Eigg, mo chridhe. We both know it. Don't make this harder for me. Go back to yer isle and live the life ye were born for."

He was still pushing her away, after everything they had both said, and she pulled back from his touch before she did something unforgiveable. Such as allowing a tear to escape.

"Harder for *ye*?" It was a foolish thing to focus on, but for some reason she couldn't move past it. "What of me? Don't ye care that I want to stay at Creagdoun—that I want to stay with *ye*?"

He swung about and marched to the hearth before expelling a tortured breath. "'Twas only by the grace of God, or sheer good luck, that ye escaped MacGregor. But on yer isle, ye would've stood a chance to defend yerself against him. I know how good ye are with a sword, Isolde. But because of me, ye were defenseless."

And finally, she understood.

She went to his side and grasped his biceps, pushing at his immovable muscles until, with obvious reluctance, he faced her.

"I was wrong," she whispered, and she cupped his jaw, his day-old beard grazing her fingers. "I always believed if I left the isle, my strength would remain in the earth of Eigg, where the blood of my foremothers has nourished the land for years without number. But ye saw the truth, William. Ye saw what I could not. It's not the isle. My skills are within me, wherever I may be, but it took MacGregor telling me how he had slain ye and would take yer castle before I could believe in myself."

His gaze roved over her forehead, where she had slammed into MacGregor's face to free herself. Tenderly, William traced a finger over the spreading bruise, before he released a jagged breath and cradled her face in his palm, mirroring her own actions.

"Ye fought him?" His voice was husky, but there was a thread of doubt as though he wasn't certain he had understood.

"Patric's taught me many tricks to escape a man's clutches that require only quick thinking and nimble feet. As soon as MacGregor released me, I used my trusty dagger to sever his ear, and then I ran."

Comprehension dawned in William's eyes as he appeared to understand where the blood on her shawl had come from. Then admiration replaced realization, and thankfully, and most importantly, the final remnants of fear in his eyes finally vanished.

"Ye bested him." There was no mistaking the pride in his voice, and a strange, pleasurable pain filled her heart. Once, she'd be so certain that the despised William Campbell would deride her skills with a blade.

How wrong she had been. About so many things.

His thumb brushed across her lips. How could so gentle a caress fill her with such longing?

"What of yer fierce Pict queen ancestor? Ye once told me ye're blood-bound to ensure her legacy endures. Can it endure beyond the

Isle of Eigg?"

The Deep Knowing whispered through her mind, and before she could stop herself, spilled from her lips. "The bloodline of the Isle must prevail beyond quietus."

All her life she'd been convinced of its meaning.

The daughters of Sgur's bloodline could not leave the Isle.

But did it really mean that? In the end, even her grandmother had questioned it, by forging an alliance with Bruce Campbell, the baron of Dunstrunage.

*The alliance is to keep ye safe.*

She still didn't understand what Amma meant by that, but one thing was for sure. Her path was no longer confined to the Small Isles.

William gave her a quizzical look but didn't question her, and instead of guilt that she had shared the secret with him, only relief washed through her, as though a burden had been lifted from her soul.

She'd been right to tell him. And although she might never comprehend the full truth of the Deep Knowing, she understood enough to know that by leaving her beloved isle, she was still following her destiny.

"I'll always be a daughter of the Isle, William. But my heritage is my own, and that will never change, wherever I may live. Her legacy will endure, and maybe it's simply time for her bloodline to reach beyond the isle she loved so fiercely."

His hand trailed from her face, along her arm, and grasped her fingers, and his smile was as potent as the first glimpse of sun after a dark winter of rain. "Could ye truly choose Creagdoun over Sgur?"

"I choose ye, William Campbell, over Sgur. Wherever we live, so long as ye're there, is my home."

He lifted her hand to his lips and kissed her fingers. His warm breath caressed her skin, and he pressed her fingers against his jaw as his gaze caught hers.

"And I choose ye, Isolde MacDonald of Sgur Castle and daughter of the Isle. Ye're so much more than I ever dreamed a bride of mine could be." Slowly, he opened his fist, and she gazed at the beautiful gold ring, engraved with sprigs of heather and set with emeralds, that lay on his palm. "Would ye do me the honor of wearing my ring, Isolde? It once belonged to my lady mother, and her mother before her." He drew in a ragged breath. "I was going to give it to ye, to take with ye to yer isle, so ye'd always have a reminder of the Campbell whose heart ye stole. But it's yers, whether ye stay or go. And so is my heart."

She gave a choked laugh and held out her hand so he could slide it onto her finger. Then she flung her arms around his neck and whispered in his ear.

"I'll never leave ye. And my heart is yers, my noble, beloved, Campbell from the sea."

## The End

## About the Author

Christina Phillips grew up in England and has always been fascinated by history and the lives of the people who lived so long ago. As a child she loved visiting castles and palaces, and ancient Roman ruins, and spent many happy hours making up stories set deep in the past.

Christina now lives in sunny Western Australia with her high school sweetheart and their family. She enjoys writing historical romance where the stories sizzle and the heroine brings her hero to his knees.

Hopelessly addicted to good coffee, expensive chocolate and bad boy heroes, she is also owned by her gorgeous cats who are convinced the universe revolves around their needs. Naturally, they are not wrong.

Christina's Website:
christinaphillips.com

Christina's Newsletter:
christinaphillips.com/pages/newsletter

Christina's Facebook:
facebook.com/christinaphillips.author

BookBub:
bookbub.com/authors/christina-phillips

Amazon Author Page:
amazon.com/stores/Christina-Phillips/author/B003G299V0

Goodreads:
goodreads.com/author/show/3216349.Christina_Phillips

PayPal email address:
christinapph@gmail.com